Mogololo

Martyn Hurst

Copyright © 2017 Martyn Hurst

All rights reserved.

ISBN:
ISBN-9781521095904

DEDICATION

For Melanie.
For my love for her and our shared love of Africa.

Chapter One

To the inexperienced eye it appeared to be a rock, a large grey rock that happened to be under a wild fig tree and it looked as if it could have been there since the beginning of time. Then it stopped being a rock and became an elephant as its trunk started to sway giving its hiding place away. It had been standing there for ages, waiting for the day to begin and it had become bored with this position and decided it was time to move on. For something weighing many tonnes, an elephant manages to move remarkably quietly. Its motion is as much a glide as a walk, and this elephant, which had been standing so still, some fifty metres from the watching observer on Mogololo Lodge's verandah, simply melted further into the bush, to get on with its elephant life - relaxed, confident and calm.

For Ralph, who happened to be that watching observer, this was always his favourite time of the day. The sun wasn't yet up but the night was over, everything was perfectly motionless and there was a strong feeling of expectation about what the day was going to bring. There was even a special smell in the air at this time of day: it was crisper, sharper; what dew there had been overnight was allowing the scents of the grasses, bushes and tiny flowers to rise into the air before the sun rises and bakes the land into an unforgiving crust once again. The guineafowl were already out and about, squawking their good morning calls to each other, squabbling in the dirt for the pick of the tiny grubs that had dared to come up out of the ground. Far off, a woodland dove was calling to a distant partner; seconds later a plaintiff, descending string of notes came back, answering the call and sharing woodland dove gossip. The air was still, chilled like great chablis and full of mystery as to what the day might bring.

Perched on his favourite rock, overlooking the valley that was still wearing its thin cloak of pre-dawn mist Ralph was warming his hands on his half pint mug of coffee, occasionally dunking an Ouma's Rusk into it and crunching off a mouthful. His buff-coloured fleece was zipped up to the neck, yet he still wore the shorts and desert boots that epitomised his game ranger life. He didn't mind the chill, as he knew that in no more than three hours time the temperature would be up around the high twenties, making his bush shirt sticky with sweat between his shoulder blades, so a little bit of early morning cold was worth it.

As the rock hard Ouma's Rusk hadn't absorbed much of Ralph's coffee, it had done its typical explosion of crumbs all down the front of Ralph's fleece as he bit into it.

"Bugger!" he muttered to himself, "well I suppose it's more for the birds to enjoy now, rather than me."

He moved off his rock and strolled back towards the verandah, brushing the crumbs from his fleece. On the way, he kicked at the leadwood logs from last night's fire, waking them up into first a glow, then a few half-hearted flames, and the fire was a living thing again. He stared at it for a while, marveling at the strength of the forces of nature; the logs had once sprung from seeds, struggled to establish themselves as saplings, survived into maturity, lived long and productive lives giving protection, nourishment, shade, oxygen and more. Then to be pushed over by an elephant, just so the elephant could get at some tender leaves that would have been out of reach had the tree still been standing, followed by another long period of giving cover to the tiny creatures that formed homes under the fallen trunk. Bleached by the sun, bark stripped off and nibbled by insects and, years later, collected by one of the cook boys, foraging for firewood for Ralph's game lodge. These were the wonderful circles of life he daydreamed about during this special morning time of his.

Then Ralph was stirred from his thoughts by a small cough.

"Morning Edison," he murmured, knowing the cough came from his tracker, fellow game ranger and life-long friend. Edison was generally a man of few words but beneath that quiet exterior was an intense intelligence and unshakable loyalty to Ralph. He was from the local Shangaan tribe, part of their nobility in fact (if you happened to understand the complex social structure of the local people). He stood a bit shorter than Ralph, but his wiry frame belied the strength that lay there.

"Hey Ralph," replied Edison. "Need more coffee? I see you've done your usual party trick with your rusk!" nodding towards the remnants of the crumbs down the front of Ralph's fleece.

Ralph smiled at his friend as he brushed away more rusk crumbs. "No, no more coffee, thanks. You got some?"

"Sure. Guests will be up soon."

"Yes," sighed Ralph. "But only two of them for the drive this morning. And they're really nice. Our Dutch couple."

"Oh, so they'll understand Afrikaans, then?" joked Edison.

"Well you can talk to them in Afrikaans if you like. You know mine is rubbish!"

Edison chuckled, knowing Ralph's inability to fully master the language of the old South Africa, yet Edison was fluent in at least four languages. "I'll get the Land Rover ready then."

Ralph heard the alarm bark of a baboon, way off in the distance, thinking it was probably worried about the presence of a leopard in the area. Then he turned his gaze to the east and marveled at the colours in the sky as the first sign of the sun made itself known, streaking pink into the morning clouds on the horizon and filling the day with promise. This is what he does and thinks most mornings, but never tires of the spiritual lift it gives him.

Finishing off his coffee, Ralph had a fleeting thought of the life he might have had: a cattle farmer, like his father and grandfather before him. The trouble was, he didn't much like cattle: stupid, smelly, clumsy beasts. While growing up he'd helped his father around the farm, of course; that's what sons of farmers did, but when his father's second heart attack struck him down (if only he'd taken the doctor's advice and quit smoking) and Ralph was left with thousands of hectares of not-particularly fertile grazing land, bordering Kruger National Park, he made the life-changing decision to follow his dream and set up the game lodge. Wildlife had always been his passion and growing up in the bush had been as much as an education for him as the rather mediocre boarding school he'd been despatched off to. He instinctively knew the rhythms of the flora, fauna and the seasons of the generally hot and dusty land that was as much a part of him as his own fingerprints. So, attempting to turn his passion into his business seemed a great idea at the time.

He thinks of the guests who will soon join him: Jan and Esther, a lovely couple from The Hague, retired but still full of life and enthusiasm. They'd been at the lodge for three nights but they would be leaving today, after their last game drive. It was great to have appreciative, interested guests; Ralph's problem was he didn't have enough of them. So far, his game lodge was not a roaring financial success.. From the sale of the cattle herd and a fairly substantial loan from the bank he scraped the capital together for the required game-proof fencing, converted the farmhouse into the main lodge building and constructed four guest bungalows, all very stylish and Africa-themed. Each of the guest bungalows was fully self contained, with one main room, vast bed, sitting area, and big glass doors overlooking a shaded outdoor verandah. There was an outdoor shower and each of the units was perfectly private, yet safely within walking distance of the main lodge building. Ralph had called it Mogololo Game Lodge (named after the farm his grandfather had started and Ralph inherited) and for the best part of a year he'd been running the business on a wing and a prayer, optimistically hoping that guests would beat a path to his door and keep his cash flow flowing.

Ralph was the first to admit he didn't have much of a head for business but he was really good with people, provided they showed more than a cursory interest in the bush and game experience he would give them. He left the catering and hospitality issues to his girlfriend Tanya.

At least, that was the plan.

Tanya, however, wasn't happy. She was good at the menu planning, ordering supplies and managing the kitchen staff; and she'd been great in the early days of designing the guest bungalows and making sure all the little touches of comfort were in place and always in keeping with the African style that Ralph had wanted to create and support. They'd met when Ralph was on one of his infrequent visits to the northern suburbs of Joburg, introduced by a mutual friend. Tanya was on the rebound from a pretty disastrous relationship and was captivated by Ralph. He never thought it but he was regarded by women as something of a dish: his hair was a mop of tight brown curls that resisted any attempt at control; he had strong facial features, the deeply tanned skin of a game ranger and a winning twinkle in his eye that was hard to resist. And Tanya hadn't resisted. The idea of a complete change of lifestyle had appealed and in the beginning, it was a novelty and fun. What she didn't like, however, was being so far away from a town for days and weeks on end. Nor had she come to terms with some of the smaller creatures that insisted on sharing her and Ralph's accommodation: the lizards and geckos, the stick insects, the bats, the moths, the occasional scorpion and, her very worst nightmare, snakes.

The previous night, after the guests and staff were all in their rooms, Tanya and Ralph barely shared a word. Ralph knew Tanya hadn't settled into the life of running a game lodge but this was his life now, this was what he did. He tried to make sure the things Tanya didn't like were kept at bay, but he didn't always succeed. Last night, a ground squirrel had found its way into Tanya's wardrobe and after Ralph had stopped her screaming, he had to catch the squirrel and banish it to the outside world. Tanya had glowered at Ralph, climbed into bed and turned away from him. She was still asleep at five thirty am, or pretending to be, and as Ralph really didn't want a full-scale confrontation at that time in the morning, he dressed and crept out of their room as silently as he could.

He was still musing on what to do about the Tanya problem when his Dutch guests, Jan and Esther strolled up to the campfire.

"Jan, Esther, good morning!" said Ralph. "I hope you slept well?"

"Ja," replied Esther. "But what was the screaming in the night? It sounded human, not like a wild creature."

Ralph laughed, "I'm afraid Tanya's not too fond of ground squirrels trying on her shoes. One took her by surprise when she opened her wardrobe and I had to get rid of it."

"Not permanently, I hope," said Jan. "It's not going to be on the breakfast menu is it?"

"No," said Ralph, "we're very conservation-minded here. I just kicked the thing out and told it to find its own bed. Now, have you had coffee? Are you ready for your drive? I always think this is the best time of day."

Ralph really enjoyed having guests like Jan and Esther; they were enthusiastic about everything he told and showed them, asking intelligent questions about the animals, birds and plants and being thrilled when Ralph spotted something unusual and made them feel as though they were the only ones who had ever seen a honey badger or wild dogs or a cheetah with cubs, or whatever it was that Ralph was sharing with them.

They strolled across the dusty ground to where the game vehicle was parked. It had started life as a normal long wheel-base Land Rover. When the game lodge idea formed in Ralph's head he had an engineering friend of his work on it and convert it into a game-viewing vehicle. There were still two seats at the front, then a slightly higher bench seat behind and a higher-still bench behind that. The whole affair was open-sided and topped off with a canvas roof or awning to give the passengers some shade. Ralph couldn't claim complete originality for the idea, he'd copied from other game lodges – but it worked, and his guests loved the thrill of being able to be high enough to see the game properly, and still be in relative comfort.

This was where Ralph was in his element: driving his Land Rover along the trails he had created, occasionally venturing into Kruger Park itself, as there were no fences between Mogololo and Kruger, but generally staying on his own land, territory that had quickly reverted to natural bush after the cattle had gone. There was no great purpose to the tracks and trails Ralph drove long. They twisted and turned round the natural obstructions of rocks, termite mounds and giant trees, occasionally climbing a rise, then dropping down again, meandering through the bush with the sole aim of encountering animals.

There was a small, fold-down seat over the front bumper of the vehicle where Edison sat. He scanned the bush with his expert eyes, reading the spoor, listening for sounds and calls, and spotting creatures even before Ralph. The bush was totally part of Edison's DNA, he had an instinct for it, an extra sense that would alert him to the presence of an animal before anyone else. Edison had serene calmness about him, he was the sort of man who didn't need to be talking all the time to make his presence felt. He spoke when he needed to, always scrupulously polite but totally comfortable in his own skin. Some thought of him as being shy but he was simply his own person, and completely at home in the bush and proud of the partnership he enjoyed with Ralph.

There was a very discreet and private sign language between him and Ralph; Edison would raise a hand, point a finger, nod his head in a certain direction. Ralph would then interpret for his guests, often whispering to heighten the drama and not disturb the animals they were watching.

The animals, of course, were used to the Land Rover and became completely blasé about their presence. Ralph was still safety conscious, however, and frequently cautioned his guests not to get over-excited or make extravagant gestures and to always keep arms and legs inside the vehicle.

On this morning, Jan and Esther's last at Mogololo, Ralph had a sort of a plan of what he wanted them to experience. He'd managed to get them great sightings of elephant, buffalo, a pod of hippo wallowing in the river and a fleeting glimpse of lion, but that was in Kruger Park territory and there he was forbidden to leave the recognized roads. On his own property, however, he was able to wander wherever he liked. There were well-worn trails and tracks and he tended to stick to those, but if Edison suggested it, he often crashed into the Mopane thickets to follow the trail of something exciting.

This was one of those mornings. He wanted to show rhino to his Dutch guests. Rhino are quite territorial and, unlike elephant, tend not to roam over vast distances. He knew there was a solitary male that liked to hang around one particular area and that was where he was headed now.

'Roads' were too grand a title for the tracks Ralph was driving. The trail was just a single vehicle width and hard-packed red earth with grass growing in the centre between the two tyre tracks; there were many ruts and bumps, some worn by the repetitive journeys of Ralph's 4x4 game viewing vehicle and others by the run-off from the infrequent but dramatic downpours that came in the rainy season. Then there were the branches and trees that got pushed over and strewn around the tracks: elephant damage. Ralph was busy negotiating round just such a tree when he was conscious of a crashing in the bush to his right. A lone bull elephant was browsing just thirty metres away, Ralph slowed right down and stopped and pointed for Jan and Esther to see. They whispered their 'oohs and ahs' and took pictures to impress their friends back home, then the elephant took exception to being interrupted, shook his massive head to flap his ears, raising a cloud of red dust from his hide as he did so, and glared at Ralph's party.

"OK. OK. Take it easy," Ralph told the elephant. "We're just passing through, old fella, we're not bothering you."

Jan and Esther were impressed with the calm with which Ralph addressed this majestic animal. In the few days they'd been at Mogololo, they'd learned to trust his knowledge, experience and feelings for the bush. They knew they were in good hands.

"Has this elephant not got a family?" asked Jan.

"Well he's certainly a mature bull elephant," replied Ralph, "but it's likely the dominant bull of the group has pushed him out as he could be considered a threat. There's only one alpha male in an elephant herd. They're not too good at sharing the females, so until the alpha male gets too old, or gets injured, or loses his strength to stand up to the challenges of the younger males, the bulls have to wait their turn. They generally form a 'boys club' of similar-aged males, but this one seems to be a loner. We'll give him some space and show some respect; after all, it's his patch of land more than ours, isn't it?"

Jan and Esther nodded their approval at Ralph's wildlife lesson. The sun was well and truly up now, the day was warming. They moved off.

Up at the front of the vehicle, Edison was concentrating on the sandy track; big animals like rhino can go wherever they like, browsing or grazing as they move, but they also like ambling down the manmade trails. Edison very discreetly gave Ralph his "slow down a bit" signal and Ralph duly reduced his speed. Edison signed, "carry on" then fifty metres later, pointed left.

"Hang on!" commanded Ralph and took the Land Rover off road, smashing through young trees and bushes and watching out for treacherous ant bear holes that could wreck his vehicle in an instant.

"Are you not damaging the vegetation too much?" asked Jan, hanging on to the rail in front of him as the Land Rover rocked over the rough ground.

"Young trees are tough," Ralph explained. "They spring back very quickly. Watch out for that thorn bush, though!" Jan did as he was told and ducked under the vicious thorns."

"We have brambles in Netherlands, and sharp bushes called gorse," ventured Esther, "but your African thorns are bigger and nasty and more dangerous."

"Indeed they are," agreed Ralph. "That's Africa for you!"

Edison suddenly gave his "stop!" sign. He was staring off to the east through thick bush. Then he extended his arm and pointed. Ralph followed Edison's direction with his binoculars, Jan and Esther followed suit with theirs.

Ralph spotted it before his Dutch guests. "About 100 metres," he whispered. "I'll try and get around it from the north, so it won't pick up our scent."

"What is it?" whispered Esther.

"Rhino."

As quietly as he could, Ralph manoeuvred the vehicle in a wide circle and approached the animal from downwind. It was magnificent. A fully-grown male white rhino. It was grazing contentedly, unaware of its sudden celebrity status. Ralph expertly positioned the vehicle to give his passengers as good a view as possible.

They were thrilled. As they busily took photographs, Ralph gave them more whispered information, "I reckon this boy is about seven years old now, fully grown, of course, and he weighs about one and a half tonnes. This is the white rhino…stupid name really because he's not white at all. It really should be "wide" rhino because of the shape of his mouth, unlike the pointed snout of the black rhino. This one's horn is magnificent and, tragically, that could be his downfall. Ounce for ounce, it's worth more than gold in the Far East. You know poaching is a real problem here in southern Africa. We're lucky on Mogololo that we haven't been bothered, but I suspect it's only a matter of time. I've known this rhino for years, he's had a few girlfriends and fathered a few young in his time, but he's pretty happy on his own. I'm so glad we found him for you this morning."

"So are we," agreed Esther. "It's criminal that such a creature should be in danger like that."

"Criminal, yes," said Ralph. "It's policing it that's hard."

They watched the rhino contentedly grazing for a minute or two more, then Ralph's mobile phone buzzed in his pocket. First he was astonished that his phone had actually picked up a signal, then he apologised to Jan and Esther for the electronic intrusion and looked at the screen of his phone: a message from Tanya. She wasn't happy.

"Anything serious?" asked Jan.

"Don't think so," replied Ralph. "Nothing I can't sort out." But he wasn't anywhere near as confident as he pretended.

"Well, thank you for introducing us to your rhino friend," said Esther.

They were motoring steadily along a dusty track when Jan suddenly cried out in alarm, followed by a squeal from Esther.

Ralph did as much of an emergency stop as the Land Rover could manage and turned to Jan and Esther, "What is it!"

Jan was holding his cheek in a bit of discomfort. "Some bug just hit me!"

"There it is!" cried Esther, pointing to the floor of the vehicle.

"Ah, it's just a dung beetle!" reassured Ralph, leaning over the back seat to pick up the source of the panic. "They don't fly that much, and when they do they're not very good at it and terrible at navigating." He was holding the creature quite carefully to show the couple and now they had calmed down they were both intrigued. It was about the size of a half walnut and as Ralph held it carefully, its legs were furiously windmilling in an attempt to break free.

"He's got pretty good armour-plating," commented Jan, rubbing his cheek where the beetle had crashed landed into him.

"So is it called a 'dung' beetle because it eats the stuff?" asked Esther.

"Well yes, they do eat it," replied Ralph. "But they also manage to roll it into a ball, move it away from the pile of dung and bury it; sometimes just for food, but the female also lays an egg inside it, buries it and when the grub hatches, it eats its way out."

"Ugh," said Esther, "not my idea of a gourmet dinner."

"More than that," continued Ralph, "they manage to push a dung ball more than ten times their own weight uphill! And they use their back legs, so they are travelling backwards most of the time, never looking where they are going. Apparently, in relation to their own body size and weight they are the strongest creatures in the world."

"What dung do they like best?" asked Jan, now fascinated by the beetle's lifestyle.

"Elephant is favourite, but also buffalo and rhino," replied Ralph. "Shall we let this guy go and see what's on our own breakfast menu?" And he carefully leant over the side of the vehicle to give the dung beetle its freedom.

The drive back to camp took another half hour or so, with Jan and Esther asking occasional questions about plants and animals, enthusing about how much they had enjoyed their trip and promising profusely they would be back.

Ralph was his usual gracious and charming self, but he'd heard these sort of promises before – the excitement of being in the bush often gets forgotten when Europeans get back to their metropolitan lives, but ever an optimist, Ralph hoped it would be true this time. The bookings diary was looking dangerously empty; he really needed more business.

The thatched roofs of the lodge and bungalows were largely hidden by the acacia and fever trees that surrounded the camp and Ralph's heart was sinking as they eventually came into view, knowing that he was probably facing a gale of abuse from Tanya –perhaps about a moth that had got caught in one of her precious face creams, or the kitchen had run out of eggs without letting her know in advance. Or, even more serious, a sleeve of her favourite bush shirt might have got snagged on a thorn and somehow, it would have been Ralph's fault.

As it turned out, it was worse than that.

Chapter Two

The camp at Mogololo was planned with care. At its heart was the old farm homestead, built by Ralph's grandfather but Ralph had remodelled it to make it much more in keeping with what he thought his guests were hoping for in their bush experience – lots of open space, thatched roof, wide verandahs, chairs to flop into and share stories and the knick knacks of 'old Africa' that had become part of the fabric of all game lodges. There were lots of books on wildlife, framed old maps, old photographs of massively tusked bull elephants and even one or two hunting trophies from days long gone when hunting was not considered so much of a crime. Thankfully, there was not a television in the place. Ralph reluctantly had agreed to an internet connection but that was in his poky office and definitely not for guests to go surfing.

Around the homestead, there were four new thatched bungalows, each identical and discreetly placed to give each visiting couple some privacy during their stay and a glorious view over the bush, yet enough security that they were not far from Ralph if his game-ranger-hero qualities were needed to deal with any intruding creature.

It was into this blissful and seemingly peaceful environment that Ralph drove his Dutch couple back from their morning game drive. All seemed quiet and Ralph wondered whether Tanya's threatening text to 'get back here. NOW' had been a knee jerk reaction to some minor crisis that had sorted itself out in the last half hour.

"It all seems remarkably quiet around here," he said, more to himself than to Jan and Esther. "Anyway, you go and freshen up and we'll see you for breakfast whenever you're ready?" His guests duly jumped down from the vehicle and went off to their bungalow. Ralph thought he'd better check in the kitchen to see why there was so little activity around the place.

He found Miriam, one of his long time helpers, in the kitchen but without much sign of any cooking going on. She was in the middle of what could have been the aftermath of an unsupervised cooking party of a dozen or more five year olds; mess everywhere, packets of opened food all over the floor, broken china, upturned pots, cartons of milk and juice sprayed everywhere and Miriam on the verge of tears. Ralph knew there had to be a story, so he gently let Miriam explain in her own time.

"Oh, Mr. Ralphie!" she started, "The monkeys got in to the larder last night. I don't know how they opened the door but they break in and help themselves. They still here this morning when Miss Tanya and me come in and she go bananas. Truly bananas, I tell you. She like a monkey herself! She start throwing things around and shouting, 'That's it! I'm not staying one more day in this – then she use a bad word – place!' And she smash a plate on the floor and throw the milk against the wall and go off and slam the door behind her. Shaaai! She an angry lady, that one."

"OK Miriam, I'll sort Tanya out in a minute," soothed Ralph, "but first of all we have to make breakfast for our guests, OK? What have we got left we can give them?"

Miriam was so relieved that someone was taking control, "We still got some eggs and bacon as the monkeys didn't get into the fridge, but there's no cornflakes or rolls or fresh bread. All gone. And not much fruit, monkeys they like fruit."

"Any bread in the freezer?"

"Yes, I think so."

"Well you get that out and we'll microwave it fast and at least we can give them bacon and eggs and toast. And once you've started that, lay the table for four people and I'll start on this mess and get breakfast under way. All right?"

As Miriam shuffled her ample weight into the outhouse where the freezers were kept, Ralph started cleaning up the trashing of the kitchen during the monkey invasion. "Bloody monkeys," he muttered to himself. "Hope to God we don't get a visit from the public health inspectors this morning." In their excitement at finding this treasure trove of food, the monkeys had left plenty of evidence of their presence around the kitchen in terms of generous droppings of monkey crap on the floor, the counters, even in the sink. Edison walked into the kitchen and quickly taking in the situation started laughing uncontrollably.

"You can shut up, too!" snapped Ralph.

"I see it's monkeys one, Mogololo nil," he volunteered. "Want any help?"

"Damn right I do," replied Ralph, now also beginning to

see the funny side, "You can see if there's any fruit juice left, and get the kettle on. Jan and Esther have paid for their breakfast, I'm going to make sure they get it."

Ralph made a valiant effort to maintain an air of serene calm during breakfast with Jan and Esther, but Esther wasn't fooled, her feminine intuition sensed that some drama or another had overtaken Ralph and he was hiding something.

"So where is Tanya this morning?" she asked.

"Umm, she's busy organising stuff for the next arrivals, I think," bluffed Ralph, knowing full well that Esther had seen right through him.

"Hmm," said Esther, "So the text you got from her was nothing to worry about? I hope we see her before we leave."

"Ja," added Jan. "We must be driving in twenty minutes, I think."

Ralph really didn't feel like volunteering that he hadn't seen Tanya to confront her about the kitchen fiasco, nor that he was covering up for the complete shambles of his own management, security, catering and hospitality skills. He just hoped a smile and a veneer of 'all-is-right-with-the-world' pretence would help him cover up. It seemed to work.

And, twenty minutes later, he was still smiling and maintaining his cheery demeanour as he helped Jan and Esther with their bags into their hire car and gave them strict instructions on how to navigate back to the main road that would eventually lead them to Johannesburg, to the airport, and to their home in the Netherlands. They, in turn, were effusive in their thanks and praise for all he had done for them, and gushed with promises that they would return next year, and in the meantime tell all their friends about Mogololo. Ralph waved them off, then turned and walked to his own bungalow to face whatever Tanya was going to hurl at him.

Surprisingly, it wasn't a torrent of abuse. She was in their bedroom, suitcases on the bed and folding her clothes with care and arranging them in small piles to be packed. Ralph could tell her mood was not good. Tanya had long dark hair that she was constantly fussing with, flicking it this way or that way, rearranging it in a very narcissistic manner. But this morning, it was severely tied back in a pony tail, and the expression on her quite angular face was set and hard.

"You'll have to go into town to get food to replace what those bloody monkeys stole and trashed, so I'd like you to give me a lift," she announced. "Sorry Ralph, I just can't take any more of this bloody place. I need some civilization, some contact with the outside world, a visit to a restaurant where real waiters serve decent food, and perhaps a long soak in a bath. Anywhere where monkeys definitely aren't!"

Ralph stood, letting the scene sink in. "So you're thinking of going for how long?"

"Forever."

"Ah." Ralph wasn't that surprised, but the fact that the conversation (or to be more accurate, the one-directional statement) was being done with a degree of calm, made him realise their relationship was facing the end. "So leaving me without a front-of-house manager doesn't tweak your conscience just a little bit?"

"Oh, you'll get along fine without me – just give the punters your game ranger smile and they'll melt in your hands. They always do. It's only me who knows how bloody singleminded, inflexible, self-centred, patronising and impossible you can be!" With that she started dumping her clothes into her suitcases, treating them with as much pent-up violence as she could, cramming shoes, tops, jeans, underwear, make up, toiletries, books and hairdryer into her bags with a ferocity that Ralph was used to being directed at him rather than her life's possessions.

"Tanya…" he started.

"Don't you Tanya, me!" she snapped. "I've had enough. Not taking any more. Ready to go. Now. You going to take me?" Ralph could only just suppress a smile at her new mode of truncated talking, leaving out all the niceties of language in order to deliver a more brutalised message. He sighed.

"OK, give me ten minutes."

In those ten minutes he had a quick meeting with Miriam, asking her what was essential to replace in the larder and listing anything else they needed. He brought Edison up to date with developments and told him he would be in charge for the next few hours. They were expecting a couple of South Africans to check in that afternoon, Ralph wished bookings were better and he longed for a time when they would have a full house and he could feel he was achieving something his father would be proud of, instead of limping along on the brink of financial collapse month after month. Edison took the news of Tanya's departure quite philosophically.

"Well, it's been lively since she's been around," he said. "Not sure having someone in a bush camp who's afraid of the bush is the best idea you've ever had. You OK with Miriam being in charge of everything domestic though? I mean she's a great cook, but she always needs to be told what to do."

"I was wondering if Grace might like to step in, just for a while, until I get something permanent sorted out, of course?"

"Grace? My wife, Grace?" said Edison.

"That's the one."

"Ayssh! She and Miriam, they from different tribes, man! They hate each other!"

"I'll stop them knocking lumps out of each other, don't worry," said Ralph reassuringly.

"I can ask," offered Edison. "Shall I do that now?"

"That would be good," said Ralph. "Don't push her into

it, though. Let her think about it for the rest of the day, at least. I should be back before the afternoon arrivals get here. Now, I'd better sort out Tanya, before she takes a baseball bat to the rest of the house and kitchen. Don't forget we've got two guests coming in this afternoon. Their names are bookings diary in the office, can you sort them out if they arrive before I get back?"

"Sure," said Edison, "I'll get Grace to help…break her in gently."

Ralph's drive into town with Tanya was frosty, to say the least. She wasn't interested in the sighting of the steenbok Ralph pointed out, nor the secretary bird, pounding its claws up and down a snake it had found. "One less snake for you to get freaked out over Tanya," Ralph muttered, more to himself than to her, but even that raised no response, Tanya pointedly stared out of the window away from Ralph for the hour or more it took to reach the small town.

"OK Tanya," Ralph said, once they had reached the start of the tidy gardens and houses on the fringe of the town, "Where do you want to go?"

"As far away from here as possible," she said. "Can you drop me at Mary's house, I'll scrounge a bed for the night and sort myself out tomorrow. The sooner I get back to Joburg the better." Mary was an old friend from school in Joburg who had happily settled in the Lowveld, unlike Tanya.

"OK, if that's what you want," said Ralph, in no mood for an argument. "Look, Tanya, I'm sorry you feel the way you do about not wanting to stay at Mogololo. I thought it really could work out well between us, but I'm not giving up, I'm not going to chase you to the bright lights of Sandton, this is what I want. I love the bush, bastard thieving monkeys and all. So they trashed the kitchen, I'll put stronger locks on the cupboards. If you can't hack it, well, maybe it's best that you move on. I know I owe you some money for the work you've put in, I'll put some money in your account at the end of the month, OK?"

"Fine," came the one word answer from Tanya who was still staring out of the side window.

And, after an awkward few seconds outside Mary's house when Ralph carried her bags to the door, but didn't know whether to kiss her, hug her or just shake her hand in goodbye, he was almost relieved when Mary came rushing out of her house, overjoyed that her old friend had come to stay.

"Tanya!" she squealed and grabbed her friend in a hug, "I was thrilled when I got your text! Fab you're coming to stay. Hi Ralph, how are you? Tanya! You've lost weight. Oh Ralph, just put the cases down anywhere. Cup of tea Tanya? Coffee? How've you been? I've got so much to tell you, you'll never guess what's happened!" The two old friends went arm in arm into Mary's house, leaving Ralph stranded on the verandah.

"Perfect", he said to himself. "Bye, Tanya. Have a nice life."

If Ralph didn't have the responsibility of driving back to Mogololo and organizing the game lodge and looking after guests he probably would have just gone to the nearest bar and had beer after beer until he'd got past caring about his troubles. He was, thankfully, a bit more responsible than that. So first of all he headed for his bank where he needed to have a word with his friend the bank manager about extending his overdraft for just a bit longer.

Fortunately in a little town like Hoedspruit, parking wasn't a problem and he was able to leave his beaten up old 4x4 outside the bank. He breezed into the branch and asked one of the young staff if Frans was in and could he see him?

"Frans?" replied the young bank person. "Oh! You mean Frans Hoffmeyer who used to be manager here? Oh, he was shifted off to Sandton about a month ago."

"Oh, right, " said Ralph. "That's a pity. Who's replaced him then?"

"Mr. Wilson. Shall I ask if he can see you? Who shall I say it is?"

"Henderson," replied Ralph, "Ralph Henderson of Mogololo Lodge, up in Sabi Sands."

"Right, take a seat Mr. Henderson," and the youngster went off into the depths of the offices, away from the customer area. Ralph thought quickly: this wasn't great news. Frans had been a school friend of his and had pulled quite a few strings to help get Ralph's business up and running; someone completely new might not have the same confidence in Ralph's abilities to make a success of the business and make the bank a profit along the way. They might also be an absolute stickler for protocol and awkward about some of Ralph's rather cavalier approaches to deadlines and timetables of repayments.

The young bank person came back into the banking area with someone who reminded Ralph of his head teacher at school. His heart sank.

"Mr. Henderson?" said the very prim and proper headmasterly bank manager, "I'm Henry Wilson, I'd be happy to give you five minutes, would you like to come into my office?"

Ralph was kicking himself for walking straight into this. He should have phoned first to see if Frans could see him. How was he to know Frans had been kicked a rung or two up the corporate banking ladder?

They entered a completely characterless, bland bank office, Mr. Wilson waving at a chair for Ralph while he settled behind his desk. "Mogololo Game Lodge, young Emily said, is that right?"

"That's me," said Ralph, hoping a smile might help win him over, "Founder, principal, 99% shareholder and head bush guide."

"Hmmm," replied Mr. Wilson, not overly impressed, "I'll just pull up your account details." He bashed away at his keyboard and concentrated on what came up on his screen.

Ralph pushed his sales pitch a little further, "We're still pretty new. We're going after a market that appreciates a very experienced, personal service, yet one which concentrates on the real essence of the bush. We're not promising spas, massages or plunge infinity pools. We give our guests a cracking good time in fabulous bush country and, so far, we've been getting good feedback."

"Hmmmm," repeated Mr. Wilson, still not bowled over by Ralph's presentation. "I see you've been drawing considerably more in cash than you've been banking from your bookings. How long is that likely to continue?"

"Ah. Yes, last month was a bit down on occupancy," admitted Ralph, "But we have two guests coming in today for three nights and next month is looking promising."

"You're not going to make money on just two guests every now and then, Mr. Henderson," admonished Mr. Wilson. "I see you are already at the limit of your overdraft. I hope you weren't going to look for a further advance, as I'm afraid the bank's position would be not to look favourably upon such a request."

Ralph thought to himself, 'What do you know about running a game lodge you stuffy old fart?' but he refrained from using language like that and put on his best, people-friendly smile. "I'm not exactly asking for more," explained Ralph, "But I was hoping we could agree to me postponing my scheduled repayment for a couple of weeks. I have actually put considerable cost saving measures in place this week. I've decided to dispense with the services of one of my senior hospitality managers, so the payroll will be reduced in future."

Ralph let this news sink in, silently patting himself on the back for turning Tanya's departure into something this walking calculator would approve of, although he hadn't a clue how he was going to manage without Tanya's special skills and touches.

"That's good to hear," said Mr. Wilson. "Cost reductions are an excellent policy when you have an overdraft as large as yours. Look, it's not in the bank's interest to see you fail, so I'll give you another 10 days to get the scheduled payment into the account, but I suggest we meet again in three weeks time to give me an update on your progress. I'd appreciate seeing your balance sheet, forecasts and business plan as well, if you could email all that to me, perhaps?"

With that, Mr. Wilson stood and extended a limp hand towards Ralph, indicating the interview was over and Ralph should mind himself in future, straighten his school tie and make sure he delivered his homework on time, and no more smoking behind the store sheds.

'Pompous prat,' Ralph thought to himself as he took the soft Wilson hand and forced a smile. "Thank you Mr. Wilson, I'll get on it as soon as I get back to the lodge."

Back out on the street, Ralph let out a sigh of frustration and kicked at the knobbly tyre of his 4x4. "Bloody banks!" he said, to nobody in particular.

His next task was the list of supplies he and Miriam had put together, at least that would take his mind off Mr.

Wilson the weasel, so he set off for the big supermarket on the edge of town.

The third thing that contrived to make Ralph's bad day even worse happened in the supermarket. His shopping list was quite comprehensive, Mogololo needed lots of things to keep it running: the food, the cleaning stuff, the toilet rolls, the booze (most lodge visitors liked a drink at sundown, and often quite a few more to toast the night skies, too). Ralph collected a trolley and started working his way up and down the aisles; it wasn't particularly methodical, of course, he wasn't used to the layout of modern supermarkets and was bemused as to why they didn't have a special section just for game lodges? Then he spent ages trying to track down some of the more obscure items, and as he was looking, he kept tossing odd things that caught his eye into the trolley. Quite soon, he discovered he had chosen the trolley with the wonky wheel. It wasn't evident when the trolley was empty and feather-light to push but the more he piled into it the heavier it got and the more uncontrollable to steer. Ralph's mood darkened with every tin, bottle, packet and product he added to the trolley's groaning load. It was also getting so piled high with the boxes, cans, packets and bottles that Ralph's shopping was in danger of toppling out of the trolley. So, in attempting to steer his by now uncontrollable vehicle around the end of an aisle it was inevitable that disaster would strike.

And it did.

To be fair to Ralph, the person he struck was crouched down at the time, way below Ralph's eyeline, trying to find a bag of caster sugar amongst rows and rows of granulated.

"Ow! Shit!" squealed the crouched-down person, now trying to defend herself from toppling packets of cornflakes and pasta that rained down from Ralph's overfull trolley.

"I'm so sorry!" cried Ralph, rushing round to see whom he had collided with and how bad the damage was. "Are you OK? Let me help you up."

"No! Haven't you done enough already? Ouch!" Ralph quickly took in that his unintended victim was a female; in her late twenties he guessed, was very pretty and was very mad. At him.

"I'm really sorry. I seem to have won the booby prize of the unsteerable trolley. The bloody thing's got a mind of its own. Are you OK though?" asked Ralph, very solicitously.

The girl checked the bits that were hurting: an ankle, her elbow, her pride. "Nothing's broken, might have a bruise or two. Bit of a shock, that's all." By now she had got over the initial impact of the collision and was standing up, fussing with her bobbed, blonde hair and brushing down her jeans and T shirt to remove any supermarket dust and dirt that she imagined might have found its way on to her clothes. Ralph didn't see any and thought he'd better stop looking at what he had noticed was a very good looking body under the clothes. In fact, everything about this girl was making a very big and very good impression on all of Ralph's senses. She was so petite, neat and almost elfin-like, yet there was an obvious strength inside. She also had the bluest eyes Ralph could ever remember seeing.

"You'll have guessed I'm not that good at shopping. I don't usually have to do it," he stumbled on, thinking of something else to say. "Don't suppose you know where the chutneys are, do you?"

"Next aisle, middle shelf," said the girl. "If you don't normally do the shopping, why are you buying so much?"

"Oh, it's not just for me," explained Ralph. "I run a game lodge and, er, we're one person short on the team at the moment and as I was coming in to town, I got lumbered with the shopping today."

Ralph decided he should attempt to prolong this encounter, "Look," he started, "I've had a bitch of a day so far and I haven't helped by bashing you over. Would you please let me buy you coffee; as a sort of a peace offering?"

"Coffee's over there, on the next aisle," she replied. "Am I turning into your personal supermarket guide or something?"

"No, I meant a cup of coffee."

The girl softened, and smiled, "Of course you did. I was just teasing." She looked at her watch. "OK, I don't have another appointment until two, and I think I deserve a cup of coffee after what you've done to me."

"Great, there's a place across the street, isn't there?"

"I know, my mother owns it, so you'd better be on your best behaviour."

Ralph bowed gallantly from the waist, "Naturally. I'll just get this lot paid for and loaded in my car. See you in a couple of minutes?"

The coffee shop was a little too twee for Ralph's taste, rather too much checked gingham curtains and table cloths and fussy, floral cushions but the girl was there ahead of him and confirmed her attachment to the place in the way she was helping her mother behind the counter. She waved Ralph over to a corner table by a window, finished off serving a customer, then came across to Ralph. He stood, politely, and extended a hand.

"I'm Ralph Henderson," he said, very formally, "Mogololo Game Lodge, on the Sabi Sands concession."

"Ella Moffat," said the girl, "physiotherapist and part time waitress at the Crumbs Coffee Shop."

"Really?" said Ralph. "A proper physiotherapist?"

"What d'you mean, 'proper'? Of course I'm proper! D'you want to see my certificates?"

"No, sorry!" said Ralph, "I just didn't realise there was a physio in town?"

"Nor do many other people. Business isn't exactly brisk,

shall we say," replied Ella. "Look, what sort of coffee do you want?"

"Oh, double espresso please."

Ella went off to play with the great shiny Italian coffee-making contraption, and Ralph was aware of a rather matronly woman eyeing him suspiciously. Obviously Ella's mother, thought Ralph, so he gave her what he hoped was a winning smile. She sniffed, hunched her shoulders dismissively and went about emptying cups and saucers from the dishwasher.

Ella came back with coffees.

"Don't think your mother approves of me," whispered Ralph.

"Oh, she's very protective of me," said Ella. "I told her I'd been mugged by a bloke in the supermarket but then he'd repented and promised to give up mugging people and was going to give all his money away to the poor and work as a nurse in a leper colony. After he'd bought me a cup of coffee, of course."

"Thanks," said Ralph, "that's a great first impression I haven't just made."

Ella giggled, "Sorry, I couldn't help it. She's very harmless really. But why were you having such a shit day? Before you bumped into me, of course."

Ralph explained how his now ex-girlfriend had left him in the lurch at the game lodge, embellishing the drama of the monkey raid on the kitchen and making it much funnier the longer the story got, then he explained his awkward interview at the bank and the worries he had about keeping Mogololo's head above water financially and all he really wanted to do was carry on sharing his love of the bush with others who would also appreciate it and then he realised he was rambling on and apologized to Ella. What he hadn't noticed was that while he was talking she was totally wrapped up in his story and had blanked out the rest of the café, the town, and the world, and was absorbing all that Ralph was saying. When Ralph stumbled to his unexpected halt and apologised that he was boring her, she shook herself out of the trance.

"No!" she said, "don't apologise. I think what you are doing is fantastic, important and you must succeed. You must!"

Ralph smiled, "Well, that's very good of you to think that. I'm glad someone agrees with me, anyway."

"I was brought up here and so I've always had the bush on my doorstep but I haven't really made that much use of it. But the way you've just been speaking about it makes it sound so wonderful. I feel I want to find out more."

"Ask away," said Ralph, pleased that he hadn't been boring this girl after all."Well first of all, what went wrong with your relationship with whatshername?"

"Oh, Tanya? Isn't hindsight wonderful," started Ralph. "Now I can see we were never going to last as a couple. It started off fine: a physical thing, I suppose. And she did have some good ideas about furnishings and stuff but she was never comfortable in the bush; too far from a hairdresser or a restaurant with crisp white linen napkins.'

"Nothing to do with living with a man who's not safe to be in charge of a shopping trolley?" asked Ella, with a big twinkle in her eye.

"Yeah, OK. I was...am...a bit single-minded, I suppose. But it comes with the territory of trying to run a game lodge, keep our heads above water, keep the guests happy and keep the staff on their toes."

"So Tanya got a bit neglected then?"

"In her eyes, yes, I suppose she must have thought that. But I was hoping for a bit more flexibility on her part, too. Anyway, enough of Tanya. She's history."

"Good. Look forward. That's what I'm always telling my physio patients," said Ella.

"Physio?" queried Ralph. "Are you sure you don't deal in phsychology, too?"

"Sometimes there's a bit of both," explained Ella. "I can help sort out muscles and tendons, but there are occasions when having the right attitude and positive approach is part of the healing process."

"I can relate to that," said Ralph. "I'm a 'glass half full' man myself."

"So what are you doing to promote the lodge?' asked Ella.

"Probably not enough," sighed Ralph. "With my tiny budget I haven't got the money to advertise overseas. I've been relying on the tourist board but they're not exactly pro-active on my behalf, and I've got a couple of travel agent contacts in Joburg who are supposed to give me bookings, but they haven't been breaking down my door with customers. Do you want to walk up and down with a sandwich board for me?"

"Can't imagine that would work. But let me think about who I know who might be able to help," said Ella.

"Well that would be nice," said Ralph. "What you must do, of course, is come and visit Mogololo. As my guest, of course."

Ella pondered Ralph's offer, for a moment, weighing up what she was rushing into, then realized she was a grown up, she had free will, she was a lady of the world and could make her own balanced, rational decisions. "Oh, that would be fab!" she gushed. Then she realised she sounded like an excited teenager, drooling over a popstar, "I'll have to check the appointment diary for my patients, of course," attempting to add a degree of seriousness and professionalism.

Ralph carefully wrote his phone number on a paper napkin for her, adding some basic directions on how to get to the lodge.

"Now," he said, "I think my vast overdraft can just manage to pay for our coffees, then I must get back to the Lodge, it's a bit over an hour's drive from here."

Ella also coyly gave Ralph one of her physiotherapist cards. "There, that's my phone number and email," she said. "Do phones and emails work at Mogololo?"

"I don't tell clients, but yes, they do. If I climb up to the top of the rock behind the store room I can just get a mobile signal and the landline is normally pretty reliable, as long as the copper wires haven't been nicked or the elephants haven't pushed the poles over."

There was an awkward moment when Ralph didn't know whether they were still at handshake stage or had they progressed to cheek kissing? He thought handshake was probably best. "And I'm so, so sorry about crashing into you in the supermarket," he added.

"So you should be!" grinned Ella. "But I hope your day gets better from now on."

"Oh it's managed a huge improvement already," said Ralph.

On his drive back to Mogololo Ralph had a lot to think about: his encounter with his new bank manager, the way his relationship with Tanya had ended, where more bookings for Mogololo were going to come from…but most of all, he thought about Ella. After not the best of starts, they seemed to click, and Ella, unlike Tanya, seemed to enjoy hearing about the Lodge and its challenges. But priorities first! Ralph needed to concentrate on getting Mogololo into profit, and that meant more bookings. While he was still cruising down the tar road, before turning off for the last dozen or so kilometres of dirt, he had a bit of a brainwave.

Email! Ella had asked if the lodge had email, of course it did, nearly all his guests confirmed their arrivals or asked questions via email. He thought he should write an email to all his previous clients, inviting them for a return trip to Mogololo, and offering a ten percent discount, perhaps. And also getting those past clients to introduce their friends to come and stay at Mogololo, also for a ten percent discount. Seemed to make sense, and what he lost on the ten percent, he knew he would more than make up on the beers and wines he would be able to charge for at sundowner and dinner time. Well, at least it was a plan.

Creating the wording for the email in his head as he drove, Ralph very nearly missed what was one of the most spectacular, and quite rare, occurrences in the bush. Just a little way off the side of the dirt road a blackbellied korhaan was in the process of performing its mating display. A slender bird with long legs and long neck but otherwise fairly insignificant compared with many other of Africa's spectacular bird varieties, the male would try to impress the female with his daredevil aerial display. From a standing start, the male bird launches himself into the air, flies up to around twenty or thirty metres and then, as if shot by some invisible silent hunter, tumbles, uncontrollably, from the sky, only to miraculously open his wings at the very last second and land on the point where he started. Impressed, Mrs. Blackbellied Korhaan? No? OK, I'll do it over and over again until you are!

Ralph watched, mesmerised for a few more moments,

thinking perhaps he should try something like it himself to impress Ella; then, in a considerably better mood than when he had left the lodge in the morning, he arrived back and parked his battered old 4x4 in the shade, noticing a strange vehicle in the space he normally used himself.

His good mood wasn't going to last.

"Oh, Mr Ralph!" It was Grace, Edison's wife who came running up to him. "We have a visitor. A visitor I wish we did not have."

"Hey, Grace," said Ralph, "What's happened? Who is it?"

"It is a man from the council. I man I know and do not like. He is not a good person," said Grace, in a very conspiratorial voice.

"OK, who is he and where is he?" asked Ralph.

"Wilfred Nokwe, from the district council," explained Grace. "He is on the verandah, drinking tea. He asked for beer but I asked Miriam to make him tea."

"And where's Edison?" asked Ralph.

"He took the two new guests on a game drive, about an hour ago, just before this Nokwe arrived," said Grace. "Be careful around him Mr Ralph, do not trust him!" she added, in a whisper. "I knew him from school, where he was the leader of a nasty gang."

"OK," said Ralph. "I'll see what he wants."

Very quietly, Ralph approached the verandah of the main

lodge, making sure he could see the visitor before the visitor could see him. He saw a big man, fat through dedicated over-indulgence rather than just having been born big. His suit was a little too tight for him, as was the not-too-clean shirt he wore. Ralph could see the back of his head; it was one of those heads that had successive rolls of fat where a normal neck would be. Not pleasant. Slumped in one of the verandah's low chairs he was busily boring into his nostril with a forefinger and then examining the results carefully before wiping his finger on his trouser leg. He had the air of someone used to getting his own way, a bully, Ralph thought.

"Mr. Nokwe," Ralph said, quite loudly. "I'm Ralph Henderson."

The big man, stirred, made an attempt at rising out of the chair, failed the first time, but then with a big effort managed to push himself upright, "Ah, Mr. Henderson, yes, I am Wilfred Nokwe, Cabinet Member, Mpumalanga Council."

"And how can I help you Mr. Nokwe?"

"It might be that I am the one who can help you, Mr Henderson. Your game lodge is very attractive Mr. Henderson. Very attractive. Is business good?"

"It could be better," Ralph replied, still waiting for the man to explain why he was visiting.

"Well, perhaps I can help with that," said Nokwe.

"In what way?" asked Ralph, with a strong suspicion that

he knew the answer.

"Well I had some business to attend to down the road with one of your neighbours, and I had heard of your lodge, so I thought I would introduce myself," explained the big man, very smoothly. "In the Mpumalanga Council I work very closely with the tourism department. I can introduce you to some wealthy guests. I am well connected, you know."

"I'm sure you are, Mr. Nokwe," said Ralph, knowing where this was leading.

"Oh yes, being a senior member of the council means I have a wide circle of influential friends," Nokwe said. "But a public servant's salary is quite low and I have a large family to support. So if your lodge was to put me on a retainer each month, I would be happy to recommend my friends visit your lodge rather than any of the others in the area."

"And, of course," said Ralph, "You would not be saying the same thing to any of the neighbouring game lodges, would you?"

"Mr. Henderson!" exclaimed the big man feigning an expression of shocked surprise, "It is you I am talking to, is it not?"

"Hmmm," replied Ralph, "I'm not entirely convinced of your loyalty, although I can clearly see your rather transparent motivation." He now wanted to get rid of this man as soon as he could. "Well thank you for visiting Mr. Nokwe, but I'd prefer to find clients my own way, I think."

"Your operating license will come up for renewal some time in the next twelve months. It would be difficult for you if there were some problems getting it approved...?"

"My license is with the National Parks Board, not Mpumalanga Council," said Ralph, "Now I think our meeting is over."

The big black man huffed and puffed, "You will be sorry for this decision, Mr. Henderson. It will go badly for you."

"I'll get by," said Ralph, and he walked off the verandah, heading for his little office, more angry with Nokwe's threat than worried by it. Throughout his adult life, he had abided by a moral code learned from his father: be master of your own future rather than be beholden to others. His father had been rather an old fashioned liberal, often at odds with the ultra right wing Afrikaaner government of South Africa, and scrupulously fair in his dealings with his team of black staff workers. He had been a strong role model for Ralph; Ralph had never shared his love of cattle, but he always appreciated the freedom his father had given him while he was growing up, indulging him when Ralph wanted to keep a menagerie of orphaned animals, snakes and birds. It was only now he was fully grown up himself that he appreciated how tough it must have been for his father bringing up a boy all on his own after his mother had tragically died when he was an infant. Tough life lessons indeed, but in this particular subject, Ralph had been an excellent student.

Ralph was still in this rather reflective mood when Grace came to quietly knock on the door of his cupboard of an office. "Has he gone?" she asked anxiously.

"Going, certainly," said Ralph. "And I hope he never comes back. What did he do at school that makes you dislike him so much?"

"He was in class with my brother," said Grace. "He was a bully then, and he and his gang used to hurt my brother and his friends and steal their food. The teachers did nothing to stop him."

"Well he can't bully me. Anyway, Grace, I just want to say a big thank you for helping out. I'll try and find someone to do Tanya's job, but you filling in until that happens is really great. Edison's really lucky to have you, so are we!" Grace blushed and giggled, "Oh,MrRalphie," she said, "As long as you keep me away from that Nokwe man, I'm happy."

Chapter Three

Life at Mogololo carried on its pattern of a few guests arriving, staying two or three nights, being enthralled by the experience of getting immersed into the ways of the bush, close to potentially dangerous wildlife, learning from Ralph and Edison's deep knowledge of their environment, and then leaving, to be replaced by new incomers and the rhythm of game drives, sundowners, night time tales, peaceful sunrises continued in its steady and satisfying circle.

It was some two weeks since the visit of the gross Mr. Wilfred Nokwe. Ralph hadn't exactly forgotten about him but he had filed him away in the back of his mind. Grace was proving to be an excellent front-of-house hostess although Edison wasn't so happy that his wife's attention was now divided between being the smiling face of the game lodge and being his wife. Edison was rather old-fashioned like that, but his loyalty to Ralph was as strong as his devotion to Grace, so he didn't bring up the subject with either Grace or Ralph.

The hinted-at conflict between Miriam and Grace hadn't materialised, or not that Ralph had noticed; Miriam was actually relieved that Ralph hadn't asked her to take on more responsibility. As long as she was up to her elbows in flour, making cakes and baking bread she was happy. And Grace was steadily overcoming her shyness and reticence at greeting new people. But she did keep asking Ralph how he was progressing with finding a more permanent front-of-house person.

Ralph had put the word out around some of the other private game lodges that he was looking for someone to be responsible for the hospitality side of Mogololo but so far no one among the few people he'd seen was quite right. He was secretly hoping that Grace would really like to carry on being the temporary manager, but he also didn't want to upset Edison.

Coming back from his morning game drive with four happy guests on board, all of them now looking forward to one of Miriam's legendary breakfasts, Ralph saw an unfamiliar car parked outside the homestead. It was the sort of car the police used. Ralph cheerily encouraged his guests to freshen up and make their way to breakfast, then he went looking for whoever had arrived in that car.

There were two of them, and yes, they were policemen; a young, uniformed constable and an evidently more senior officer in plain clothes. He was overweight, perspiring, and Ralph imagined he was the type likely to have high blood pressure and be a potential diabetes sufferer. The young constable drew the attention of the other man to Ralph's approach.

"Ah, you must be Mr. Henderson," he said, "I am Inspector Thoko Masiwa, Hoedspruit Police."

"Good morning, Inspector," said Ralph, "What can I do for you?"

The inspector didn't answer Ralph's question immediately. There was an arrogance about him Ralph didn't like, the way he was pulling and stroking his earlobe in an absent-minded manner, weighing up whether he was going to bother to speak or not.

"Well now, Mr. Henderson," he eventually began, "I am a personal friend of Mr. Wilfred Nokwe, he came to see you a couple of weeks ago."

"Mr. Wilfred Nokwe came looking for a handout," answered Ralph, "and I was disinclined to give him one."

"'Disinclined', yes that's an interesting word," said the policeman. "It implies a certain degree of refusal but perhaps not a permanent rejection."

"Oh, it was permanent all right," said Ralph firmly, "I'm not in the habit of bribing public officials, or being bullied by them."

"Mr. Nokwe did not see it that way," Masiwa said, "He was talking of a more business-focused arrangement."

"It was a feeble attempt at getting cash out of me and I wasn't having any of it," said Ralph, "And what's it got to do with you?"

"Oh, think of me as an envoy, Mr. Henderson," said the Inspector, "An ambassador to encourage you to consider the future of your enterprise."

"Inspector Masiwa," said Ralph very firmly, "I hope you didn't come all this way just to deliver an unwanted message from your fat friend. You've had a wasted trip."

The Inspector refused to rise to Ralph's dismissive tone,

"Oh I have to co-ordinate with the anti-poaching team in the Park; we've received some intelligence that I need to discuss with them."

"You've made quite a detour if you're heading into the Park," Ralph commented. "We're clear of poaching in our area; we all check regularly for the signs."

"But the poachers are getting cleverer and cleverer," the Inspector said, smugly. "You never know when they will strike. It would be to your benefit to co-operate with me to ensure your guests do not get upset by the aftermath of a poacher's kill."

"I don't believe I am obstructing you in your duty, Inspector," Ralph said.

"There is co-operation and co-operation," the Inspector replied, very cryptically.

"Are you inferring that I should 'co-operate' with you in the way your friend Mr Nokwe wanted? Bribing you? Protection money, or would you call it insurance? Cash in brown envelopes every time you visit?"

"I would hope we can be professional in these arrangements, Mr Henderson."

"There are no arrangements, Inspector! Not now, not in the future, not ever. Got it?" Ralph fumed. "Now I have some guests to look after. You know the way out."

The young constable who was with the Inspector looked deeply embarrassed. He was not used to seeing his boss spoken to like that, and the Inspector himself, with nothing left to say to Ralph barked at the poor frightened young man to get in the car and he stormed off, with the constable trotting behind him.

Ralph watched him leave, then walked on to the homestead verandah to make sure his guests were being spoiled by Miriam and one of her magic breakfasts.

He joined the two British couples who were working their way through a mountain of scrambled egg, bacon and mushrooms, with Miriam fussing around them like an old mother hen, offering more toast, coffee, orange juice, jams, marmalades, and everything else she could think of. Ralph held himself back and had just one slice of toast. If he wasn't careful, he would indulge every morning and end up the size of that loathsome Wilfred Nokwe or even Inspector Masiwa.

The breakfast time conversation covered all sorts of wildlife, bush, flora and fauna questions that Ralph was so polished at answering, providing just the right amount of information without blinding his audience with too many scientific facts or even boring the pants off them. They were all on their second or third cups of coffee when Ralph noticed one of the men was holding his head in a slightly strange position and occasionally rubbing his neck quite vigorously.

"George," he started, "Got a neck problem? You seem to be in a bit of discomfort."

"Oh, I don't think my head's going to fall off or anything," said George. "But it does seem to be getting stiffer and stiffer."

His wife, Alice, said very sympathetically, "I think you must have just slept awkwardly, dear."

George now owned up to his real condition, "No, I think it's a bit more than that. I feel as though I've really tweaked something. But I don't want to make a fuss."

"If you'd like," started Ralph, "I happen to know a physiotherapist in Hoedspruit. I was looking for an excuse to invite her out to Mogololo. Would you like me to give her a call?"

"Oh I think a couple of Ibuprofen will sort it out, won't it dear?" volunteered Alice.

"I wouldn't mind," said George, dismissing his wife's offer of pills.

"I'll go to the office and give her a call," said Ralph, enormously pleased with himself for finding an excuse to get in touch with Ella – an excuse that was professional rather than just ringing her up for a date like an over-eager teenager.

Fortunately for Ralph (and George with the sore neck) Ella was free the following day so she agreed to make a "house" call by driving out to Mogololo to look at George's problem and possibly give him some treatment.

"I'm not sure what I'll be able to do in one session," she

guardedly told Ralph when she had got over the surprise of Ralph's call and listening to the symptoms George was showing. "I'd be happy to give it a try though."

"And it is a good excuse for you to come and see Mogololo," added Ralph.

"There is that," agreed Ella. "You won't be in charge of any shopping trolleys though, will you?"

"Not even a wire basket," promised Ralph.

Ella was the epitome of professionalism when she arrived at the Lodge, complete with a small suitcase full of the bits and pieces that were essential to a physio's life. She was dressed in a crisp white uniform of tunic and trousers, but expressed her individuality with a pair of the brightest dayglow orange canvas shoes Ralph had ever seen. Ralph, secretly delighted that he had an excuse to talk to Ella again, and had put on his very best clean bush shirt and shorts that morning, made the introductions between George and Ella and suggested they went off to George and Alice's bungalow to see what could be done to ease George's discomfort.

Ralph fussed around the camp, pretending to be busy while George was being pushed, pulled, prodded and massaged. He turned all the bottles on the bar so they were lined up properly, with labels facing outwards. He polished glasses, he rearranged ornaments, he made sure the visitors' book was open at the space for the next entry, he plumped up cushions that were already fully plumped. "God, I'm behaving like a girl," he told himself.

Thirty five minutes later, George, Alice and Ella emerged and found Ralph on the shaded verandah.

"The girl's a marvel!" announced George.

Ella blushed, "Well, I did my best. You might be a bit sore later, but I think I've eased the problem for you."

"I can't thank you enough," said George and then quite discreetly to Ralph, "Will you add Ella's fee to my bill, Ralph?"

"Oh, sure, yes, no problem," said Ralph, not quite sure of the protocol.

Alice and George said their thank yous and goodbyes to Ella and went off in search of their other friends, leaving Ralph and Ella in a slightly awkward silence on the verandah.

"Well," started Ralph, "You've made a hit there. What did you do?"

"He'd trapped a nerve; a bit of manipulation, massage, he'll be right as rain now. What was he whispering to you?"

"Oh, he wanted to know how enormous your fee was going to be, and if he'd have to sell his wife into slavery to pay it," joked Ralph.

"Well, house calls this far out are usually triple my normal fee, and there's the petrol, and the time to get here…" started Ella, then seeing Ralph thought she was being serious, she laughed, "Oh, goodness, I'm only joking, is five hundred rand OK?"

"Bargain," replied Ralph. "Tell you what, I'll throw in a personal game drive, for free, right now. OK?"

"I thought you'd never ask," said Ella. "I brought my camera and binos just in case."

"Perfect. You go and get them, I have to get some paperwork to the Head Ranger's office in the Park, we can go the roundabout route and see what we find on the way," said Ralph. He picked up a brand new baseball cap with Mogololo's logo discreetly embroidered on it and offered it to Ella, "You'd better have this, too. Courtesy of the management."

It was one of those drives where, if you hadn't known better, you'd have thought Ralph had stage-managed everything just to show off. With Ella sitting beside him, he was able to show her a couple of young bull elephants, pushed out of the herd and not quite ready to challenge the dominant male for the right to breed with

the females. There was a shy honey badger he spotted, not normally seen in the middle of the day. Then there were the birds: carmine bee eaters, lilac-breasted rollers, yellow-billed kites, fish eagles, hornbills and so many more.

Even though she was an all-South African girl, Ella wasn't that familiar with the bush and was fascinated by everything she saw, asking lots of questions and was intrigued by one particular tree she saw.

"Ah, that's an exceptionally nasty one called Euphorbia Damarana," Ralph told her.

"Nasty?" asked Ella, "In what way?"

"It's not normally found here but my dad had this hare-brained idea of raising gemsbok on the farm, some thirty years ago. He imported half a dozen of them from Namibia when it was still South West Africa, and the gemsbok is the only animal that eats the leaves and seed pods from this type of Euphorbia, very common in Namibia. When they arrived, they must have had some seeds in their gut, dropped their dung, the seeds germinated and we've got a few Euphorbia trees on the property. It can be deadly poisonous."

"What, is it poisonous to humans as well as animals?" asked Ella.

"Yup, gemsbok is the only creature that can tolerate it," answered Ralph.

"And the gemsbok who accidentally brought it here?" asked Ella.

"Bad idea of Dad's," Ralph replied. "The lions got them all."

Ella particularly loved giraffes and when they came across a group, Ralph explained the behaviour of one particular couple; there was a large male and a smaller female, sticking really close to each other. "You see how the male is shadowing her every move?" Ralph said, "It's obvious she's getting close to the peak of her fertile season. She's almost ready to mate; he knows it, she knows it, but she teases and teases, leading him on but not quite allowing him to satisfy himself or her. It could go on like this for days."

"Seems like he could do with a cold shower," commented Ella.

"Oh, he knows patience will pay off in the end," said Ralph, leaving his comment to hang in the air, hoping the underlying meaning of his thought would not be lost on Ella.

On the way back from the Head Ranger's office in Kruger Park, and once they were on his own property, Ralph went a slightly different route. He wanted to show Ella the rhino, his rhino, as he liked to think of it. He was pretty confident he knew which area it would be in and they found it on an open plain, contentedly scratching its side on an old tree trunk. His tiny eyes were closed and his face, had it been human, would have shown an expression of pure bliss, as he pushed backwards and forwards, rocking against the stump of the tree.

"His favourite rubbing post," said Ralph. "I often see him here. He's great, isn't he?"

"Magnificent, " agreed Ella, with her camera up to her eye.

They continued watching it for a few moments, the rhino sensing that something or someone had strayed into his territory, but he wasn't too bothered about it, he was having too good a time scratching his crusted hide.

"I'm glad I found him for you," said Ralph, "He's my best animal, I think. I know we shouldn't humanise game like that, but I am very fond of this old boy, I like to tell him my troubles. He's a very good listener!"

"Troubles, Ralph?"

"Running Mogololo really isn't easy, Ella. It's full on, all the time. And with the bank on my back, staff issues, keeping clients happy, remembering to order enough fuel for the vehicles, beer for the bar, toilet rolls for the bathrooms, it never stops."

"Poor Ralph," sympathized Ella. "But can you think of a better place to be miserable?"

Ralph burst out laughing, realizing he was being teased. "OK, I give in. Yes, it is paradise. Now I'm afraid we have to get back, I've got visitors to look after and staff to keep on their toes."

Ella reached across and touched his arm, "Ralph, thank you so much for taking me out and showing me this. It's all so wonderful. I think you're very lucky to have Mogololo."

"Well, we'll have to make sure this isn't your one and only visit, won't we?" said Ralph, leaving the unspoken promise hanging in the hot, African air.

Chapter Four

Life at Mogololo continued in its reassuring and steady African rhythm and Ralph put the visit of Inspector Masiwa out of his mind. He had more important things to manage at the Game Lodge than a grasping policeman, looking for a soft-touch hand out. Things like his staffing problems. Nothing had actually been said but he could sense there was a growing tension between Miriam and Grace, the two key people responsible for his guests' comfort and contentment. He raised his concerns with Edison, while they were cleaning the Land Rover to get ready for an afternoon drive.

"Has Grace said anything to you about the way things are going in the lodge, Edison?"

"You mean is Grace worried Miriam is going to put rat poison in her tea?" Edison chuckled.

"Oh dear, are things not great between them?"

"Well, when Tanya was here, Miriam knew Tanya was the madam and she had to follow her instructions. Now Tana is not here and Grace is in her place, Miriam thinks Miriam should be the one making decisions about the food and dishes for the guests. But Grace says to her that Mr Ralph has put her in charge. Aieee! Two women wanting to be boss! " And with that, Edison collapsed into a fit of giggles.

"Oh, come on Edison!" said Ralph, "What am I going to

do then?"

"Well, you could get the two of them together and get them to talk to you about what they feel. But I bet they wouldn't be really honest with you. Or you could talk to them separately and see what is troubling them. But again, it's unlikely they would really tell you their feelings."

"What would you do?" asked Ralph.

"Well, you know that story how an ostrich is supposed to bury its head in the sand…" started Edison.

"Which isn't true, of course," interrupted Ralph.

"Yes, but do not let the truth get in the way of a good story!" joked Edison. "Perhaps you could just ignore the situation and hope it gets better by itself."

"Don't think that's a very good idea, " said Ralph as he was sloshing water over the mats of the Land Rover to get rid of the worst of the dust. "I thought you Shangaans were supposed to be wise and fair in your dealings with everybody."

"Oh we are," said Edison, very defensively. "But these are women we are talking about, are we not?"

Ralph couldn't help but laugh at Edison's response, and inwardly reflected on the way his friend had neatly avoided being drawn in to the issue, as his own wife, Grace, was involved. No more was said, but Ralph filed away in his mind the instinctive diplomacy his friend had demonstrated in the way he answered, or avoided answering, Ralph's dilemma.

It was one of those lowveld afternoons when the heat descended on you like an unwelcome electric blanket. The air was hardly moving. Even what shade there was offered little respite from the soaring temperature. Gaze at the horizon and the light just shimmered as it teased you with mirages of pools of water that weren't there, or upside down trees, or zebras standing on clouds. The animals and birds were still, sensibly saving energy for when they would all need their wits, reactions and strength. The team at Mogololo went through the motions of doing all that needed to be done to keep the lodge in perfect condition, but even they all felt their energies being sapped by the heat.

Into this baking environment, a new group of visitors arrived at Mogololo. They had booked direct through Ralph's website and there were six of them in total. There's always a moment of anticipation and uncertainty when new guests arrive, especially those who Ralph knew were coming from the city. They are often tired, hot and uncomfortable from a long car journey; they are on unfamiliar territory and unsure of where they should go; they can't decide whether they should unpack their stuff from the car now or leave it a little while as they explore their new surroundings, so Ralph always tried to be there when a party of new guests turn up to put them at their ease and establish a relationship with them right from the start. Of course, it was just as uncertain for Ralph; would he get along with these newcomers? Were they really interested in the bush? Or did they just want to slob around the camp and drink beer all day long?

As he walked towards this group of six as they decanted themselves from a thankfully well-airconditioned minibus, Ralph made a snap decision that this group should be OK. Middle-aged, three men, three women, dressed for the bush…ah! apart from one female who was just a bit out of place.

She looked like she was dressed more for lunch-with-the-ladies than a long weekend in the bush. Her clothes, while understated looked ultra expensive, she jangled with jewellery, bracelets, earrings and her designer handbag was big enough to accommodate most of Ralph's own clothes collection. While the rest of her party bustled around with rucksacks, water bottles, sunglasses and mobile phones, this lady stood, slightly apart and under her wide brimmed and thoroughly impractical sunhat surveying her new surroundings with the air of someone unused to doing much for herself. Ralph forced a welcoming smile onto his face and approached the group.

"Good afternoon everyone!" he said, brimming with genuine good cheer, "And welcome to Mogololo. I'm Ralph Henderson and you must be the Wilson party."

"Ah, yes, Gerry Wilson," said the driver of the minibus, stepping forward to shake Ralph's hand. "My wife Linda, that's Fanie and Esme, Dick and Miranda."

Ralph tried very hard to absorb this barrage of names but knew he would probably fail, "Well, welcome to

Mogololo all of you", he said, "Now, let's get you settled in. Here comes my team, Edison and Grace; Edison, you look after .. er…Fanie and Esme; Grace, you take Dick and Amanda…"

"Miranda!" snapped the lady from underneath her wide-brimmed hat.

"Of course, so sorry, Miranda," apologized Ralph. "…and I'll look after Gerry and Linda."

Bags were unloaded and the couples were led to their respective lodges, with Ralph brightly chatting to Gerry and Linda, while he was secretly hoping that Grace would be OK with prickly Miranda. Ralph had every confidence in Grace, but when confronted with a powerful and potentially confrontational personality such as Miranda, she may find it difficult to know how to handle the situation. Grace was used to the simple life of the bush; the so-called sophistication of someone so evidently from the city might be challenging.

Ralph suggested to the party that they meet a little later for tea on the verandah, then he'd take them all on a game drive. He retreated to his little haven of an office. Before long, however, Grace came to find him. She wasn't happy.

"Ralph," she started, "That lady is very difficult! All she does is criticise. She think we are a five star hotel, not a game lodge. She want special tea brought to her room, she wants me to iron her clothes, she tell me I am not doing my job properly. Then she ask why is there no bath in her room, just outside shower? I say all the lodges have outside shower because most guests like it."

"Good for you, Grace," said Ralph, 'what did she say to that."

"Nothing. She gave me a big sniff and toss her head away and start complaining to her husband about something else."

"Oh dear, poor Grace," said Ralph.

"Well, I would rather not have to deal with persons like this," said Grace. "Ralph, are you going to find someone else to be doing this job I am doing? I do not think it is right for me., and I am not right for this job."

"Oh Grace," said Ralph, "I know I said it would only be temporary, and I did mean it. But finding someone who is right for Mogololo isn't easy, you know. And I really appreciate all that you are doing, I really do."

"And then there is Miriam," added Grace. "I find she is being difficult with me as well."

"Ah," said Ralph, very quickly, "Here come some of the guests, we'll talk about this another time, OK?"

The guests all gathered in the main homestead and Miriam came with a tray of tea and biscuits.

"Have you earl grey tea?" demanded Miranda.

"We have Five Roses and Rooibos, Ma'am," responded Miriam, quoting the local brands of tea. Miranda sniffed and carefully studied her nails.

Ralph thought he had better get to work to settle this new party into life at Mogololo. "Sorry Miranda," he said, "we are a bit out in the sticks here, but Miriam makes fantastic biscuits, I promise they are delicious! Now, I hope you'll all enjoy your tea. I'm just going to get the vehicle ready for our game drive. We'll have a stop for sundowners, so does anyone have any preference for anything apart from beer, wine, gin and tonic, soft drinks?"

Gerry spoke for the group, "Ralph, I'm sure whatever you've got will be fine."

Ralph breathed a sigh of relief and went off to check the Land Rover with Edison.

"Hey, Edison" he said, "We'll have to work hard with this bunch. Grace has already had a problem with Number One lady. She's a bit of a princess, so when we are on the drive, anything you can do to impress her would be appreciated."

"Sure," replied Edison, in his usual, laid back manner. "We'll find something."

Ralph went to round up the party and gave them his usual briefing about what to do if they encountered any of the more dangerous animals: keeping quiet; not putting arms or legs outside the vehicle; not standing up; and reassuring them that he had a rifle, a two-way radio, and lots of experience.

The guests were happy. They climbed into the vehicle, sitting on the tiered seating of the specially adapted Land Rover. Edison took up his normal position on the little seat right perched on the front bumper and Ralph drove.

They went off into the bush and saw most of the usual animals such as zebra, impala, wildebeest, water buck, giraffe and warthog. Ralph was hoping for something more spectacular to impress this group. There was a single elephant, but too far off to see properly. Edison studied the narrow track for spoor but didn't spot anything significant. After an hour and a half, Ralph pulled up at the top of a small hill and stopped the vehicle at his favourite spot for drinks.

Edison helped him set up a table, complete with table cloth, and they set out drinks and snacks. The guests thirstily gathered around. Everyone had a drink apart from Miranda.

"Do you have a Campari and soda?" she haughtily enquired.

"Ah," said Ralph, "Terribly sorry, no. I can do you gin and tonic? Brandy and coke perhaps?"

"Oh, I suppose a gin and tonic will be OK," sighed Miranda.

Ralph poured her drink, making sure she wanted lemon and ice, and offered it with his best smile.

It was a magical part of the day; cooler than it had been earlier and thankfully, the guests were appreciating the lengthening shadows and the changing colours in the sky as sunset approached. It was a magical spot, with wide vistas across the game reserve and the still air was frequently punctuated with bird calls and the alarm bark of baboons. They sipped drinks, chatted and Ralph began to feel that even icy Miranda was beginning to thaw, just a little. Edison was helping with the drinks and passing round snacks and when he thought the guests were sufficiently supplied for the moment, he whispered to Ralph, "You OK on your own for a second?"

"Sure," whispered Ralph in reply, "where you going?"

"Just wait." And Edison slipped away from the party and walked quietly towards the bushes. Ralph continued answering the guests' questions about wildlife, the big five, the dangerous encounters he might have experienced. (Guests always wanted to hear about the near-death experiences, but then needed reassurance they wouldn't have to face them themselves.) Just then he noticed that Edison, now a good 50 metres away, was reaching up into a thick bush. His knowledge of Edison's experience in the wild kicked in, and he inwardly smiled. "Look!" he said to the guests, pointing at Edison.

Edison came walking back to the group, carefully holding his right hand in front of him. Perched on his wrist, a chameleon was balanced, gripping his outstretched finger tightly with the claw of one leg, delicately pointing forward with its other front leg. It was a vivid green, a small crest behind its head and weird, multi-directional eyes that swiveled independently of each other. It was quite calm, making no attempt to escape.

"Ladies and gentlemen," announced Edison, "may I introduce you to my friend, the Chameleon." The guests gathered round, fascinated by Edison's find.

"It's exquisite!" said Miranda, animated for the first time. "How did you find it?"

"Ma'am, I've been around the bush all my life," explained Edison. "I am used to knowing where creatures like to stay, to hide, to live. I spotted this little character in the mopane bush as we stopped. He is an adult chameleon. If we put him on a different background, he might just change colour for us." And with that, Edison offered his arm to Miranda. "It's OK. He won't bite and he grips very gently with his feet." She was a little nervous at first, but Edison encouraged the chameleon to move off his arm and onto hers. Everyone was enthralled by the slow, measured movements the creature made as it rocked backwards and forwards a little, measuring up its new surroundings.

"Let me tell you a story about the chameleon," Edison started, "when the Creator made the earth, he was quite pleased that he made humans, but after a while, he noticed the skins of the people were getting damaged and did not look so good as when he first made them. So he called the chameleon to him and said, 'Here, I want you to take a package to the humans, a gift from me. But do not tell any of the other creatures or they will become envious.' And he gave the chameleon a little parcel. The chameleon rushed off because in those days he could move really fast. On the way, his cousin the snake saw him and called, 'Hey, cousin chameleon, where are you going in such a hurry?' 'Oh, I am on an errand for the Creator, I am delivering a gift to the humans from him,' said the chameleon. 'I must not stop and chat with you.' 'Oh, but it's been so long since we have seen you, my wife will want to give you some supper before you carry on your journey.' Well, the chameleon was quite hungry and he thought he still had plenty of time to deliver the package to the people, so he agreed to go with the snake and have something to eat. True enough, the wife's snake had made a lovely supper but the snake was crafty and he made sure the chameleon had plenty of beer to drink with the food and before long the chameleon was asleep. While he was sleeping, the snake took the package the Creator had given to the chameleon to deliver and discovered it was a set of new skins. 'Oh', said the snake, 'I think we can make use of these smart new skins,' so he and his wife put them on. When the chameleon woke up he was angry that the snake had taken the precious parcel but the snake would not give the new skins back. So the chameleon crept away, afraid and ashamed that he had let the Creator down. And from that day, the chameleon always moves slowly and tries to hide himself by changing colour to match his background. And, also, perhaps that is why people do not like snakes, because the snakes can shed their skins and grow new ones, which is what the Creator had planned for people."

"Oh!" exclaimed Miranda, "that's a delightful story! Thank you so much for telling it. And look, he's no longer just green, he's become a little blue on his body, as well."

"Matching your shirt, Miranda," offered Ralph.

"Now, should I put our friend back where I found him?" asked Edison, putting his arm next to Miranda and encouraging the chameleon to come to him, which it did.

"Do you know," said a smiling Miranda, "For me, that was better than coming face to face with a lion."

"Glad you enjoyed it," said Ralph, "Now come on everybody, back on the vehicle, let's see what else is out there."

Edison was the last one to take his seat, he turned to catch Ralph's eye and they shared a conspiratorial wink between them; a group of happy guests and a sigh of relief for Ralph.

The relief, however, was short-lived. It was dusk when Ralph pulled into the parking space at the Lodge and he urged his guests to go and freshen up and join him for a drink on the terrace before dinner in fifteen minutes or so.

As he walked past the main lodge where dinner always took place he could hear raised voices coming from the kitchen. He walked through and discovered Grace and Miriam facing each other across the vast kitchen table, Miriam clutching a rolling pin like a club and Grace with a frying pan raised above her shoulder.

"You can not tell me what to do in my kitchen!" shouted Miriam.

"I can when I think you are making big catering mistakes!" responded Grace.

"All the guests like my cooking!" screamed Miriam.

"But you have to give them more fresh vegetables and fruit," yelled Grace.

"I don't have to do what you say!" replied Miriam, increasing her volume with every word. "This is my kitchen and you have no authority here!"

"But why won't you listen to reason," pleaded Grace.

"Because the person I am looking at, I do not consider to be reasonable," hissed Miriam.

Ralph intervened, "Shut up, the two of you!" he commanded. "What is going on? I heard you half way across the game reserve!"

"It is this person who thinks she can tell me what to do in my kitchen," snapped Miriam. "I will not be told what to cook by a person who is the shape of a stick insect and obviously knows nothing about food."

"I know a lot about proper balanced diets!" retorted Grace, "And you are giving the guests heart attack foods day after day. You will kill off all of Ralph's guests and give Mogololo a bad reputation with your meat and cream sauces and dumplings and pies!"

"Girls! Enough!" said Ralph, as sternly as he could manage without laughing. "Now stop it, both of you!"

Miriam and Grace both calmed down a little at Ralph's admonishment. "That's better," said Ralph, "Now, I know what this is really all about. You both need someone to replace Tanya, don't you? Well I'm sorry it's taking so long, but you've made me realise I must try harder to find someone. In the meantime, Grace, perhaps it's better if you do leave Miriam in charge of menus and the food preparation. And Miriam, you are doing a really great job and everyone loves your food…but perhaps a few more salads and green vegetables might be an idea? Just as an option?   Grace, I know you're under a lot of pressure and I appreciate that you're not completely happy doing the 'front-of-house' job, but it's really good for me to know you're there until I can find the right person to step in. Is that OK girls?"

Both ladies looked a bit sheepish and nodded. Grac"Riughtquietly put down the frying pan on the kitchen table and Miriam replaced the rolling pin in the big pot where she kept most of her cooking utensils. "Right," said Ralph. "Quick shower and change for me, and then there are guests' drinks to look after. Grace, I'm counting on you to keep up the good work that Edison started on the game drive. He was a marvel and the difficult lady you met earlier has turned into a pussy cat. Trust me!"

Chapter Five

During dinner with the guests that evening, Ralph operated on autopilot. He was his normal affable and attentive self, helping guests to drinks and passing dishes down the table, but his mind was wrestling with the problems he was having with the women in his life, particularly Grace and Miriam. He smiled inwardly at the thought that he never had such issues or problems with animals, and his relationship with Edison was forever solid. They could have days when they never said a word to each other, but they didn't need to. There was mutual trust and respect, with no egos or personal agendas getting in the way. But women! There was the Tanya situation that had left him high and dry, there was the difficult Miranda client whom Edison had single-handedly managed to charm and win round, but who might there be causing disruptions in his life tomorrow? Next week? Next month?

He snapped himself back to reality and his task to keep the smiles on his guests' faces and ensure their experience at Mogololo was all he had promised it would be. He believed passionately in what he was doing: his love of the bush, the sights, smells and experiences of the privileged life he led sharing this wonderful place, first with nature itself and then with his guests. He so wanted to make a success of the farm his father had struggled with all his life; the dusty, unforgiving land was ingrained in his skin, but he wasn't prepared to put up with the problems of being a cattle farmer and hence his move to make the land work for him as a game lodge, where he was able to encourage wildlife to share his territory (though he readily admitted it was always theirs in the first place and he was the newcomer intruder) and, hopefully, make a living at the same time.

It was the 'making-a-living' part that was proving difficult. Bookings at Mogololo were steady but not spectacular, there was extra capacity to fill and after Ralph's run-in with his new bank manager he knew he had to do something to make the figures look better, but even before that, he had to stop the bickering between Grace and Miriam and get someone to take over the meeting-and-greeting role. But who?

It was Edison who gave Ralph the nudge he needed. In the soft and chilled atmosphere of dawn, he and Ralph were getting the vehicle ready for the guests' early morning drive.

"What happened to that nice lady who came here a couple of weeks ago? The physio who sorted out one of the guests who had a stiff neck?" he asked.

"Ella?" replied Ralph, startled that Edison had brought up the subject. "Why

"Oh, it just seemed that you were rather impressed by hr, that's all," grinned Edison.

"Impressed?" blustered Ralph, taken aback by Edison's perception, "Well I don't know much about physiotherapy but she certainly helped out, er … what was his name?"

"George," said Edison, "but that wasn't the way I thought

she made an impression on you."

"Well she was a very impressive physio. Not that I know much about physios, mind you."

"It was more the chemistry between the two of you that seemed to have made its mark."

"You wouldn't be trying to influence my personal life, would you Edison?" said Ralph, trying to deflect the interrogation.

"Well it's about time somebody did," retorted Edison. "Now, you'd better get these guests of yours organized for this game drive." And he walked off, cheerily whistling, *'The bells are ringing for me and my gal…'*.

The morning drive was a fabulous experience. The guests were all in the same relaxed mood as the previous evening and even Miranda had retained her sense of humour and, of course, Edison was now her favourite person in the world. She insisted on sitting in front, next to Ralph so she could be the first to sense Edison's game-spotting skills from his tiny seat right at the exposed front of the vehicle.

"Is he really safe perched out there in the front?" she whispered to Ralph.

"Well, I haven't managed to kill him off yet," replied Ralph, "And we've been doing this for a while now. No, Edison knows the bush better than anybody. And he has a healthy respect, too. If we came across a particularly awkward elephant, or lions that were defending their young, he'd come in the vehicle with us pretty quickly. But out there at the point, he's in the best place to scan the bush for us. He's not too happy if I go charging through thorn bushes without letting him know first! But Edison and I grew up together; he's like the brother I never had."

"So lucky," responded Miranda wistfully, "to have a relationship like that."

Their conversation stopped there as Edison had spotted something through the scrubby mopane trees. He held up his hand to get Ralph to slow down and pointed off to his left. Ralph quietly stopped the vehicle and looked through his binoculars, not sure what it was Edison had spotted. Edison's focus was locked onto something 80 or so metres into the bush. He pointed, helping Ralph follow his line of sight.

"Got it!" he said, as much to himself as the guests who were straining to see what Edison had spotted, but didn't know what to look for. Ralph turned to speak softly to them all. "About 80 metres off the track, by that pointy termite mound, there's a family of wild dogs. I've spotted four, there may be more. They're normally very shy and there are very few of them in the reserve, so we're incredibly lucky to see them. Can you all spot them now?"

One or two of the guests were straining to see what Edison and Ralph had seen, but when their eyes eventually managed to separate the bushes and the grass from the animals, they were elated and thrilled. Ralph offered his binoculars to Miranda and directed her where to look. "Oh!" she squealed with delight, "there's babies, too! Two of them! Oh, Edison! Thank you for finding them for us!"

Edison smiled back, humbly acknowledging her thanks, but saying nothing. Ralph, happy that they had managed to find something extra special for the guests, also said nothing, but his thoughts played back the time he had been driving with Ella and they'd come across the rhino, and the way Ella had responded with such joy at the sighting. He determined that yes, he would get in touch and maybe, just maybe, if her physiotherapy wasn't keeping her as busy as she wanted, she just might like to become involved with Mogololo?

The guests bombarded Ralph with questions about wild dogs: what did they eat? How many puppies in a litter? How long before the young can fend for themselves? How far do they roam? Is there one alpha male or do all the males get to mate as they like? As Ralph was fielding the questions and telling all he knew about wild dogs, their habits, the colourings on their coats, how the Africans relate to them, he thought how strange it was that most of the questions revolved around sex. Some basic human instinct for curiosity about other species, he supposed, but it brought into focus how non-existent his own sex life currently was. He smiled wryly to himself and was about to start the car and move on when Miranda caught his eye.

"What's that private grin for Ralph?" asked Miranda.

"Oh, not so private really," said Ralph, "Just coming to a big personal decision I suppose."

"Really?" probed Miranda, sounding very intrigued.

"Mmmm," continued Ralph. "I was wondering whether I would go for fried eggs or scrambled, at breakfast this morning. I've decided on fried!" And with that he started the Land Rover, gave Miranda a winning smile and thought to himself, 'I'm damned if I'm sharing my private life with this princess!'

After breakfast that morning, with the guests happily settled into their books, their conversations, their sunbathing, birdwatching or just sitting and soaking in the bush atmosphere, Ralph took his mobile phone up onto the hill behind the kitchen, the only place in Mogololo where the cellular signal had a chance of reaching this remote part of South Africa. As he trudged up through the rocks he was nagging himself that he really ought to do something about improving the communications – he piggybacked on one of his friendly neighbours for an internet connection, he had a two way radio that linked into the National Parks Board system, but otherwise he felt pretty cut off. The trouble was, he knew it would be expensive to get decent connections, money he currently didn't have. So he continued his climb, checking the screen of his phone until the screen confirmed that he had one bar, two bars, yes! three bars of signal strength. Enough to make a call.

"Hello, this is Ella Moffatt. I'm sorry I can't take your call right now, but if you'd like to leave a message or make an appointment for a treatment, please talk after the beep and I'll get back to you, Thank you."

The beep sounded, Ralph spluttered and hesitated, he'd built himself up for a real conversation, not a disembodied statement into an electronic memory. "Oh, hi. Ella. This is Ralph. Ralph Henderson? Mogololo? I just wondered how you were getting on, you must be busy with lots of patients, I suppose. Anyway. I'd like to talk to you about something, just an idea I had. It's difficult to get a signal out here, I'll try and call you again. Bye."

He stared at the screen of his phone as if it was to blame. "Pathetic!" he told himself. "Worse than a love-struck teenager. No wonder I'm turning into a sad impression of a monk." He stood on the top of the hill, idly wondering how the Afrikaans language managed to turn "hill" into a weird word like "kopje" and was marveling at the endless space unfolding in front of him, pristine bush at its best with hardly any human intervention, just how it should be, when he was pulled right back into the twentyfirst century as his cellphone started ringing.

"Hello?"

"Ralph, it's Ella."

"Wow, that was quick!"

"I'm helping Mum out in the café and couldn't get to my phone in time, thanks for leaving me a message. I was wondering when I'd hear from you. How have you been?"

"Oh, OK, thanks," said Ralph, trying not to sound over-excited. "And you?"

"Oh, so-so, you know. Not many patients, so I spend more time wrestling with the coffee machine than manipulating back muscles. So what's the idea you want to talk about?"

"Well…" began Ralph. "Hang on, I'm just going to scramble back up this kopje to get a better signal. How's that? Can you hear me?"

"A bit crackly…but carry on," prompted Ella.

"You'll probably think it's daft and you wouldn't touch it with a barge pole, and you'd be quite right to dismiss it out of hand, and you've got your physio practice to build up of course…"

"Ralph!" chided Ella, "Get to the point! What's the idea?"

"Um…do you want to come and help run Mogololo?"

"But that's your job."

"Yes, it is. But there are some parts of the job that I'm useless at, and I think you'd be really good."

"Oh?"

"And if you'd like, perhaps you could come out to Mogololo and we could talk about it? You becoming involved in running the lodge, I mean."

"Of course," said Ella, very quickly. "On a purely professional basis."

"Naturally," said Ralph. "So when can you come?"

"Ummm, tomorrow?" replied Ella.

"Terrific!" enthused Ralph, although he tried to sound more matter-of-fact than he felt. "We've only got two guests in tomorrow, so you'll have a lodge all to yourself and we'll have plenty of time to talk. "

"OK, till tomorrow then, I'll get to you after lunch. Bye."

Walking back down the hill to the Game Lodge, Ralph had a grin splashed all over his face. The first person he bumped into was Miriam.

"Oh, Mr Ralphie!" she exclaimed, "I haven't seen you looking so happy for a long time. What's been tickling your feathers?"

"Hello Miriam," said Ralph, still grinning. "Oh, just a bit of good news, I hope. I'll have a special guest joining us tomorrow night. What will you be making for dinner?"

"Special?" said Miriam. "I expect it's a special 'lady guest' then?"

"Might be."

"Well, I had better think of something special. I expect your special lady guest likes green vegetables," said Miriam.

"We'll find out tomorrow," said Ralph, then he went off to his own bungalow to avoid any more of Miriam's questions.

Ella turned up at Mogololo in the middle of the afternoon the following day. Ralph was busying himself with the generator that was kept discreetly away from the main camp to minimize the noise it made. The camp didn't have an electricity supply from the main grid, so running a diesel generator was the sole source of power. Some baboons had been trying to break into its little hut and Ralph was making it more secure. So as Ella pulled into the camp she was greeted by Edison.

"Welcome, Miss Ella," he said. "I am Edison."

"Yes, I know, Edison, and thank you," said Ella. "Ralph has told me lots about you, and I don't think I need to be 'Miss' Ella. Ella will do just fine."

"I think Ralph will be back in a minute, he's just fixing the generator hut. The baboons seem to think there is food inside, but it's just diesel. Not very tasty."

"So," said Ella, "Is the Lodge not so busy at present?"

"Not really, we have space for more guests. I know Ralph doesn't want to get too big like the other commercial lodges, but we really could do with a few more bookings. Not my department, though. I'm just a humble tracker."

"Oh, Edison, I know you're a lot more than that!" smiled Ella. "Ralph couldn't manage without you, I'm sure."

Edison was saved from more embarrassment by the arrival of Ralph's pick up and Ralph, looking very dirty and disheveled, tumbled out of the cab.

"Oh Ella!" he said, "How great to see you, and here's me looking like a builder's mate's assistant!" He attempted to clean his grubby hands on his even grubbier shorts and shake her hand, but Ella diffused his awkwardness by leaning up and kissing him on the cheek.

"Hello Ralph," she grinned, "Glad to see you got dressed up for me."

"Give me five minutes," he pleaded. "Edison, could you organize a cup of tea for Ella while I shower and change? And we've got a young couple staying who will be having a game drive soon, would you like to come along?"

"Try and stop me."

The game drive was one of those magical two hours when the animals just seemed to appear on cue and put on a performance for them. The young couple were honeymooners and although Ella offered the front seat in the Land Rover for them, they were happier holding hands together in the back. But they were very attentive and interested and appreciative of everything Edison and Ralph found for them.

First there were the zebra; quite a big family group of a dozen or more and there were two little foals shyly trying to hide behind their mothers. Ralph was concerned about one of the adults who seemed to be limping. He slowly manoeuvred the vehicle around them and saw this particular zebra had great gashes down the side of one of its hind legs. "Probably a lucky escape from a lion," explained Ralph, "But it won't be lucky next time. Its leg looks infected and will severely slow it down. If a lion doesn't get it, the hyenas probably will."

"Is there nothing we can do?" asked the young honeymooning girl.

"No. It wouldn't be fair to intervene," explained Ralph. "This is just nature at work, I'm afraid."

The mood in the Land Rover was a little dark for a moment, but it was not long before Edison raised his hand a sign for Ralph to slow down. He pointed off to the left in the direction of a giant wild fig tree. "Ingwe!" said Edison in a loud stage whisper.

"What?" asked Ella.

"Leopard!" replied Ralph. "Look, on that branch about 20 feet up from the ground." The group in the Land Rover sat transfixed as the leopard's tail twitched, ever so slightly. It appeared to be asleep, legs dangling either side of the big branch, with its head nestled on the smooth bark of the wild fig.

"Is it asleep?" whispered Ella.

"Resting, perhaps, but certainly not asleep," replied Ralph. "It looks like an adult male. He can stay like that for hours. Leopards are pretty lazy when you think about it. A bit of hunting, stash the carcass somewhere safe from hyenas and lion, eat a bit, sleep it off, eat a bit more; not a bad life, is it?"

"While the women are left all alone to look after the children," commented Ella in response.

"Yes, there is that," conceded Ralph. He turned to the newly-marrieds in the back of the vehicle, "Look, I don't want to disturb him, but shall I move the vehicle round to the other side? You might get better pictures."

The young couple nodded enthusiastically, too awed by being in the presence of a wild leopard to actually speak. Very slowly, Ralph took the Land Rover around the other side of the tree where the leopard, keeping its eyes on them, very obligingly followed their progress; slightly curious, but not sufficiently interested to move more than he had to. As if on cue, the leopard yawned, showing off spectacular teeth. Cameras clicked, whispered questions asked and answered, Edison constantly scanning the bush for any signs of danger or potential problems.

"Ralph!" warned Edison, "Hyena." And he pointed to a clump of bushes fifty metres ahead of them. With that he deftly hopped down from his little perch at the front of the vehicle and scrambled into the very back of the Land Rover, behind the young couple.

"Are hyenas a threat to humans?" asked Ella, impressed by the speed of Edison's change of seat.

"Edison?" asked Ralph, "Are hyenas a threat?"

"They are to me," grumbled Edison.

Ralph laughed and then explained, "Many years ago, when Edison was still a boy, looking after his father's cattle he had a run in with a couple of hyenas. He was on his own, no gun, nothing but a stick to protect him. He was facing down one of them while the second got behind him and took a bite out of his bum. Not surprisingly, that made him really mad and he walloped one of them with his stick and lashed out at the other with his bare feet. Hyenas are pretty cowardly and they ran off but since then Edison's never felt safe around them. Is that right Edison?"

"They've tasted me once and I don't trust them not to want to try again," replied Edison. "Though so far, I only see one here now. But there will be others, somewhere close."

With that, the hyena Edison had spotted moved into the open, with its eyes on the leopard and, more specifically, on the remains of the young impala that the leopard had stashed in the tree. The leopard, now fully awake and in no mood to be intimidated by a hyena, sat up in its tree, bared its teeth and spat a fierce warning at the hyena.

The hyena pretended to take no notice but it carefully avoided any eye contact with the angry big cat. It was then joined by a second, and a third hyena, slinking out of the bushes, circling the fig tree and looking as menacing and as ugly as only hyenas can.

"I can see why Edison doesn't like them much," whispered Ella.

"Not exactly cuddly, are they?" agreed Ralph. "But they have their role to play in the great scheme of nature. Along with vultures, they're the garbage collectors of the bush, cleaning up all the left overs and keeping the place tidy.

They will make their own kills, of course, but generally, they like to pick off other predators' left-overs. They won't have any luck with this one, though. That leopard's not going anywhere."

They watched the stand-off for a few more minutes, then Ralph said they should move back to camp or Miriam would give them all a ticking off if they were late for her dinner.

Ralph found them a spot at which to gaze in wonder at a magnificent African sunset while they enjoyed some drinks, then drove down dusty tracks that criss-crossed the bush, wending their way back to Mogololo.

"How long did it take you to learn to navigate your way around in the bush?' asked Ella.

"I'm still learning!" said Ralph. "No, seriously, it does take a while. All these tracks probably look much the same to you, don't they? But as I know them so well, I can find my way almost with my eyes closed. I know the ant hill shapes, the rocks, the big trees, and knowing where the sun comes up and goes down helps. Now, unless I'm making all this up, the camp is just the other side of this rise." And it was.

Miriam had created a wonderful dinner for them and she fussed around them like a mother hen making sure they all had what they wanted and blushed with enormous pride when Ella praised her skills and asked for a little more of her Malva pudding. Ralph noticed the exchange between them and was hugely relieved that Miriam seemed to like

Ella.

After dinner, left to themselves, Ralph thought he had better talk to Ella about his idea for her to help be part of Mogololo.

"So, how would you like to run the Lodge for me?"

"Well, that was subtle Ralph," said Ella. "I suppose it's too much of a pun to say you're not one for 'beating about the bush'?"

"Sorry," said Ralph. "I suppose that was a bit blunt, wasn't it. But look, I really need someone to add the touches that I'm so bad at…"

"You mean the feminine touches," interrupted Ella.

"Yes, and I can see you've made a hit with Miriam, which Tanya never did, and Grace is going to be so relieved that the pressure will be off her. Do you need me to tell you what the job specification is, or shall we make it up as we go along?"

Ella laughed, "Ralph! You're never going to be a captain of industry, are you!"

"Heaven forbid!" blurted out Ralph.

"I think making it up as we go along is a good start, but a few basic ground rules…"

"OK," said Ralph, "such as..?"

"I imagine I can look after all the housekeeping, catering,

staff welfare, guest hospitality, booking admin and feedback ... and you look after the game drives and getting the guests to book in the first place."

"That sounds good to me."

"But don't forget I'm still a physio. If I have a patient who needs me, I'll have to dash back to town and help them, will that be OK?"

"Absolutely," said Ralph. "In fact I had an idea about that: you could actually promote your services around the other camps, looking after guests' problems like you did with that character George, who was here."

"That's a good thought," agreed Ella.

"I'm sure you'd pick up some patients, but I suppose we should talk about that very vulgar subject of money."

"Ralph! I can't afford to pay you!" teased Ella.

"Don't think it works that way," smiled Ralph.

"What did you pay Tanya?" asked Ella.

"More than she was worth, in the end," grumbled Ralph. "Look, I've got an idea, you write down a figure and I'll write down a figure and we'll see how far out in our thinking we are from each other. How's that?"

"Are we talking per month?"

"Exactly."

"Got a pen?" Ralph went behind the little bar and found a

ballpoint pen and an old notebook. He pulled out two pages and handed one to Ella.

"Here you are," said Ralph. You go first."

Ella furrowed her brow for a few seconds, thought carefully, counted on her fingers for a few seconds more, as if she was attempting some complicated mental arithmetic, then, shielding her writing from Ralph's curious gaze, she wrote, folded her paper and passed the biro back to Ralph. Ralph didn't take more than ten seconds to write down his figure and folded his paper. "Right!" he announced, with a degree of self-assuredness he didn't really feel, "Let's see!"

They swapped their pieces of paper, looked at them, and they both immediately burst out laughing.

"See!" exclaimed Ralph, "I knew you were perfect for the Lodge; your figure's just below mine, so we'll go with mine and by the way, there's a profit sharing scheme for everyone."

"You've got to make a profit first," chided Ella.

"With you on board, that will be a breeze," said Ralph. "Can you start next week?"

Chapter Six

Ralph often compared the running of Mogololo to one of those variety show acts where a juggler attempts to keep plates spinning on sticks; as soon as one begins to slow and show signs of crashing to the floor, it needs its stick to be revived and whipped up to speed again, while the other plates are in imminent danger of disaster. Just keeping the show on the road was a daily challenge for Ralph's non-existent management skills. So having Ella on board was a breath of fresh air for the running of Mogololo. Ralph felt as though a weight had been lifted from his shoulders; Miriam was happily singing in the kitchen as she created wonderful food for everybody and Grace was glad she no longer had the main responsibility for the Lodge; she was quite happy to help and be Ella's assistant. Ella had begun to shape plans and schedules and divide roles and tasks; she even got Ralph to be better disciplined with his own administration.

Ralph also turned his attention to generating more bookings for the Lodge. He emailed past guests, using that idea he had of offering a discount for a return trip and attached some wonderful photographs of recent game sightings in the hope they'd spark great memories of their own game drives. He urged past clients to spread the news among friends and relations and tempted them with a discount, too. He nagged his travel agent contacts in Johannesburg. He tiptoed through the minefield of bureaucracy at the Tourism Department in an attempt to get them to feature Mogololo in their publicity. He called an old journalist friend to ask his advice on how to raise the Lodge's profile. (As the journalist friend specialized in crime reporting, he wasn't much help.) But with Ella's assistance and encouragement, bookings slowly began to increase and Ralph was no longer living in daily fear of a summons from the bank to discuss his overdraft.

It was all going so well. Until that Thursday morning.

That particular Thursday, Ralph was driving with Edison, to check the fences around the south of his property. Sharing an open border with the main park was great, but Ralph had responsibility for the line between Mogololo and his farming neighbours; neighbours who were not over keen on having a vast array of wildlife either trashing their fields, consuming their crops or terrorizing and eating their livestock. The fence was pretty sturdy, even an angry bull elephant would have trouble breaking it, but there were lots of burrowers who would dig under the fence to get at some tempting opportunity on the other side of the fence. Warthogs would often start the tunnels; once they had broken through, hyenas would invariably follow, plus honey badgers, small cats like civet and caracal, there seemed to be a bush telegraph of news that would spread throughout Mogololo that there was a break in the fence and rich pickings on the other side. So it was a regular and necessary patrol that Ralph and Edison would make, loaded with shovels and spare fence posts and wire to make and mend any problems they found along the fence line.

They were making slow and steady progress along the fence when Edison's sixth sense alerted him to something away from the fence, maybe a kilometre or two towards the east.

"Ralph," he said, "Over there, to the left of that big kopje, something's happened." Edison was pointing into a fairly thick section of bush but he had spotted vultures circling in the sky and dropping, one by one to perch on the branches of a dead tree. The vultures were anxious and unsettled, hungrily anticipating their turn in the food chain to feast on whatever it might be that had caught their attention...and Edison's.

"Let's see," responded Ralph, and he turned up the next track to head in that direction. His first thought was lions, and that he would be able to bring guests on the next game drive straight here. But his first thought didn't last long.

"It's an odd place for a kill," said Edison. "Too much cover for the cats."

"Wouldn't be a rogue pride, muscling in on the territory?" ventured Ralph.

"It's unlikely," said Edison, "Not in this part of the park, there's too many small mopane trees for the grazers and difficult for the lions to hunt. Watch out for that ditch!"

Ralph saw the danger just in time and wrenched the vehicle round, narrowly missing a termite mound and bouncing over a fallen tree.

"You charge extra for the white-knuckle theme park ride?" asked Edison.

"Okay, okay," said Ralph, "Now, where are we looking?"

"Oh-oh," said Edison, "Not only looking, but smelling. Follow your nose."

Edison was pointing to the left, and Ralph cautiously pushed the Land Rover through the scrubby bush, taking a round-about route to avoid the bigger trees but not worrying about the smaller ones he drove over, he knew they were tough enough to spring back.

"Can you smell it?" prompted Edison. "That way," pointing further into the bush.

Ralph concentrated and was aware of a smell he didn't really want to experience: a metallic smell of blood, and of death. He steered the Land Rover round a big rock and saw it. The rhino. His rhino. Dead.

"Shit!"

The carcass of this magnificent animal was lying on its side, one front leg trapped in a cruel wire snare, congealed blood all around the tight loop that had cut into its short stumpy leg, with the snare securely anchored to a milkwood tree, some ten metres away. It was evident the rhino had thrashed and crashed its way around the limits of the snare's wire, the grass was flattened, with clumps of earth churned up. Apart from the pain, the rhino must have been desperately confused as to why it was trapped in one place. The worst thing, of course, was its face. A bloody mess of gristle, sinew, muscle and bone, hacked to pieces to remove the horn. A horn that had taken years to grow to maturity, a natural material known as keratin, similar to horses' hooves, and totally useless, unless you were a rhinoceros. Or you were a ruthless poacher, tempted by the huge rewards that were there for the taking in the far east where rhino horn was valued, gramme for gramme, above gold. A stupid, awful trade in death to satisfy vanity and ostentation of those who would show off their knife handles or trophies, fashioned from this oh-so-precious and fast-disappearing material. Or the completely superstitious oriental health-remedy market where it was supposed to have mythical, magical powers. All unproven, all crap. If only the end users could see what Ralph and Edison were witnessing here: the demise of a magnificent beast that quietly kept itself to itself and until today, lived a trouble-free life.

There was a mass of flies that reluctantly rose from the rhino's face as Edison and Ralph got down from the Land Rover and approached the carcass.

"Bastards!" muttered Ralph. "You poor old boy," he said to the rhino. "You never harmed anyone, did you? How did they kill him Edison?"

Edison walked around the dead animal, shaking his head and tutting. "Slowly, I think, Ralph," he said. "Once he was caught in the snare, they must have stabbed him with spears, probably poisoned. Look, you can see the holes in his side. And then hacked off his horn with pangas"

The vegetation around the rhino was flattened. "Well I hope he put up a fight," said Ralph. "How long ago, do you think?"

Edison thought for a while, looking carefully at the wounds on the rhino, "Not long. Maybe last evening? And there's no sign of another vehicle so they must be on foot."

"So we could get them?"

"We could try," agreed Edison. "I doubt they'd go straight to the fence, it would take too long to get to the location, and I bet that's where they're headed. Let's find tracks."

Carefully, both Ralph and Edison walked around the killing area, swatting at the persistent flies that thought they might also provide some sort of nourishment, as an alternative to the dead rhino. Edison's sharper eyes found the trail first.

"Here you go Ralph, this way," he called, pointing at the sandy soil where he had found a collection of footprints. "Two, at least," he said, "possibly three, going north, towards the location."

"Well that's where we'll go," said Ralph through gritted teeth. "Let's get the bastards."

Edison took up his "game-spotting" position on the little folding seat at the front of the Land Rover, concentrating on the ground for signs of the poachers. Ralph drove cautiously, but as fast as he could in an attempt to catch the poachers. He was seething with anger and was desperate to catch them and attempt to extract some form of personal revenge, though he didn't quite know what. Edison kept him on the right trail, following the footsteps in the sandy track, and guiding Ralph with one arm, while he clung on to the vehicle with his other hand. After fifteen minutes, they reached a large marula tree and Edison held up his hand for Ralph to stop.

"What is it, Edison?" asked Ralph, but Edison was already off his little seat and moving quickly into the bush. Ralph turned off the engine and followed Edison. Behind the trunk of the huge marula tree, they both stopped and gazed at a pathetic sight of three young men, lying on the ground, evidently dead and it looked like they had not died peacefully in their sleep. There were no signs of violence, but the bodies were all curled in the foetal position, tumbled on top of one another, and close by, was the remains of a fire.

"Wow," exclaimed Ralph. "What happened to them? ... Not that I'm all that sorry."

"If it's what I think it is," said Edison, "We shouldn't go too close, that fire isn't properly out yet."

"What do you mean?" started Ralph, then a sudden thought came to him, "What? Did they start a fire with Euphorbia?"

"Looks like it," agreed Edison. "Not exactly experienced in the ways of the bush, were they?"

Ralph looked at the pathetic little group of bodies on the ground. Three young black men, probably not yet out of their teens, dressed in a jumble sale of odd clothes, their deadly pangas on the ground, a couple of home-made spears and, wrapped in a dirty, blood-stained old towel, their poached trophy: the rhino horn. Ralph picked it up, it weighed quite a few kilos. "I guess they thought this was going to give them each a BMW and a new mobile phone," he said. "Though with all the middle men and traders along the line their take would have been pretty small in the end. And what did they really get? A horrible death breathing in poisonous smoke from a tree that doesn't even belong in the park. It's all my Dad's bloody fault! Him and the gemsbok from Namibia! Mind you, if he hadn't planted those Euphorbia Damarana trees these poachers would have got away with it. Their poor bloody luck they lit a fire with it. "

"So what do we do with them?" asked Edison.

"Well, if we leave them here, the hyenas and vultures will get them; maybe that's what they deserve, but I guess we'd better take them to the police," said Ralph. "I'll take some pictures while we're here, just in case the police want to follow it up."

So Ralph snapped away with his camera phone, covering the angles he thought the police might be interested in, making sure some shots included the remains of their deadly fire, then he and Edison loaded the bodies into the back of the Land Rover, together with their pangas and spears.

"Edison," said Ralph, "We can't both go off and leave Mogololo, there are guests coming in today. I'll drop you off at the Lodge, then go on to town and sort out the police. Knowing them, it might take some time, so can you hold the fort?"

"Sure…I don't envy your conversation with the police," said Edison.

Ralph grunted and was lost in his own thoughts as they made their way back to Mogololo. He drove slowly into the parking area and Edison hopped out. "Tell Ella not to worry," said Ralph. "I'll be back as soon as I can. You can look after the afternoon drive, can't you?"

"Of course, good luck."

Driving through the park, with his very unwelcome dead passengers, Ralph went over and over the details of the day so far, knowing the police were bound to want to know why had he moved the bodies from a crime scene? Why Edison, the other witness, was not with him? What items they had taken? He was dreading the interviews he would have to go through, for the sake of the police 'following their procedures.'

In the end, it wasn't quite as bad as Ralph feared. He explained his story to a uniformed constable on the desk who stood, wide-eyed and horrified, at the story of three dead men in a Land Rover outside. The constable quickly passed Ralph up the line to a sergeant who made notes in a slow and deliberate fashion on his lined A4 pad. When Ralph got to the part about the Euphorbia Damarana, he had to spell it out three times for him. The sergeant tut-tutted at the implausibility of men dying so quickly from breathing in poisonous smoke, but Ralph was adamant that's how they died.

The story had to be told a third time, to a detective, who rather than take notes about Ralph's story, chewed bubble gum throughout Ralph's monologue, punctuating certain points by blowing disgusting pink bubbles with the gum and, when they burst, folding the mess back into his mouth with his prehensile tongue.

He only had one question for Ralph, "So where is this rhino horn?"

"In the Land Rover," replied Ralph.

"We will need it as evidence," said the detective.

"I can appreciate that," replied Ralph, "But I would like a receipt for it, if that's all right with you?"

The detective bristled with indignation, "A receipt?! Why? Do you not trust us?"

Ralph diplomatically avoided the direct question by saying he would just need a receipt to show the Kruger Park authorities who were bound to want to open a file on the poaching for their own records. The detective snorted dismissively and pushed back his chair so it screeched noisily on the concrete floor and left the interview room. He was back a moment later with a scrappy piece of paper with a police stamp on it and a handwritten scrawl to say it was a receipt for rhino horn. Ralph's name was misspelled but at least it was something, so they went out to the Land Rover as it stood baking in the sun in the building's compound and Ralph retrieved the horn from under the passenger seat and handed it to the detective. The other cargo in the Land Rover, the three bodies, had already been collected and they were on their way to the mortuary for further investigation.

"Don't suppose any of you knew those guys, did you?" Ralph asked the bubble gum blower.

The detective gave Ralph another of his dismissive stares and said nothing.

"Just asking," said Ralph, attempting a smile, although he certainly didn't feel like smiling after the events of the day so far.

"OK, you can go now," said the detective. "But I expect my boss will want to talk to you once I have given him my report."

"Your boss?"

"Yes, Inspector Thoko Masiwa."

Ralph silently groaned at the mention of this particular name, but tried his best to keep an expressionless poker face. "I see," he said. "Well, he knows where to find me."

Ralph drove back to Mogololo with a big black cloud hanging over him. The brutal slaughter of a rhino really sickened him, especially 'that' rhino, the one he had known for so many years. He'd watched it come to maturity, he was aware of the battle scars it carried from scraps with other rhinos when attempting to establish his territory. He'd seen it face down lions when they were opportunistically trying their luck to intimidate him; they had failed. His rhino was a stubborn old boy and not susceptible to intimidation. He'd discreetly watched him singling out female rhinos when he sensed they were ready for mating. He wasn't much of a parent though; once the female was pregnant, he quickly lost interest and carried on his solitary existence.

And now he was gone. The scavenging hyenas, jackals, vultures and marabou storks would eat his remains. In a few weeks, there would be no sign of him at all, not even a smudge on the red earth, just a few scattered, bleached bones that even the hyenas couldn't manage to break.

He got back to camp and wearily got out of the Land Rover. Ella had heard the vehicle coming and had come out to greet him.

"I think you need a hug," she said and promptly wrapped her arms around him.

"Whoa!" said Ralph. "That's really welcome, but I'm probably in need of a shower!"

"Don't care," said Ella, still hanging on to him. "You've had a shitty day and deserve a bit of hugging. Was that the special rhino?"

"I'm afraid it was," he said, " And it's probably not over. There's another policeman who's not my favourite person – nor am I his – who's going to be nosing around."

"What else do they want to know?" asked Ella.

"Well, a while ago, this particular cop tried to tap me up for a bribe and I wasn't having any," said Ralph. "I showed him up in front of one of his constables and I can't imagine he's forgotten the encounter. So he'll probably want to make a point and be as difficult as he can, going over the details I've already given them, time and time again."

"Oh dear," said Ella. "Well, he won't be turning up this evening, will he?

We've got some delightful guests who arrived while you were in town. Go and have a shower, then come and have a drink with them. Go on."

So Ralph did as he was told and a little while later he was freshened up, drink in hand, with his best 'game ranger smile' on his face, meeting and greeting the guests. Ella was right, they were delightful and the evening just about managed to diminish the hurt and anger he was feeling over the day's events. The poached rhino wasn't mentioned; Miriam's cooking was praised; the stars shone; a male lion was calling, thrilling the guests with eager anticipation of the sights and experiences they would share tomorrow.

Ella managed the evening perfectly, being solicitous and a perfect hostess to the guests, but also keenly aware that Ralph needed some extra-special attention, too. Although seated at opposite ends of the big yellow stinkwood table, with six guests between them, she managed to catch Ralph's eye quite frequently, but as discreetly as she could, giving him looks of tenderness and support. Ralph thought how lucky he was to have her and the distraction of her regular eye contact made him ponder over their relationship. Since she had arrived at the Lodge a couple of months ago, everything between them had been perfectly and strictly professional and there had never been a question of anything more. But now, this evening, with all that had happened today, he was questioning his own feelings and coming up with surprising thoughts as to how much he wanted her. So much so that he was rather distracted and completely thrown by a question from the lady to his left.

"Tell me Ralph," she had said, "Is there a mating season for elephants?"

"Mating with Ella?" blurted Ralph, "Oh, I think that depends…hadn't you better ask her?"

"Is Ella an expert on elephants?" asked the lady.

"Oh! Goodness, I'm sorry!" said Ralph, "I completely misheard you…'elephants', of course! No, female elephants can come into season at any time of the year. The male elephants know when, of course, and they show their eagerness to mate by the secretion of what is known as 'musth'. They get an over-abundance of testosterone, they get quite aggressive and they secrete the musth from a gland close to their eyes. It makes them look as though they are crying. Can be very dangerous to humans when they are in musth. "

"Hmmm, I wonder of humans show the same traits?" said the lady, quite cryptically, looking down the table and smiling intuitively at Ella.

Ralph, now totally confused and discomforted by the way

this conversation was going, managed to extract himself, just, by commenting, "Well, we'll have to see if we can find you some elephants tomorrow on the game drive."

The lady smiled and turned to Edison who was hovering at her shoulder, offering to top up her wine glass. Ralph was saved from further embarrassment.

Dinner ended, the guests withdrew to their lodges and the Mogololo crew began clearing up the table and getting ready for the following morning's breakfast. Ralph made a major decision. "Edison, Miriam, Grace: go on off to bed, all of you. Ella and I will look after this, there's not much more to do."

Ella looked quizzically at Ralph, but said nothing.

"Don't forget to put on the pink rubber gloves when you are washing up, Ralph," joked Edison. "You don't want to spoil your hands, do you?"

"Get out of here, Edison! Before I change my mind." Edison laughed and followed the two girls, leaving Ralph and Ella on their own.

"Well, that was subtle, Mr Henderson," said Ella, loading a tray with glasses from the dinner table.

"Hmmm?" responded Ralph, knowing what Ella meant, but putting off actually making a comment.

"Getting rid of the staff so you can do the washing up?"

"I thought they deserved an early night."

"Nothing to do with giving us some time just to be alone?"

"God Ella! Am I that transparent?"

"Yes, actually, you are. Now are you going to put those plates down and come here, or not?"

Ralph smiled and did as he was told, putting a pile of plates back down on the table then walked around it to where Ella was standing, smiling, in the soft light of the candles and kerosene lamps. He took the tray of glasses from her and put that on the table and then folded his arms around her and buried his face in her sweet-smelling hair. She returned his embrace and traced her hands up and down the bumps of his spine, her fingertips forgetting their duties as belonging to the hands of a physio, but purely enjoying the passion of shared excitement.

"This was bound to happen, wasn't it?" she whispered.

"I think it was," replied Ralph. "I think I've known it ever since our encounter in the supermarket."

"Who'd have thought it was a display of canned fruit and me looking for caster sugar that would bring us together?"

Ralph didn't want to continue talking, he wanted to kiss and explore and make up for the time he knew he'd wasted, and Ella was as enthusiastic as he was to show that she, too, was ready to share and enjoy and plunge into the future she imagined for them together. Clearing the rest of the dinner table was forgotten as they kissed and clung to one another and arms and bodies entwined and pressed harder together. Breathlessly they attempted to talk but the passion of the moment was too urgent for either of them to make any sense.

"Shall…" "Yes…yes!" "Now?" "Mmmmm" "What about..?" "Don't care…" "What if…?" "Come back later…" "What?" "Tidying up…"

Ella eventually took control. "Ralph! For goodness sake! Let's go to your lodge. Now. Please. I can do all this in the morning."

Ralph smiled and looked lovingly into Ella's eyes. "Of course."

So they left the table as it was, and walked, surprisingly slowly, arm in arm, away from the main building and down the dirt path to Ralph's bungalow. There were fireflies and moths, geckos and frogs, guiding their way, as if the wildlife knew that a new romance had started. Inside Ralph's room, they kissed, more tenderly and slowly now. They both knew they had all the time in the world, but they clung to one another as Ralph manoeuvred them towards his bedroom, almost afraid to break the spell.

"Pretty tidy for a batchelor," said Ella, as Ralph managed to light a kerosene lamp to give the room a little more light than the almost-full moon was throwing through the mosquito-meshed window.

"Not having many possessions or clothes probably helps," replied Ralph. "But this isn't the time for a kit inspection young lady. Please come here."

Ella moved gracefully towards him and they found themselves lying on their sides, face to face, on Ralph's bed. Very gently, Ralph found buttons on Ella's shirt to unfasten, and she also did the same to him, tugging Ralph's shirt from his smarter-than-usual bush shorts that he wore to have dinner with guests.

Ella shrugged off her shirt, unfastened her bra and Ralph gasped with awe and wonder. Very tenderly, he stroked and caressed and loved the little whimpering noises that Ella unconsciously made. Soon, all of their clothes were an untidy pile on the floor and Ralph pulled the mosquito net curtains together around the bed. "Now I've got you, I'm damned if I'm going to share you with the mozzies."

Later, loving hours later, Ralph and Ella were still wrapped in one another's arms and legs but nowhere near sleeping, Ella wanted to know more about this man she was now committed to emotionally, as well as practically in terms of her earning a living.

"Ralph, tell me how it all started?"

"What? 'Birds and the bees' sort of started? Didn't your Mum tell you? Or school?"

Ella snorted and found a free hand to lightly slap his shoulder. "Mogololo, I mean! The Lodge, what gave you the idea?"

"Ooh, growing up here in the farm, I was always aware of how precarious it was for Dad. The rains were always unpredictable, there were all sorts of diseases, poaching, problems with elephants trashing the fences and helping themselves to the crops, not to mention Mum's garden, predators taking young stock. It wasn't easy to scratch a living. Grandpa had started it and he was either a better farmer than Dad or he was lucky, because I do remember it being great to grow up when I was really little, but Grandpa died, Dad took over and it always seemed to be more of a struggle then. I was packed off to boarding school, then had to do my bit in the army and it was when I was in the army I decided if ever I got the chance I would love to be more involved with wildlife and the bush. Poor old Dad died before I came out of the army, Mum had already passed away and I was determined I wasn't going to be a farmer but I had this great lump of land to my name. I had some offers from neighbouring farms to take it over, but also I could see what their real motive was: they wanted it because I had all this shared fence with Kruger; they could see the opportunity for traversing rights. Well, I'd already worked that out so I decided to turn the whole place into a game lodge."

"And you did it all by yourself?" asked Ella.

"With a bit of help from the bank – I had a friend who was a bank manager then, I wish he'd told me he was leaving."

"Oh yes, your meeting on the morning you bumped into me for the first time."

"Yes, that was the best bit of that day, for sure."

"But carry on about how you got Mogololo going," urged

Ella.

"Well, the money from the bank nearly all went on game fencing; we just tore down the fence between us and Kruger, once I'd done all the paperwork with the Park authorities. And the cash I got from selling what was left of the herd went on building the lodges and adapting the main homestead. We started small and didn't have much money to advertise ourselves, but by chance, a travel journalist from one of the big London papers heard about us and wrote some very nice things, so that got us going."

"And where did the notorious Tanya come into the picture?"

"Oh, to be fair, Tanya was a big help in making the lodges comfortable. I probably would have just put in army camp beds and a folding table and chairs, but at least Tanya made them all pretty and homely. But she got bored and was never cut out for the bush in the first place. Anyway, she's gone and good riddance, because now I've got you.

"And I've got you," whispered Ella.

"And I couldn't be happier," added Ralph. "But we've got guests to look after in a couple of hours, so I really think we should sleep a little bit, don't you?"

"Mmmm," came a sleepy response.

Chapter Seven

The morning was one of those perfect Mogololo mornings where the air was crisp, still and had a clarity that only Africa can deliver. The Lodge was slowly waking up but some of the occupants had enjoyed more sleep than others. Ralph and Ella were still intoxicated with the emotions and physical pleasures that had exploded between them and sleep had not been a priority – but for the sake of appearances and discretion, they had both been out of their shared bed before dawn to ensure the whole Lodge was presentable for the guests. Even though he hadn't slept much, Ralph was flying on a wave of euphoric adrenalin, masking the anger he still harboured over the death of his rhino.

They busied themselves with clearing the table and getting the coffee, cool drinks and biscuits and rusks ready for the early morning game drive snacks, occasionally giggling like teenagers when they accidentally-on-purpose bumped into one another. They were unaware that Edison had been hovering on the threshold of the Lodge for a minute or two.

He coughed, discreetly. "Well, good morning. I see the clearing up of last night is taking a little longer than you thought."

"Yes, good morning to you, Edison," replied Ralph with a smile. "I guess you could say we got …er…distracted."

Ella flicked Ralph with a tea towel.

"Such distractions are to be applauded," said Edison, in his most imperious tone. "Long may the distractions continue. I'm very happy for you both."

Ella came around the table to give Edison a hug. "Well, thank you Edison," she said, "That means a lot. Honestly."

"Well, come on young Edison," said Ralph, "Time we got ready to show these guests of ours what we do best."

"You mean driving into ant bear holes, having punctures and running out of fuel?" suggested Edison.

"It's a good job I'm in a good mood, or I'd fire you for insubordination!"

"And I'd hire you again immediately, even if he did," said Ella.

Before their banter could descend even further into farce, the first of their guests drifted down to the verandah and exchanged greetings, good mornings, praise for the wonderful day and were full of anticipation of the game drive they were about to enjoy. When all of them were gathered, Ralph shepherded them to the vehicle and managed to get them all seated and made sure they had their cameras, binoculars, sun hats, sun screen creams and patiently listened to their questions and requests about what they'd love to see on their drive. Taking great care to avoid as many potholes and thornbushes as he could, Ralph set off on the drive.

At the Lodge, Grace and Miriam, through typical African intuition, knew exactly how the Ralph and Ella relationship had developed over night. They were full of probing questions that Ella was not too keen on answering.

"Miss Ella," started Miriam, "Mr Ralph, does he make you happy?"

"Of course, Miriam," Ella replied, as non-commitally as she could manage.

"Very happy?" added Grace.

"Like you are drawn together by fate and share one heartbeat?" prompted Miriam.

"I bet he has very strong hands," voiced Grace.

"I can see he has strong legs," giggled Miriam.

"Girls, if you think you are going to get me to give you details of what has happened between Ralph and myself, I am afraid you will be disappointed. We work together. We are friends. Well, maybe more than friends. But that's all you're going to hear from me. OK? Now, we have breakfast to prepare for six hungry guests after their game drive, so shall we concentrate on that?"

Grace and Miriam giggled but did as they were told. Ella went off to the Lodge office to try and concentrate on the next order of supplies from town, but her peace and quiet did not last long, as Grace rushed into the office to warn her.

"Miss Ella!" she said in a very loud whisper, "That horrible policeman is back."

'What horrible policeman?" said Ella.

"The one who is horrible," responded Grace with unarguable logic.

"Sorry Grace, you're going to help me out here," said Ella very patiently. "You need to tell me who and why you think he is horrible."

"It is that Inspector Thoko Masiwa from town," said Grace. "He was here before and he and Mr Ralph had a big argument. Mr Ralph would not give him what he wanted."

"Why, what did he want?"

"A bribe, of course. Mr Ralph would not give him one and made him look small in front of his constable policeman who was with him."

"Hmmm," said Ella. "Just what Ralph would do. OK, we'd better see what he wants."

Ella went from the little office to the verandah, not at all sure what she would encounter. First impressions were not good. There, slumped in one of Lodge's squishy chairs was a great lump of a man, overweight, sloppily dressed in not too clean trousers and a garishly striped shirt, idly flicking through one of the coffee table books on game photography.

"Good morning," began Ella, with a strong voice of efficiency.

Her tactic to immediately establish the moral high ground

didn't work on this individual. He paused his rather disinterested perusal of the book for a second, glanced up at Ella, and carried on paging. "Who are you?" he demanded, dismissively not giving her any attention.

"I'm Ella Moffat, I help run Mogololo. Who are you?"

Now, he slowly turned his attention on Ella, looking her up and down in a patronising and demeaning way. "I am Inspector Thoko Masiwa from South African Police and I am here on a very serious matter. Is Edison Ngoveni here in your camp?"

"No," said Ella, "Not at the moment. What do you want to talk to him about?"

"It is a serious police matter that I will not be discussing with you," said the Inspector, very dismissively. "When do you expect him?"

Ella checked her watch, "Oh, in maybe an hour, perhaps an hour and a half."

"I will wait."

"Well, I'd rather you didn't wait here," said Ella quite bravely, "We are expecting more guests to arrive this morning and I would prefer not to have a police welcoming committee for them." The young uniformed police constable who was accompanying the Inspector looked wide eyed with horror and amazement that someone was talking to his boss in this way.

"Really?" replied Masiwa. "And where would you suggest

we wait?" adding a rather a menacing edge to his question.

"There's a pleasant lookout point over there," said Ella, pointing to the raised decking, beyond the lodge. I'll get Grace to bring you some tea, shall I?"

The promise of tea seemed to defuse the situation and the big inspector heaved himself up from his comfortable chair and nodded to his constable to follow him in the direction Ella suggested. "And plenty of sugar in the tea," was his parting comment, to make sure he was still scoring points in this conflict of wills.

Ella had to use all her powers of persuasion to get Grace to take a tray of tea and rusks over to the lookout deck for the two policemen.

"No, Miss Ella!" she complained. "We should not be giving tea to that man. He is not a nice person."

"Well, " said Ella, "I agree he is not very nice, but we don't want to make matters worse. I wonder why he wants to talk to Edison? It was Ralph who spent so long at the police station yesterday. Now please try and be polite to him … and no spitting in the teapot out of spite, do you hear?" This last comment made Grace collapse into giggles at the very thought of it, but she complied with Ella's instructions.

An hour dragged by. Ella restlessly tried to attend to things in the office but her heart wasn't in it. She was listening, listening, for the drone of the Land Rover engine returning to camp, but all she could hear were the calls of the birds and the occasional snorting honk of a zebra. "Come on

Ralph," she muttered to herself, "Hurry home and let's get this awful man off the property."

After what seemed an age, she eventually heard the vehicle returning to camp. She alerted Miriam and Grace that guests would be ready for breakfast in just a few minutes, then hurried down to greet the returning game drive.

Ralph's delight at seeing Ella was soon clouded by the look of concern on her face. "What's up?" he whispered.

"That policeman you had a run in with: Masiwa, he's here and he wants Edison."

"Edison?" blurted Ralph, making the man himself look up, and so Edison came to join them.

Ella diplomatically guided the guests towards breakfast and then carried on telling Ralph what she knew, in as whispered a manner as she could, "Yes. He wouldn't say why. I've parked him on the lookout deck."

"Good girl," said Ralph, patting her comfortingly on the shoulder, "Come on Edison, we'd better go and see what the cops want with you."

Ralph and Edison walked over the red earth to the lookout deck. They could see the inspector slumped in one of the deck chairs used by guests, while behind him, stood his young constable, evidently nervous. The inspector was asleep, snoring quite loudly and the constable was in two minds as to whether he should attempt to wake up his boss, or allow these two men to do it. The decision was taken from him: with a grunt and a great twitching of his legs, the big inspector woke up.

"Ah, Mr Henderson," said the inspector. "And you must be Mr Ngoveni?" he added with a very unsubtle emphasis on the 'Mister'.

"Yes," replied Ralph. "What do you want with Edison?"

"I read the statement you made about the bodies of the so-called poachers you brought to the station yesterday. I am not satisfied with your story and I require a separate statement from Mr Ngoveni."

"What do you mean, 'not satisfied with my story'?" snapped Ralph.

"In my professional opinion, Mr Henderson, your statement is full of conjecture, fabrications, assumptions and other nonsense. A tree that when you burn it, the smoke can kill? Whoever heard such rubbish!"

Ralph managed to contain his anger and said, "Inspector Masiwa, your ignorance is barely eclipsed by your arrogance. It is very apparent you know nothing of wildlife, nature, the bush or the environment in which you live. It is a proven fact that the Euphorbia Damarana, when burned, gives off a lethally toxic smoke. Something that neither you, nor your three dead poachers were aware of."

"Well, we are awaiting the autopsy report to show whether your fantasy story has any truth," said Masiwa, "but I, for one, have never heard of it, nor do I believe it."

"So you're rewriting the laws of nature, are you?" said Ralph, very sarcastically.

"When the laws of our country are being flouted, it is my responsibility to investigate," retorted the Inspector with as much pomposity as he could muster.

"Then you're a bigger idiot than I gave you credit for!" shouted Ralph.

Edison thought he ought to diffuse the tension between these two warring buffaloes. "So, Inspector, what do you want to know from me?"

"I want you to come into town and give me your statement."

"Why can't you interview Edison here?" protested Ralph.

""Because I am the Police Inspector and it is my wish that the interview takes place at the police station."

"Ridiculous!" exploded Ralph. "Complete waste of time!"

The Inspector ignored Ralph's outburst and said to his constable, "You go with Mr Ngoveni in his vehicle and follow me back to town."

"Ah, so Edison has to be a chauffeur to your man, does he? Using Mogololo fuel?" complained Ralph.

"It's OK Ralph, " soothed Edison. "The sooner I go, the quicker I'll be back."

"I still think it's bloody ridiculous that you won't talk to

Edison here! Not that he will tell you anything different from what I said yesterday."

"Mr Henderson!" warned the big policeman, "I suggest you do not obstruct the police in the pursuance of their enquiries!" The two men stared at each other, locked eyes and waited for the other to blink, neither prepared to be the first to back down.

Ella cleverly broke the impasse by declaring, "Edison, just give me two minutes and I'll get you a bacon roll to eat on the way into town; you haven't had any breakfast today."

"Thank you Ella," said Edison very graciously.

"I'm sure the Inspector and his Constable had a good breakfast before getting here, and they've had tea and rusks, so they won't be needing any, will they?" And with that, she turned away and marched briskly towards the kitchen.

"I need Edison back here by 2pm," said Ralph. "I have a business to run and he's a vital part of my team."

"And I have the deaths of three young men to investigate," retorted Masiwa, and then, to his Constable, "Let's go."

Edison shrugged his shoulders in submission and began to walk towards the Lodge utility vehicle, grinning to Ralph as he passed him and whispering,

" 'Vital part of your team,' I like that."

"Get back here as soon as you can," growled Ralph, but also with a smile on his face, just for Edison to see.

Ralph grabbed some breakfast for himself in the kitchen, amazing Miriam with the speed at which he made the left over scrambled eggs and bacon disappear.

"Mr Ralph!" she exclaimed, "You should not eat so fast. It cannot be good for your digestion."

"Don't worry Miriam," he said, between mouthfuls. "I had to learn to eat at top speed at boarding school. If you didn't wallop down what was on your plate quickly, the boy next to you would grab what he could if he had finished his. It wasn't what you would call, a 'refined' boarding school. Now, I need to get going and look after these guests of ours."

Ralph found the guests, relaxed and happy on the verandah, soaking in the calm and warmth of the mid-morning bush; some reading books, others with binoculars to their eyes looking for birds or whatever might be hiding in the bush.

"Hello again everybody," started Ralph, "Sorry I couldn't join you for breakfast, we had a 'bit of a situation' with our local policeman that needed sorting out." The guests looked up in alarm, but Ralph continued, "Nothing to be concerned about. Yesterday, Edison and I came across a dead rhino, he'd been killed for his horn and it was pretty recent when we found it so we set off after the poachers. We found them pretty easily, but they were dead."

"Dead?" gasped one of the guests.

"Yes, afraid so," carried on Ralph, "They must have been pretty clueless. They'd lit themselves a fire using a type of wood that gives off a deadly smoke. Doesn't take more than a few breaths and you're a gonner. Anyway, I took their bodies to the police station and expected that would be it, but this morning this Inspector Masiwa turns up and wants Edison to go and give his statement at the police station. Why he couldn't just do it here is beyond me, but there we are."

"Gosh, life's never dull around here, is it?' commented the lady who had been sitting next to Ralph at dinner last evening, smiling rather conspiratorially at Ralph. Ralph, for all his game-ranger bravado, picked up the unspoken reference to Ella and blushed like a teenager caught smoking behind the garden shed.

As if summoned by an unseen thread, Ella chose that very moment to join the group on the verandah. "Hello," she said, "Edison all sorted. I'm sure he'll be back as soon as he can."

"I've just been explaining to our guests all the excitement we had yesterday, before they arrived," said Ralph. "But we're not going to let it spoil their enjoyment of Mogololo, are we? I would quite like to head out for a walk, who's up for a stroll in the bush with me? Nothing too arduous, just an hour or so; perfect for working off breakfast and building up an appetite for lunch!" Three of the male guests jumped at the opportunity, and two ladies also agreed to go. The very perceptive lady who had worked out what was going in between Ralph and Ella said she would rather stay put and enjoy the view from the verandah. She smiled very sweetly at Ella, "I'm sure you can find time to have a cup of coffee with me, my dear?"

So as guests went to put on their walking boots and collect cameras and binoculars, Ella made up a tray with coffee and biscuits and returned to sit on the verandah with her new mature friend, Patricia, and see what she had in mind to talk about.

"Now Ella," started Patricia, once she had helped herself to coffee, "I can see you and Ralph have something special going on…"

"Well, it's early days…" responded Ella.

"I know. I wonder if those 'early days' started last night?"

"Goodness, was it that obvious!" spluttered Ella.

"I doubt anyone else spotted the signs that were sparking between the two of you. I've had some experience in these matters and I have to say, you are simply glowing, my dear. Don't worry, no one else has a clue what's going on."

"I think the staff do!" said Ella, "But I'm glad none of the other guests have found what's going on between Ralph and myself distracting."

"Oh, my husband Brian is oblivious to these things. All he cares about is his golf, his priceless collection of snuff boxes and making sure the government doesn't do anything too illegal!"

"Oh, is Brian an important lawyer?" asked Ella.

"Sort of," said Patricia. "He's an advisor to the Minister of Justice. It all sounds very boring to me, but it keeps him occupied. More than occupied in fact. You've no idea how much trouble it was to get him to come away for this long weekend!"

"Well I'm so glad you managed it."

"Me too. Now, tell me more about Ralph. I'm dying to know more."

So Ella, still in the flush of teenage-style excitement over her new love chatted to Patricia about how she and Ralph had met and how Ralph had been left in the lurch by a previous girlfriend and how he'd been such a perfect gentleman and how she'd been longing for him to make a move and was almost wondering how forward she should be in prompting them to become an 'item' but it the end, it was the upset of the rhino poaching that had been the trigger.

"Well, just you make sure you hang on to him," advised Patricia. "I can tell he's one of the good ones."

"Well I'm certainly not going to tell Ralph that," laughed Ella.

The day passed by; another blissful, hot African day, full of the sounds and scents of the bush. Yellow-billed hornbills clacked their bony, extended beaks together, gossiping with their mates in between searching for grubs or scrounging for scraps around the kitchen, baboons far off in the distance barked with bad-temper at one another, and wheeling eagles were mere dots in the sky as they circled on the thermals rising from the baked, dusty earth. As the time for the afternoon game drive came closer, Ralph kept anxiously looking and listening for Edison's return from the police station in town. He didn't come. Ralph called young Jackson, a relative of Edison's who had been working at Mogololo as a trainee game ranger, gardener, luggage porter, waiter and barman.

"Come on Jackson," instructed Ralph. "Baptism of fire for you this afternoon; load up the coolbox with the sundowners and then hop up on the seat at the front of the Landy; you're my spotter on this drive. You've seen Edison work with me, so you know what to do."

"But Boss," complained a worried Jackson, "I've never done it before!"

"Great time to start then; show me what a great tracker you're going to be!" grinned Ralph, teasing young Jackson probably more than he deserved. "Don't worry, I need you to be looking out for antbear holes just as much as big cats and elephant."

"OK Boss," said Jackson, standing at ramrod straight attention like a soldier, full of pride at his new status.

So with Jackson perched like a mascot at the front nearside of the Land Rover, and with six guests happily aboard, Ralph set off on the afternoon game drive, ready with his running commentary on the flora and fauna, and ever-patient with guests' questions about what they were seeing and experiencing.

They hadn't gone too far before the two way radio crackled and sparked into life. The radio was really kept for emergencies, Ralph didn't want it to become the norm that game drives were interrupted by constant radio chatter. They shared frequencies with other game lodges in the area, of course, and Ralph always had half an ear open to pick up news of sightings other game guides had made but this time, the transmission was just for him. It was Ella, back at Mogololo.

"Yes Ella?" he started, very formally, knowing that other guides would probably be listening in.

"Ralph, just to let you know I've heard from Edison. He'll be delayed in town for a little bit. He's OK, but thought you ought to know."

"OK. Thanks Ella. Out." Ralph pondered over Ella's cryptic communication. Why had she even bothered to call if there wasn't really anything to say? Patricia, who was sitting in the front beside him, caught his mood.

"Everything all right Ralph?" she quietly asked.

"Hmmm, not sure," replied Ralph, grateful that Patricia was being as discreet as possible inside the open Land Rover. He needn't have been concerned, as the passengers behind him were all sharing some private joke and were oblivious to their game guide and Patricia's conversation. But even before Patricia could probe even further, Jackson suddenly shot up his right arm and Ralph brought the vehicle to an abrupt and dusty halt.

Ralph waited for Jackson to indicate what he had seen. He waited…and waited, Jackson gazing with great concentration deep into the bush to his left, with his own body doing a good job of obscuring Ralph's view of what he was looking at.

Eventually, Jackson turned to whisper to Ralph, "Leopard, Boss. On the ground, under the big acacia tree over there."

Ralph turned to address his vehicle full of guests, "Our lucky day, folks. Jackson's found us a leopard. All stay quiet and I'll try and get us closer."

He put the vehicle into first gear and slowly eased forwards, turning off the dusty track and into the bush. He'd only gone a few metres when he stopped, "Jackson!" he whispered, "Get back here!" Then turning to Patricia he said, "Better be safe than sorry. It could be a female with cubs and I wouldn't want Jackson to be the cubs' lunch. He is a bit exposed out there in front." Jackson sprinted back and clambered up to the top tier of the Land Rover's seating.

"Now," said Ralph, "Let's see this leopard." He gently edged the vehicle forward, doing his best to avoid termite mounds and the thorn trees, but driving over the top of the mopane saplings, knowing they were tough enough to spring back and continue their struggle to survive and thrive. Ralph's passengers hung on to the grab rails in the vehicle, ducked under overhanging branches and all looked and looked, wanting to be the first to see the leopard Jackson had sighted.

But Ralph was first. "There it is!" he announced, in a stage whisper. "Fifty metres ahead, under the acacia, lying down, facing away from us. Well done Jackson. Tricky to spot from where we were on the track." Jackson beamed a huge toothy grin and puffed out his chest with pride. Ralph continued creeping forward, to give his party a better view.

The leopard was magnificent. It was actually a mature male, not a female and Ralph explained it had probably recently made a kill, had enough to eat for the time being, had stashed the remains of the carcass up a tree and was happily resting in the shade. The guests made witty comments about being a typical man: lying around doing nothing; sleeping all day; too lazy to help with the kids or the housework. Ralph indulged their remarks with good grace, but was keen to stress that in an instant, the leopard could change its demeanour and become a deadly adversary. The leopard politely obliged and supported Ralph's remarks by languidly raising its head, looking at the group in the Land Rover with its piercing yellow eyes, then it made one, vicious snarl, baring its wicked-looking teeth and it sprang up and bounded off into the bush, its camouflaged coat helping it disappear almost immediately.

Ralph's sympathies were with the leopard. But his thoughts were also with the radio contact Ella had made. What was happening with Edison?

Edison and the police constable had made the drive into town in good time. On the way, Edison had tried to draw the young constable into conversation, they were both Shangaans, from the same tribe but different villages. Edison was keen to know if they knew similar families or had attended the same schools. The constable, however, seemed to live in fear and dread of his Inspector and was reluctant to be talkative, so Edison just followed the dust cloud of the Inspector's car ahead of him and munched on the remains of his bacon roll.

In his vehicle up ahead the Inspector was driving too fast through the game reserve. The roads were dirt, over time they had become corrugated and that made the suspension of vehicles judder and shake for a very uncomfortable ride; just going faster over the surface was not the answer. While the Inspector's car was spewing up huge clouds of dust, dust that would make the grass and shrubs adjacent to the road very unpalatable to the browsing and grazing animals until the rains came, Edison was far more considerate, managing to avoid potholes and the worst of the corrugations and kept his dust trail as small as he could. He pointed out bird varieties to the constable, but the young man stayed passive, his eyes fixed on the distant cloud of his superior's car, up ahead.

They arrived in the ittle town of Hoedspruit and made straight for the police station. The police station itself was an old fashioned collection of small buildings at the edge of town. It had its own dusty compound, surrounded by chain link fencing and a South African flag hung limply at the top of a flagpole. Once there had been an attempt at growing flowers in a bed, but the weeds and lack of rain had defeated the gardener's ambitions. Everything about the place looked tired and neglected; Edison had driven past it countless times, but apart from getting his license or other papers stamped officially, he had never had cause to go beyond the front desk.

Today, however, was different. Once parked, the constable led Edison into the main building and ushered him into an interview room. The room was not welcoming. A concrete floor that wasn't particularly clean, one small, high, barred window, walls that had been painted an indeterminate colour of beige many years ago and had been thoroughly neglected since. There was a small metal desk, firmly secured to the floor, one chair on one side of it and two on the other. That was it. The constable left Edison in this room and shut the door. So Edison waited, and waited. Thirty minutes went by, then an hour. Edison realised it was a tactic to make him uneasy and unsettle him, but Edison was made of stronger stuff than that. So he endured the wait with calm and patience, focusing his mind on the game drives he had recently enjoyed at Mogololo. Edison was employed by Ralph, but though he would never admit it, as long as he was fed, housed and clothed, he would have worked for free. The game lodge and the bush was his life. He let his mind meander along the sandy tracks that the game drive Land Rover took twice a day; there was a cobwebbed network of them, cleverly criss-crossing all of Ralph's property, without seeming to cover the same territory, and then venturing into Kruger National Park itself. Edison knew all these tracks: the bumps, the bends, the rises and dips; crossing dry river beds and skirting giant ant hills; he thought of the favourite early morning coffee and drinks-at-sundown stops where he played the part of waiter and barman, always discreet and polite, offering hot coffee and fresh muffins in the morning and iced drinks and snacks in the lengthening shadows of red orange sunsets. Mogololo was his life.

But not today. Eventually the door to the interview room burst open and Inspector Masiwa crashed into the room carrying a folder under his arm and a scowl on his face. The folder was crashed down on the table, intended to intimidate Edison and establish the superiority of the policeman. In Edison's opinion, it failed. He languidly looked the policeman in the eye, waiting for him to start. Masiwa slumped down in the seat and indicated for Edison to sit opposite.

"So, Mr Ngoveni," started the policeman, "I need to establish the truth of what happened to the three young men whose bodies your employer brought here. There are some very disturbing aspects to this case: the fact that Mr Henderson saw fit to remove the bodies from a crime scene; the lack of witnesses to the event; the ridiculous claim that it was smoke that killed them; Mr Henderson's rather dismissive attitude towards the severity of this case; do you appreciate what I am saying?"

"Inspector," replied Edison, very calmly, "Had we left the bodies where we found them, there would be no bodies at all by now. The hyenas and vultures are extremely efficient at being the garbage collectors in the bush. In one day's time, all that would be left would be a brown stain on the sand and a few rags of torn clothing."

The policeman shrugged his shoulder dismissively, "Be that as it may, the interference in, and a corruption of, a crime scene is a very serious matter. He could have radioed for assistance, so someone could have guarded and secured the scene."

"I think Mr Henderson was more concerned with the welfare of his guests rather than three common criminals who were already dead, Inspector."

The Inspector sniffed loudly, "Now look, Ngoveni, Henderson is a white man. Why are you bothering to protect him? We can write your statement so you are not implicated in their deaths. You could have been elsewhere and not at the scene of the crime. Do you know what I am saying?"

"I see exactly what you are saying Inspector. But no. I will not perjure myself for the sake of your prejudices." Edison stared at the policeman, long and hard. The Inspector was the first to break the eye contact.

"Well, let me come to the manner of their deaths," blustered the big policeman. "This claim that they were overcome by poisonous smoke: totally unbelievable!"

Very calmly, Edison said, "I presume, Inspector, the bodies have gone for autopsy? I think the pathologist will confirm what both Mr Henderson and I know to be an unfortunate, but nevertheless incontrovertible truth: those men died from inhaling the smoke from a fire made from Euphorbia Damarana wood."

"Rubbish!" shouted the Inspector. "You killed them! You

and Henderson! You did it to discourage poaching on Henderson's property. The autopsy will show how you killed them; they were just boys, the two of you could easily have overcome them, and you had a rifle."

Edison sighed, "No, Inspector. They died breathing in that smoke. It's the first time I've come across it personally, but I believe it's quick, but very unpleasant and painful."

"No. Not good enough. Edison Ngoveni, I am holding you under arrest, pending further investigations of the deaths of three males, yet to be formally identified, murdered on the property known as Mogololo Lodge; anything you say may be used in evidence against you in future."

Edison shook his head in disbelief. "You can't be serious!"

"I am not satisfied with your story and I have the right to hold you under arrest and that is what I am doing," said the Inspector, very smugly.

"Can I phone Mogololo to let them know of your ridiculous action?"

"You may make one phone call," said Masiwa. He stood up, opened the door and yelled for his constable to take Edison to the front desk and supervise the single phone call that he was permitted.

Edison's heart sunk at the prospect of spending more time in this awful police station.

Chapter Eight

Ralph got back to the Lodge and once he ensured his guests were happy and would be ready for drinks and dinner in an hour or so, he went off to find Ella.

"What's happened?"

"Well, about an hour ago I had a very awkward phone call from Edison at the police station," explained Ella. "He said Inspector Masiwa had arrested him while they investigated the deaths of the poachers…"

"Arrested Edison! They can't do that!" shouted Ralph. "Those poachers died of that bloody smoke!"

"Of course," soothed Ella, "but that stupid policeman wants to get at you, doesn't he? So by holding on to Edison he knows he's upsetting you."

Ralph groaned, looked into the distance while he thought for a bit and then said, "Ella, you're medical, how long does an autopsy take?"

"Crikey!" said Ella, "I've never even seen one done. I'm not that medical!"

"But don't you know someone who does autopsies? What are they called, pathy-dologists or something?" asked Ralph, grabbing at straws.

"Pathologists. I have a doctor friend who might know someone. Let me make a call."

"Right. You use the landline and I'm going up the hill to get a mobile signal. I'll call my lawyer friend to see what he can do about getting us Edison back."

Ralph and Ella did their best to keep the mood at Mogololo as light as possible and guided the chat around the dinner table to the game and bush experience rather than the difficulties being encountered by Edison in the police station. Perceptive Patricia, however, was keenly tuned in to the tension, but was careful not to allow her Miss Marple-like deductions cloud the conversation with the rest of her party. Her husband Brian wanted to know more about how elephants arranged their social structure, drawing parallels with his feelings about women dominating the child-rearing and discipline duties while the males went off to work, to play golf, to light barbecues and drink beer.

Ralph very diplomatically accepted the analogy but stressed that within the elephant world, there wasn't much golf to be played. He did, however, relay a lovely story about once seeing a young male elephant who had come across a marula tree that was shedding its plum-like fruit as much of it was over-ripe and had actually begun to ferment. The elephant gorged itself on this wonderful, sweet-tasting harvest, not knowing that the fermentation would continue inside its gut, building the alcohol content and after a while, the elephant was really quite drunk. It staggered around for a bit, bumped into bushes and trees and was thoroughly confused about what had happened.

"Goodness," commented Brian, "Imagine an elephant-sized hangover!"

When the laughter had died down and the wine bottles circulated the table again, Patricia, who was seated at Ralph's left, quietly asked, "And what's the situation with your colleague Edison?"

"Well, getting more complicated is the honest answer," replied Ralph. "This stupid policeman has got it into his head that Edison, and no doubt he'll be back to try and rope me in as well, was responsible for the deaths of those three poachers and he's gone and arrested him!"

"Oh my!" said Patricia.

"I've got a lawyer friend of mine on the case and I'm sure we'll get Edison back tomorrow. It's utterly daft! Those boys died from smoke poisoning. Not a mark on their bodies. How Edison and I were supposed to have killed them is a pure invention on the part of that fat police inspector. According to a doctor friend of Ella's, the autopsy should be done tomorrow and then the police will have to let Edison go."

"I do hope so," said Patricia. "But if it gets difficult, I am sure Brian could ask a few questions on your behalf. He might look like a boring old lawyer, a bit like one of those old elephant bulls you were talking about, but his brain is still as sharp as a tack. And the Minister of Justice listens to him, that's the important thing!"

"Well, thanks Patricia," said Ralph. "Let's hope sense will prevail before we need to send in the heavy guns."

The following morning was the last day of Patricia, Brian and their friends' long weekend stay at Mogololo. They had an early morning game drive, a slightly smaller and faster breakfast than previous days and were packing their vehicle ready for the long drive back to the northern suburbs of Johannesbsurg. Patricia found time to have a quiet word with Ella.

"Tell me, has the lawyer friend of Ralph managed to get Edison released?"

"It should be happening right now," said Ella. "The pathology report on the three poachers should also be through by now, so that stupid policeman will have to act on that."

"It would appear that he was really getting at Ralph rather than his proper search for justice," said Patricia.

"Exactly. I imagine he's going to have to be eating humble pie for quite a while when everyone knows the full story," said Ella.

"There are some people who don't know how humble pie is cooked. But look, Ella," added Patricia, "You've got our number. If you need any help, I'm sure Brian can go over this Inspector's head and get him put in his place."

"That's very kind Patricia," said Ella.

"Think nothing of it, my dear. I just want to see you and Ralph happy and successful. I feel very privileged to have been in at the start of your relationship."

"Bit like a fairy godmother," joked Ella.

"Precisely."

Then, their conversation was interrupted by the arrival of Brian, their friends and just about everyone at the Lodge to see them pile into their vehicle, be waved goodbye and the Lodge prepared for the arrival of new guests, new stories to be told, new game sightings to be experienced and sunrises and sunsets to be gazed at and admired.

Chapter Nine

Edison came back to the lodge a little while after Patricia, Brian and their friends had left. He hadn't slept well, he was in the same clothes that he'd left the day before but took his treatment at the hands of the police with the normal, dignified stoicism that epitomized this quiet, gracious African.

Naturally, both Ralph and Ella bombarded him with questions about what had happened after he'd left the lodge yesterday. Edison's responses were carefully measured, fair and he showed not an ounce of bitterness towards the way Inspector Masiwa had dealt with him.

"The man is not blessed with a particularly high level of intelligence," he said. "When I asked him how he thought I had managed to kill three young, fit men, without leaving a mark on any of their bodies, he just dismissed my question as a mere trifle; he wasn't interested in details he said. I'm sure he simply wanted to get me locked up because he knew it would inconvenience you, Ralph."

"And it certainly did that," said Ralph.

"What about when Ralph's lawyer friend came to the police station this morning?" asked Ella.

"Well, fortunately, it was quite early – too early for the Inspector to be at his desk. The lawyer, Mr Sheldon, insisted on my immediate release on bail. He very kindly lodged the surety himself. I said you would reimburse him,

Ralph."

"Of course Edison," grinned Ralph. "I think you're worth it."

"But Edison," continued Ella, "Who was in charge of the police station when Mr Sheldon came to rescue you?"

"Just the desk sergeant. I was still locked in a cell but I could hear the argument taking place at the front desk. Mr Sheldon is not a person who is intimidated by uniforms or authority, is he?"

"Chris Sheldon is an old mate of mine," explained Ralph. "We were in school together and played rugby for the same house team. He once got sent off for arguing with the referee over some decision the ref had made. But Chris was right! The linesman had spotted the same thing Chris had seen but the ref wouldn't back down and Chris had to go off. That same day, Chris argued his case by writing a letter to the headmaster, there was a brief inquiry and that ref was never invited back to the school again! Yes, Chris can be very forceful when he needs to be."

"But this won't be the end of it, will it?" said Ella.

"No," sighed Edison. "It won't be."

"Well, the autopsy result will be with the police this afternoon, so perhaps that will convince Masiwa once and for all," said Ella.

"Hmmm," muttered Ralph, "I'm not convinced our Inspector Masiwa takes much notice of the truth getting in the way of his theories."

"Death by asphixiation due to the inhalation of toxic fumes probably produced by the smoke of burning wood from a poisonous tree such as euphorbia damarana", announced Ella to Ralph and Edison the following afternoon, once she had managed to get through to the pathologist.

"How did you manage to get the number?" asked Ralph.

"My doctor friend in Hoedspruit," said Ella, "He gave it to me."

"And the people in the lab gave you that information?"

"Well, they were a bit cagey," admitted Ella, "But I told them I was working with Chris Sheldon, the Lawyer, and they seemed totally in awe of his name, so they read out the results to me."

"Terrific!" said Ralph.

"Yes, I am very grateful," added Edison. "Very grateful, indeed."

"It doesn't necessarily mean Masiwa will let it drop, however," cautioned Ralph. "But I'll give Chris a call now. I'd better let him know that he has a new, unpaid member of staff who's been making phone calls on his behalf. He'll be thrilled, I'm sure!"

"Ralph," complained Ella, "Didn't we all want to see Edison is in the clear as soon as possible?"

"Yes, all right," said Ralph. "But I wonder if that's really the last of it?"

"Masiwa wouldn't be able to question the path. results, would he?" asked Ella.

"I think the man sees himself as being a law unto himself," suggested Edison.

"Welcome to the new South Africa, everyone," grumbled Ralph as he went off to the office and the phone.

Chapter Ten

Being in the lowveld of South Africa, the heat at Mogololo could sometimes get intense and oppressive. It was if the air had been superheated in a pizza oven and just left to hang, breathless and inert. The early afternoons were the worst. The sun had enjoyed five or six hours of uninterrupted baking and by noon, there was very little shade to be found anywhere. In the Lodge buildings there were fans that hung listlessly from the ceilings and rotated slowly like dancers around a maypole: full of good intentions but with very little result. Ralph refused to install air conditioning as he said he couldn't stand the noise of the units interfering with the sounds of the birds, so they suffered in silence, but hot silence. At least it was a clean, dry heat with no humidity to speak of, but God it was hot! And with hardly any breeze to take the edge off the temperature. But everyone at Mogololo was used to it and they paced themselves accordingly, choosing to do tasks in the afternoon that kept them away from the glare of the sun and, generally, out of one another's hair.

Although for Ralph and Ella, still in the first flush of their relationship, they wanted to be in one another's hair, all the time.

"Ralph? Why are you in my office, hanging around, when you are normally stuck underneath the Land Rover's bonnet at this time of day?"

"So when did it become 'your' office, then?"

"Well I spend the most time in it, but of course, it's 'our' office, too."

"Land Rover's fine. Nothing else to do until game drive time, I suppose."

"Well, what you could do is think of a way of getting us more guests next month. Bookings are looking pretty thin, you know."

"Hmmm, email our past guests, do you think? Special offer for a three night stay?"

"Worth a try."

"Or…"

"Yes?" said Ella.

"It's high time the tourist board did something for us. I pay them an annual fee – for what, I'm not sure – but I've never had a go at nagging them to spread the word about Mogololo, perhaps that would be an idea?"

"Yes, but I doubt they'll do something in time to get bookings in next month," said Ella. "Why not do both?"

"You mean I've got to do TWO things? At the same time?"

"It's called multi-tasking, darling. We ladies have to do it all the time."

"Can't I just go and pretend to fix the land Rover?"

Ella glared at him and tried to look disapproving…but

burst out laughing instead.

For a farmer's boy, Ralph was really very creative. English had always been his best subject at boarding school and when he wasn't managing things at Mogololo every waking hour, he read as much as he could. So creating a letter to each and every one of the past guests who had left an email address was a task he quite enjoyed. Naturally, it had to look as though each communication was personal and before long, he had sent out more than 100 invitations for guests to repeat their Mogololo experience – and enjoy a tempting discount.

Writing to the Tourist Board to encourage them to be more pro-active was more challenging. He didn't know anyone personally at the department that would look after game lodges, so he was starting from scratch. He'd identified the "difference" he could talk about: Mogololo was smaller, more intimate, much more 'hands on' than many of the bigger, neighbouring lodges; and where they offered extras like spas, yoga lessons and all sorts of massage options, Ralph concentrated on making guests feel as though they were his personal guests for the weekend, or a few nights, or however long they stayed. And he promised and delivered a full immersion into the real African bush experience. Some lodges tended to be quite superficial in the way they managed to get their visitors ticking off the species they found. Ralph, however, concentrated on helping his guests understand the ways of the wild. He often spent ages getting his guests enthralled at the struggle a dung beetle would have trying to push his prized ball of elephant droppings up a slope, or he would enthuse about the natural order of things in the way the scavengers were the rubbish collectors of the bush and again, there was a hierarchy of species that took their turn in cleaning up carcasses and just leaving bleached bones. It was a formula that worked with nearly everyone who visited but Ralph had been so busy delivering the personal touch he hadn't had time to develop a campaign to tell the world about it.

So he slumped into his favourite chair in the office, the one that had been his father's favourite chair, too; worn brown leather that had seen hundreds of backsides and arms ease themselves into it; the one with the nick where Ralph, as a naughty schoolboy, had been practicing opening his penknife like a comic-book assassin and stabbed the leather arm by mistake; the one with the dozens of little burn marks where Ralph's father's pipe had fireworked sparks and cinders on being lit and the scars were still there to see. So this was Ralph's 'thinking' chair and that's where he was now, with A4 pad on his knee and felt tipped pen in hand, doodling while he thought about how he should get what he wanted from the Tourist Board, without being pestered by salespeople and bureaucrats trying to get him to do what they wanted, instead.

"Are you sure we don't know anyone at the Tourist Board, Ella?" he asked.

"I don't. But you know lots of Parks Board people, don't you?"

"Yeah, but that's to do with game and conservation, not getting bookings."

"Then, sorry. Can't help," said Ella, turning her attention back to her computer screen and wrestling with the work schedule of the staff.

"I tell you who I do know, though," said Ralph, suddenly sitting up and looking much more alert and eager.

"Who's that, darling?" said Ella, not looking up from her screen.

"My mate Danny, in Jo'burg. Have I never mentioned him?"

"Danny who?"

"Danny de Villiers," said Ralph. "He was the one who introduced me to Tanya, but let's not hold that against him. No, he runs a TV production company and I bet he could make a great programme about what we're doing here. One of those fly on the wall documentaries."

"Or a mosquito on the wall, even?" suggested Ella.

"OK! Poke fun if you want to…but I think it's a great idea."

"And how, do you imagine, that's going to get us a full camp next month?"

"Oh, OK, I know it's a longer term plan than we need right now, but I think it would be terrific for us, and you'll look wonderful on TV!"

"Oh no! I'm not going anywhere near a camera!"

"Come on, it'll be fun. Anyway, let's not get ahead of ourselves. I've got to sell the idea to Danny, first."

"You just keep me out of it, Mr Henderson!"

Ralph started by writing a long email to Danny, outlining his ideas and promising him full access to everything that goes on at Mogololo, in the hope that Danny would see the potential for a really edgy, topical and entertaining documentary. He invited him to come and see the lodge for himself and stay a night or two, so he would really get a feel for life in the bush and what Ralph's team do to make the experience for their guests extra special.

Sometimes, fate, luck, prayers, or good fortune just seem to slot into place and make things happen with seamless ease. Or that's the impression, anyway. Ralph was not a particularly religious man but when an email response came in from Danny the very next morning, Ralph did have a private moment when he closed his eyes and said a silent "thank you." Danny responded very positively to Ralph's idea of filming at Mogololo and said he'd be there in a few days time, with his producer, so they could work out whether Ralph's idea was feasible and if Danny thought he could make a series that TV stations would want to buy.

"Of course TV stations will want it!" said Ralph enthusiastically. "And what's more important, it will put us on the map with thousands of people wanting to come and visit."

"Um," said Ella, "Isn't there something about carts and horses or counting chickens and eggs?"

Ralph tried to put on a serious, headmasterly face in response…and failed. "All right, I shouldn't get over excited, but it's great that Danny is interested, isn't it?"

"Yes, and we've had a couple of very positive responses to your email campaign to past guests: two couples for next week and two more the week after."

"Well, in that case, I'll go and wash the Land Rover," announced Ralph.

Four days later, Danny arrived with his producer, Billy, and Ralph gave them a tour of the Lodge, the guest accommodation, the kitchens, the office, introducing them to everyone they came across and explained where they fitted into the Mogololo team. One of the last to be introduced was Ella.

"And this is Ella," said Ralph. "My … er … my … Ella? What are we going to call you?"

"Ella is fine for starters," said Ella, helping Ralph out of the hole he was digging for himself. "Danny, how nice to meet you. And Billy."

There was an awkward silence while Ella waited for Ralph to fill in some of the gaps and when he seemed too embarrassed to be forthcoming, Ella explained, "Danny, I'm not going to say I'm the new Tanya…I'm not the "new" anybody. I'm me. But you've probably gathered that Ralph and I have more than a working relationship; we are, what I believe is often called, "an item". Is that OK Ralph?"

Ralph let out the breath he'd been holding while Ella had done her explaining, "Lovely girl, that was beautifully put, and in so few words. All clear, Danny?"

"Crystal. Cut glass. Perfect," replied Danny. "So when do we get one of your famous game drives Ralph?"

"We've got three 'real' guests who'll have a drive in about half an hour. So tag along."

Ella gave Ralph a knowing smile and left all the unspoken things that Ralph had failed to explain hang in the air like fireflies dancing weightlessly in the night.

On the game drive, Ralph was very solicitous to his three genuine guests and made sure they had the best seats and as much of his attention as possible. Edison was perched on his usual spotting seat at the front of the Land Rover and Danny and Billy took up their positions in the top tier of the vehicle's special seating and Ralph couldn't help but notice that Danny had a very impressive-looking, but quite small camera with him.

Ralph pointed out the usual mix of game they encountered as they rolled steadily along the sandy tracks; even though Ralph could drive these trails blindfold, he never grew bored or complacent about the privilege he felt just being there, among the natural wilderness of the bush. Whether it was golden orb spiders constructing their complex webs between trees or a family of warthogs snuffling in the dirt for roots, it was all part of Africa's amazing jigsaw, where in the end, everything had a place and a relationship with each and every aspect of life under the sun.

Danny and Billy were deep in a privately whispered conversation at the back of the Land Rover when Edison suddenly indicated that Ralph should stop.

Edison pointed to his left and Ralph quickly picked up what he had seen.

"Lion," he said in a low, assured voice, "Fifty metres that way. Two young males it looks like." All eyes followed Ralph's outstretched arm.

The lions were suddenly alert, heads up and staring at the Land Rover with their piercing yellow eyes. For a few seconds it was uncertain whether they would be interested in the Land Rover, be aggressive, be dismissive, or just couldn't care. The lions knew they were under no real threat, the biggest issue was whether they would take umbrage at being disturbed; after all, it's hard work being a lion, lying around in the bush for eighteen hours a day, with nothing much else to do than swish your tail to keep the flies away. These two young-men-about-the-bush decided they were not going to pose for these intruders on their territory so they both rose, as one, turned disdainfully and disappeared into thicker bush that Ralph and his Land Rover would not be able to penetrate.

"Ah well," said Ralph to his passengers, "A fleeting glimpse, but we saw them." And he continued slowly down the dusty trail, half hoping that the lions might make another appearance for the sake of keeping his guests delighted with their bush experience.

He really needn't have worried, his three paying guests were thrilled with the excitement of being in this wonderful wilderness and Danny and Billy, viewing the world with their televisual eyes were also entranced with the possibilities. They stopped for sundowners at the highest point of Ralph's property, a rocky outcrop that gave wonderful views over both Mogololo's land and Kruger Park and, of course, of the sunset that was in the process of performing its daily spectacular show, painting the clouds with pinks, oranges and reds in an ever-changing, moving tableau of wonder.

While Edison was busily serving drinks to the guests, Danny said to Ralph, "It's just awesome, Ralph. I can see why this place has such a hold over you."

"Even though I don't seem to be able to make it pay," replied Ralph.

"Well, if you can manage to hang on in there for a few months longer, if we do a programme about you; a series of half hour packages, probably, that's going to raise your profile enormously and you'll be swamped with people wanting the Mogololo experience."

"A few months?"

"Well," explained Danny. "There's a lot of hoops to jump through. Making the programmes is the easy bit. It's getting the programme commissioners on board, that's the tricky part. They have their schedules mapped out months in advance. I'm confident we can impress them with a teaser of the programmes we'll do, but they are the ones who have the cheque books and the say so on what gets aired, and when."

"Are we talking South African telly?"

"Oh to begin with, yes. But I can see a much wider audience internationally. There's a number of international jamborees where programme makers go and tout their wares to sell shows; we go to them every now and then, and this will be one of those shows we'll be pushing. It doesn't mean you'll be seen in every country in the world, but it could be pretty extensive. If, and it's a big 'if', we can pull it off."

"Wow!" said Ralph. "So what happens next?"

"Well, don't get too excited yet. There's so many things that can scupper great programme ideas, but Billy and I will have to start plotting out a budget, it will be our money we'll be outlaying and it could be a long time before we see a return, so it's got to be viable. But we'll also start doing some shooting tomorrow. I've got my small digi-camera kit with me, Billy can do sound, and we'll just spend the day around the lodge, on a drive with you perhaps, seeing how Mogololo goes through its day. Nothing too structured, it's got to be real and believable. We'll put a short pilot together, knock on the door of the head of factual at the TV station and don't leave him alone until he buys it. Then we can really schedule a proper shoot, just a small crew, we don't want to spoil the immediacy or intimacy by overwhelming you with people and kit. And then we're off to the races."

"It all sounds straightforward, then,' said Ralph.

Danny laughed, "Don't you believe it matey! I'm a salesman. All my eggs have got two yolks and the sun always shines on me. It could all go to the worms very easily. We've normally got three or four ideas in development at the same time, the success rate is never more than fifty per cent, and that's if we're lucky!"

"OK, I get the picture," said Ralph with a big grin, "But I'm still excited as hell!"

The sun did its daily, showing-off-departure beneath the horizon, and Ralph encouraged everyone back onto the Land Rover. Now the sun had gone, the whole atmosphere of the bush changed as the light quickly faded and the shapes of trees, rocks and anthills took on a more sinister aspect. Edison, still sitting on his perch at the front of the vehicle, had a powerful torch ready that he would sweep to and fro into the bush, searching for the reflection of wild eyes that would shine back at him. But for now there was still just enough light to see without it. They were still travelling quite slowly when there was a sudden rush and crash and a warthog came squealing out of the bush and across the track, closely followed by a young lion. The warthog was clearly sprinting for its life and was making good headway until, out of nowhere, a second lion crashed into it from the side, as a perfect piece of lion hunting teamwork.

Ralph had emergency-stopped the Land Rover and there were gasps of amazement from the guests on board at what they were witnessing. It was quick. It was bloody. It was merciless in its brutality, but it was nature. The warthog struggled for a few seconds, kicking its stubby legs and attempting to break free but the lion which had been lying in wait had it by the throat and it stood no chance. The second lion was, by now, overpowering the poor warthog's hind quarters and it was all over within twenty seconds. The warthog struggled no more. The two lions were now growling and grumbling at each other while they tore into the carcass, squabbling with each other to get at the easiest, softest parts of the animal. Everyone, including Ralph, on board the Land Rover was holding their breath. Edison quietly and sensibly, made his way into the vehicle, rather than sit exposed at the front.

Danny was using his video kit, the other guests clicking with their cameras; it was one of those bush moments when no one really needed to say anything. Until, that is, Danny broke the silence, "Are you sure you didn't organize that, Ralph?"

A ripple of laughter spread through the vehicle. "Just for you, Danny," Ralph quietly replied.

Ralph always thought it was extraordinary how quickly the vibrant life of one animal changed from a living, breathing entity into a messy, bloody carcass that was ripped to shreds first by predators and then by scavengers. It wasn't long before first a black-backed jackal came trotting into the killing arena, skittishly keeping a respectful distance from the lions, but chancing its luck and looking for opportunities to dash in and grab a scrap while the big cats were concentrating on their ripping, crunching, growling and eating as fast as they could.   Then came an ugly, hairy, loping hyena; skirting the edges of the small clearing, ducking behind bushes, looking, sniffing, baring its awful teeth but still being submissive towards the lions. The lions took it in turns to keep the hyena at bay, snarling and growling their hate in its direction. One rushed at it and made it retreat at top speed and while the second lion watched this action, the jackal darted in to steal a strip of bloody warthog hide.

The party on the Land Rover watched and video-recorded, still too excited to talk much about what they were witnessing. The lions' heads became more and more bloody, they had virtually cleaned out the cavity of the warthog body, cracking ribcage bones with their massive teeth and devouring the soft viscera with speed and enthusiasm. Then they started on the legs, tearing at fur and skin to get at the muscle underneath. They ate, and ate.

After maybe forty minutes, Ralph said, "Folks, we should get going. They'll be thinking of sending search parties out soon."

With great reluctance the passengers all settled themselves back in their seats, and Ralph started the vehicle. "We'll come by tomorrow morning and see what's left, shall we?"

Chapter Eleven

Back at the Lodge, the talk that evening was all of the lion kill and Danny and Billy shared their video of the event with everyone on Billy's laptop. Ralph had to admit it was grippingly spectacular and Danny's camerawork was impressive.

"This will cut together beautifully," said Danny. "Great start to the project!"

"Well, we'll go there first on our game drive tomorrow morning and see what's left," said Ralph, "But going from experience, the most we can expect will be a bunch of moth-eaten vultures and maybe a caribou stork."

"Worth getting though," said Danny. "And I'll want to do pick up shots around the camp. Nothing structured, I just want to see you all doing what you would normally be doing."

"You won't want me, though, will you?" ventured Ella, very tentatively.

"If you're going to be nervous about it, of course we'll respect your feelings," said Danny. "But it would be a shame. I can sense you're the most important person here at Mogololo. Much more essential than Ralph!"

"If Ella's uncomfortable, we'll keep her off camera, OK?" said Ralph.

"Understood," said Danny.

The following morning, the game drive went speeding to the spot of the lion kill. Finding it was easy, there were vultures slowly gliding around the area and coming to land on branches of trees, too wary to come straight in on the remains of the kill. Not that there were that many remains. As Ralph had described the previous evening, the lions had eaten all they need, the hyenas had come in to rip and tear at what was left, with a wily black-backed jackal or two opportunistically trying their luck as well. By the time the vultures had their turn, there was little left. But vultures manage to eke out their existence on very little. They would peck and squabble over the bits the others missed; they would find their way into crevices of the shattered skeleton, even inside the skull to scrape away at brain and gristle. The warthog was no more, just a dark stain on the dirt and flattened grass and even that would disappear in a day or two.

Billy was using the camera now and filmed what he could, also including Ralph and Edison in his shots, as well as the three genuine guests who were quite happy to be included.

Billy wanted to get down from the vehicle and film from a different, lower angle, but Ralph forbade it. "More than my life's worth," he explained. "I'd have my licence revoked in an instant. Sorry Billy."

A grudging shrug of the shoulders from Billy acknowledged Ralph's firm stance and authority and that was the end of the matter.

While the party on the Land Rover was witnessing the very real facts of life in the South African bush, Ella was struggling with crises back at the Lodge.

Miriam had come to her morning and declared that she had run out of eggs.

"I don't know what I am to do!" she wailed. "How will I make breakfast for all these people if I have no more eggs?"

Ella attempted to calm Miriam's hysteria, but she was quite concerned herself. They were trying to make the very best impression on Danny and Billy while they were filming at the Lodge and here was a self-made problem that should have been avoided. But Ella knew how Miriam could get unreasonably upset over seemingly trivial issues, so she managed to keep her frustration in check.

"Did you not notice yesterday that you were running low?"

"Well I did, " explained Miriam, "And I wrote it down on a piece of paper, then I lost the piece of paper somewhere, and I forgot it."

"Oh, Miriam!" said Ella, "What are we going to do with you? Writing lists and losing them! OK. Hurry and find Jackson and tell him to rush over to Fig Tree Lodge in Sabi Sands in the truck and borrow some eggs from them. He's to tell them we'll replace the eggs later today. Tell him to get a dozen if he can and to rush back here. Now-now! Go on!"

So Miriam went as fast as her voluminous frame would allow her, waddling like an overfed goose, relieved that Ella had managed to take ownership of the problem and had come up with a solution. Ella checked her watch and calculated that it would take Jackson thirty minutes to get to Fig Tree Lodge and back, assuming he didn't get delayed by herds of buffalo, stroppy elephants, punctures, or even the pretty new reception girl at Fig Tree Lodge itself. So, she calculated the game drive vehicle would also be returning in thirty minutes, but it was Mogololo custom that breakfast would be virtually ready and on the table by the time they got back. It called for a bit of delaying tactics.

She got on the radio to Ralph.

"Yes Ella?" he responded, his voice crackling through the static of the ancient radio system.

"Umm, just wondered where you were? We had a report over the radio network that some cheetah had been spotted up towards our border with the Park; wondered if you wanted to take the guests up there to see?"

"Funny," said Ralph, "We didn't get that broadcast."

"You must have been out of range," bluffed Ella. "Just thought everyone might like to see cheetah. There's no rush to get back, is there?"

"Just that we've got some hungry people on board – but OK, we can go and take a look, it's not much of a detour. Out." And with that Ralph clicked off his radio and relayed the news to his game viewers that they were off chasing cheetah for a few minutes, so everyone help Edison spot them, please!

Ella breathed a sigh of relief that she had bought a bit more time and breathed another one, just twenty minutes later when Jackson returned, with a big grin on his face, clutching a tray of a dozen eggs.

"Jackson, I could hug you!" declared Ella.

"Oh, Miss Ella, you'll have to wait in the queue, " grinned Jackson. "I have just made a date with the pretty new receptionist at Fig Tree Lodge. She is the Number One I shall be hugging."

"No wonder you got there in record time, then. Anyway, thanks for scrounging the eggs. No doubt you'll want to be the one to take the replacement eggs back to them , as well?"

"It will be my pleasure, Miss Ella," beamed Jackson.

"Well in that case, you can do the shopping trip into town immediately after breakfast. Now got those eggs to Miriam please!"

A little while later, Ralph returned with the game drive party. As they were all getting down and heading over to the verandah for breakfast, Ralph asked Ella, "What was that all about seeing cheetah, over the radio?"

"Did you not find them?" Ella responded, sweetly.

"No. Were there ever any cheetah anyway?"

"Well, we had a bit of an egg crisis and I didn't want you back here too soon before we were able to cadge some. I couldn't dream of having a post-game-drive breakfast without eggs, so I sent Jackson over to Fig Tree Lodge. We owe them a dozen eggs."

"So sending us on a needle-in-a-haystack hunt for non-existent cheetah was your problem-solving solution?"

"Afraid so."

"Ralph, Ella, this is absolutely priceless!" declared Danny, who, unbeknown to either Ralph or Ella, had heard every word of their exchange. "That's just the sort of story I want for your programme. It's natural, it's totally unstaged, it's wonderfully human and I wish I'd been here to capture it. Ralph old friend, we're on to a winner. I can feel it in my bones!"

"There we are then," said Ella. "Now I think it's time for breakfast. We have plenty of eggs."

After breakfast, Ralph's paying guests had to pack up and leave. There were hugs and handshakes and promises of swift returns and they were seen off with Ralph and Ella waving the final goodbye.

"Right," said Ralph, "Has Jackson got his shopping list?"

"He has. And he has strict instructions to drop off one dozen eggs at Fig Tree Lodge, plus a box of chocolates to say thank you, and he has to come back to us without dawdling and drooling like a love-sick puppy over the new receptionist over there."

"What?"

"Don't ask. You don't need to know. Now, why don't you go and check on the fence where the wart hogs were burrowing you were telling me about? Can't have our precious wildlife going walkabout, can we?"

"Yes Miss Ella," said Ralph, highly amused by her brisk efficiency. "Would you like me to look out for any cheetahs while I'm over there?" He ducked her playful punch and went off to find Edison to accompany him on his fence-mending, hole-filling mission.

As the morning drifted towards noon, the temperature rose and a still descended over Mogololo. The air was oven-hot, but thankfully humidity-free. There was a shimmering heat haze towards the horizon, birds were resting in what shade they could find, a couple of listless impala pulled at the dry grass, hoping for a little nourishment. Their ears twitched in attempts to dislodge the ever-present flies and even through the heat of the day they were wary and always on the look out for potential danger. The staff at Mogololo went through their daily tasks of room-cleaning, bed changing, food preparing, always at an African pace: steady, but never fast. It was too hot to go fast and if it took a few minutes more because you walked and moved quite slowly, what did it matter? There was always time.

The noon day peace was broken by the arrival of a vehicle.

Ella furrowed her brow and checked her bookings chart on the office wall, there were no incoming guests due today, so she closed the lid of her laptop, made sure she shut the door behind her to keep out marauding vervet monkeys, and went to investigate.

Then she wished she hadn't sent Ralph off on his trip to repair the boundary. It was Inspector Masiwa, the odious policeman from the poaching incident. He had parked his battered vehicle in the space Ralph liked to keep free for the game viewing vehicle, and he was attempting to extricate his obese frame from the driver's seat. His excessive weight made it quite a struggle.

She bravely put on as welcoming a greeting as she could muster, "Inspector, good afternoon. What brings you to Mogololo?"

"Is Henderson here?" he demanded.

"Mr Henderson is not here at the moment, Inspector. He may be away for one or two more hours I'm afraid."

The Inspector snorted his frustration at this news. "And Ngoveni? Is he here?"

"He is with Mr Henderson."

"You people think you are so clever, hey?" Masiwa started moving towards Ella and it was only as he began to move that she realized he was drunk. He started gesticulating wildly, and pointing his accusatory finger in Ella's direction. "You think you get out of situations by calling in your lawyers and knowing the names of poisonous trees, but let me tell you, I know your game!"

"What game would that be, Inspector?" said Ella, not feeling as brave as she sounded.

"I am going to get your boss and Ngoveni for the deaths of those young boys! You think just because the pathologist agreed with Henderson that the smoke killed them that is the end of the matter? No way! I am not letting this case go. You tell that to your boss. OK? I know they did it. For sure. I'll get them." With that, the fat Inspector stumbled and swayed and wiped his none-too-clean face with the back of his hand. He made a grab to the door of his car and had quite a lot of difficulty opening it.

"Inspector," started Ella, 'Do you think you are OK to drive? Would you like a glass of water or something?"

The huge man turned on Ella, "All I want is justice for those poor boys who were killed on your property!" His words were slurred and he staggered as he wrestled with the door handle.

"Inspector! You really shouldn't be attempting to drive!"

"Nah!" responded the drunk policeman. "Don't you tell me what I cannot or can do! I am the officer in charge here!" And with that he just about managed to get his bloated body into the driving seat of his car. The suspension sagged under his weight and the door hinge complained with a rusty squeak as he slammed the door shut. He poked his head out of the window and shouted at Ella, "You tell that Henderson! You tell him from me!"

By now, Ella was prepared to stand her ground, "And just what should I tell Mr Henderson, Inspector?"

"The case is not closed. Not closed at all! I still regard him as the Number One Suspect!"

Ella sighed. "Very well Inspector, I will deliver your message. Mr Henderson will be delighted to receive it."

With more than a little complaint, the Inspector's car came to life, over-revving under the very heavy right foot of the policeman, he grated gears attempting to engage one that would move him forwards, eventually found one and made a very undignified exit from Mogololo.

As Ella was breathing a very big sigh of relief, Billy the TV producer came up to join her. "Well done Ella. Beautifully handled. And I know you said you didn't want to be shown on this programme, but I couldn't resist, I've got it all on tape. The sound quality won't be great, but that drunken oaf of a policeman gave a priceless performance!"

"You mean you filmed what he was accusing Ralph of?"

"Exactly."

"So we could use that as evidence against him?"

"Don't see why not."

"Oh Billy, that's great!" She flung her arms around him and gave him a huge hug. "And I know just the person to send it to! Just wait till I tell Ralph!"

Ralph and Edison came back from their fence-checking expedition and listened carefully to Ella's story of Masiwa's drunken visit. Ralph was inwardly groaning until Ella got to the part where she revealed Billy had filmed the whole episode.

"You mean we've got him abusing you on camera? Being drunk and everything?" Ralph asked.

"Let's ask Billy to show you," suggested Ella.

They all went to find Billy and Danny who had temporarily set up their production office in the corner of the main lounge.

"Billy, please show me what happened," asked Ralph.

Billy smiled, "Of course. Let me just load the footage onto my laptop."

A few cable connections and clicks on his keypad later, and the footage began to play. There were general views of Mogololo Lodge and camp first of all, then Billy had spotted the arrival of Masiwa's car. Not wanting either Ella or Masiwa to know they were being filmed, Billy had kept back, zooming in as far as his lens would allow, and as the camera was hand-held the footage was a bit shaky. But the confrontation was real, and although the sound quality was poor, with Masiwa's drunken shouting at a high volume in the first place, it was just enough to demonstrate the confrontation and the aggression the policeman was showing.

"Wow!" Ralph exclaimed, "What a bastard. Ella, you handled him perfectly."

"Thanks," she said, without any great enthusiasm.

"Ralph, we can't use any of this in a programme," Danny commented.

"Oh, I know," said Ralph. "But I'm just so grateful to Billy for getting this. I'm not sure what we're going to do with it though."

"I am," said Ella, very firmly.

"What?" asked Ralph.

"Remember Patricia? The guest who was here a few months ago? Her husband, Brian, is a legal advisor to the Minister of Justice. If I send a copy of this footage to Patricia, and ask that her husband shows it to the Minister, I am sure that would be the end of our friend Inspector Masiwa."

"You don't take prisoners, do you, my love?" said Ralph with a smile. "Billy, can you do us a copy of that enchanting scene starring the Inspector and Ella?"

"I can write you a DVD in under two minutes," said Billy. "Think of it as a 'thank you' present for your hospitality over the last couple of days!"

"Great. And Ella, perhaps you should write an accompanying letter to your friend Patricia?"

"I'll enjoy that," said Ella with a smile.

During all this interchange and the watching of the video, Edison had made no comment. He was used to thinking and considering carefully before joining any discussion. Only when he and Ralph had walked back to the vehicle to unload their fence-mending tools did he voice his opinion.

"Ralph," he started, "You have a cast iron case to get that Masiwa dismissed from the police force. But he does have some influential friends. Might it not be better to hold back? To keep your evidence as ammunition for the future rather than bring the man down now. I can't see him leaving quietly without trying to get revenge."

"I see what you mean Edison. But for the sake of Ella, I can't just let him get away with what he did this morning. The man was pissed as a newt, he never should have been driving, he was threatening towards Ella, he's accusing you and me of things we never did. No. It's completely unforgivable, unacceptable, he's a disgrace to the South African Police."

"OK," said Edison. "But watch your back."

Chapter Twelve

Danny, Billy and a cameraman called Moses returned to Mogololo a couple of weeks later. Ella had posted her letter to Patricia, together with the incriminating DVD and was waiting for a response. Letters, of course, did not actually get delivered to Mogololo. There was a post office in Hoedspruit and all mail had to be collected from a PO Box there, so unlike email, correspondence via letters and envelopes could take weeks to receive an answer. But Ella and Ralph were prepared to be patient.

The film crew, however, were eager to get their work under way. Ralph had set some guidelines for them such as not wandering off beyond the perimeter of the Lodge and camp on their own, not getting out of the game-viewing vehicle unless Ralph or Edison said so, and never to disrupt the enjoyment of the guests' experience of being at Mogololo.

As they wanted to show every aspect of life at Mogololo, they started by going behind the scenes, to areas that guests would never see, like Miriam's kitchen. To begin with Miriam was not at all happy. She was shy and nervous and would turn her back every time she was aware the camera was on her. But Moses, the cameraman was used to teasing out performances from reluctant subjects and Miriam was rather taken with the handsome young African cameraman.

"Miriam, my baby," he crooned, "My camera wants to

love you. It has seen how beautiful your hands are and wants to record how they make bread. Will you let my camera look over your shoulder while you mix everything together? "

"If I let you do that you will capture my soul and it will no longer be mine!" complained Miriam.

"No," said Moses, "It's not like that. The camera simply wants to see how clever you are. It can't take your soul away. I wouldn't let it."

Miriam blushed coyly, listening to Moses's flattery. "Well, if you will be careful not to let your camera steal anything from me, OK, you can watch me make bread."

"And will you talk to me while you are making it?" coaxed Moses, "tell me what you are doing and why."

Miriam giggled shyly and then began, "Oh, I just mix the ingredients until they are all together, then I work the dough with my hands until it is just right, and sometimes I sing to it to make it happy before I leave it to rest and rise. That is the special yeast making it work, you see. It is the yeast that tells the dough to rise and make light, tasty bread."

"So nothing to do with you?" prompted Moses, still looking through his camera viewfinder and concentrating on getting great images onto his digital disc.

"Oh, Moses, I just introduce all the ingredients to each other: the flour, the salt, the warm water, the yeast, maybe some special seeds sometimes. Then my hands will do some mixing and pushing and pulling until the dough decides to behave itself and when it knows that I am happy that it has done enough exercise, I will leave it alone in a nice warm place and it will grow to twice its size."

"And what then?"

"Oh this is the special time. I take the dough and give it just a little more working. Not too much or it will get too tired out and all the air it has taken in will escape, just like a balloon that has been pricked by a thorn. Then I will separate the dough into loaf size portions, put them into tins which I have greased with some butter, sprinkle a little flour on top and let them rest a little bit more before I pop them all in the oven. Then the guests will have fresh bread for their breakfast."

All the while Miriam was talking, Moses carefully moved around her kitchen to record the action, and with great skill, he also captured Miriam's description of her breadmaking: how she would try to push a wayward strand of her curly hair away from her brow with the back of her hand, leaving a floury smudge on her forehead; how she so skillfully manipulated the lump of dough with her strong, capable hands; how she knew just how much effort was needed, but no more. "You're an artist," he quietly told Miriam as he eventually hit the "stop recording" button on his camera. "That was brilliant."

Danny, who had been silently hovering in the background, watching the images on a little portable monitor that fed back instant footage from the camera patted Moses on the shoulder, "Great start Moses. This is going to be a winner."

The crew moved around the camp, looking for the general views and pick-up shots that would be needed when the whole programme would be edited together. They captured scenes of cheeky hornbills who were always on the lookout for scraps from either Miriam's kitchen or the dining area. Then the vervet monkeys who were forever chancing their luck but also knowing they were as safe as anywhere in the park while they were hanging around the lodge buildings. (Their mysterious humanoid cousins would ensure no predators found their way into the camp). They found small lizards sun bathing on rocks, but who would skitter away into cracks at the first signs of interruption. On their own, the shots and images were insignificant, but the production team knew they would all add to the atmosphere of the story they were telling.

That story began to take on more shape and structure when the TV team came across Ralph and Edison wrestling with a jack, attempting to change a wheel on the game viewing vehicle. Being brought up on a farm, Ralph was used to the need to turn his hand to most things mechanical, and Edison, despite his slight build, had enormous reserves of strength. Both of them, however, were finding this particular wheel resistant to their efforts.

"Bloody thing!" shouted Ralph, "Who changed this wheel last, Edison? I can't shift this one bloody nut at all."

"Jackson, I think," replied Edison, highly amused by Ralph's struggling and straining with the wheelbrace. "Want me to have a go?"

"Go on then."

Edison took over from Ralph and fitted the wheelbrace over the nut. He planted his feet firmly either side of the wheel and gripped the brace with both hands andattempted to heave it to the left. Nothing. Veins were standing out on Edison's arms, his neck and his forehead with the effort. The nut wouldn't budge.

"Come on Edison," urged Ralph, "Jackson's not stronger than you, surely?"

"Don't call me Shirley," responded Edison, still straining on the brace.

"Hold on," said Ralph, "There's a short-ish bit of scaffolding pole in the workshop, we can put that over the wheelbrace so we can use a bit of extra leverage."

"Leverage? Oh, so you did listen in your physics lessons at school then?"

"Ha-ha," said Ralph scathingly. "Got a better idea?" And he went off to the workshop to fetch his pole.

Moses had been filming this exchange without either Edison or Ralph noticing, but now, still filming, he prompted a question, "Edison, how much time do you and Ralph spend on maintenance jobs around Mogololo?"

"Too much," was Edison's very brief response. "We are game guides, not mechanics. But someone has to look after the machines and vehicles. We can't just call out a rescue service from town."

"What else do you look after?"

"Oh, pumps and generators, fridges and freezers, plumbing, that sort of thing. When you're this far out from town, you just have to fix things yourself. It's the bush. It's life."

Ralph came back with a length of scaffolding pole. He repositioned the wheelbrace and got Edison to steady it as he put the pole over the arm of the brace.

"Not too much effort Ralph," cautioned Edison, "We don't want to shear off the bolt and be left with a vehicle we can't use."

"OK Edison, no need to nag."

Ralph carefully applied his strength to the scaffolding pole lever and with a loud complaining metallic squeak, the bolt loosened.

"See?" said Ralph, "Bit of science gets there in the end."

"Better than brute force and ignorance then," said Edison.

Having loosened all of the wheel nuts, Edison put the jack under the axle and began to pump the arm of the jack up and down to raise the wheel off the dusty ground. It inched up, and was eventually clear of the ground. The wheel nuts were spun off and the wheel with its chunky tyre removed.

This prompted a question from Moses, "So what was wrong with the wheel?"

"Slow puncture," said Ralph. "Goes with the territory around here, we spend a fortune on tyres every year, but the thorns are relentless. I bet when we check this one over we'll find a nasty long thorn has found its way in between the deep treads; they're as tough as steel nails some of them. At least the termites don't eat rubber, that's one consolation I suppose."

While he'd been talking, Edison had replaced the wheel with a fully inflated spare, put back the wheel nuts and released the jack. The vehicle bumped back down to earth and Ralph tightened the nuts…but only enough to make them secure, without needing the extra effort of a scaffolding pole to undo them next time. "Right Edison," he said, "I think we'll leave the tyre repair to Jackson, don't you? Serve him right for over tightening the nuts in the first place. And make sure he puts the spare spare wheel on the Land Rover bonnet, OK?"

"He'll be thrilled!" chuckled Edison, "Getting these tyres off the rims and back on again is one of the worst jobs in the world. Would you like me to tell him?"

"Sure," agreed Ralph, "And let the film crew know when you do. It should be quite entertaining to see his reaction."

Whatever Jackson thought of the task he had been given rather paled into insignificance with what he had just given Ella. Jackson had been on the run into town to fetch supplies for Miriam and, of course, he had been to collect mail from the Mogololo PO Box. Among the letters from the bank, the electricity supply company, the insurance company, the fuel supply people and the dozens of useless circulars, was a handwritten envelope for Ella.

"It's from Patricia," she said as she opened it and quickly scanned its content.

"Wow! Patricia showed the DVD to her husband Brian; he showed it to the Minister of Justice and Masiwa was hauled up in front of the Commissioner of Police and he's been suspended."

"Quite right too," said Ralph.

"Will that be the end of it Ralph?" asked Ella.

Ralph thought for a moment, "He's a nasty, unpredictable bully. We've just been responsible for him being fired from the police, his power base. He'll be madder than a baboon cornered in a drain gully by a bunch of hyenas. Frankly, no, I don't think that's the end of it. So we'll have to be on the look out for a visit or some sort of revenge, I'm afraid."

Ella re-read the letter from Patricia again, to see if she had missed anything.

"Patricia just says 'suspended' so he can't be under arrest or anything."

"No, the police will protect their own to a certain extent, I expect," said Ralph. "We haven't brought charges or actually accused him of anything, we just happened to have evidence of his drunkenness and awful behaviour that we brought to the attention of his superiors. It's not a hanging offence, yet."

Danny had been listening to their conversation and offered, "I could always send the clip on to a mate of mine who's a senior producer on the news desk of the TV station?"

"Nice thought Danny," said Ralph, "But I don't think we're ready for that yet. Let's just lie low and be aware that Masiwa might be looking for some sort of comeback. That means you, Billy and Moses will have to watch out, too. He must know it was one of you who caught him on camera."

"In which case, the more footage we get now the sooner we can be out of here and leave you to the prospect of a visit from your angry old bull buffalo of an ex-policeman!"

"Thanks mate," said Ralph, "You're a big help! Game drive in an hour, OK?"

Before the game drive, Ralph and Ella were on the verandah, sharing a tray of coffee and some of Miriam's famous shortbread biscuits. Moses approached them and politely asked, "Is it ok if I just shoot around you for a little bit?"

"As long as you make sure it's my back to camera, most of the time," cautioned Ella.

"Yeah, go ahead," agreed Ralph "It's not going to be very exciting though, Ella wants to talk staff schedules, I think."

"It's important, Ralph!" chided Ella.

So Moses busied himself setting up one small camera fixed on a tripod for a constant wide shot, while he operated his other camera hand-held, slowly moving around the couple as they chatted. This way, he had useful editing points which would make the conversation appear seamless when they cut out all the superfluous, unnecessary comments.

Ella started, "Actually it's nothing to do with staff schedules, it's more of a staff bonus scheme I've thought of."

"Ella!" responded Ralph, "If this is going to cost me money the answer is no. You know we're really strapped for cash as it is, we can't even think about increasing our overhead without being sure of generating more revenue."

"But my love," said Ella sweetly, "This will increase revenue, I'm sure of it."

"Go on then," said Ralph, sounding not at all convinced.

"Well, you know that most guests are really generous with tips when they leave Mogololo, they either ask me to add something to their bar bill for the staff, or they leave some cash in their rooms for them…"

"…And a lot of people want to tip Edison for the game he always manages to find for them," added Ralph.

"That's right, and all the tips are pooled and divided at the end of each month according to seniority."

"That works OK, doesn't it?"

"To a degree, yes, But what I was thinking that if we get the staff together and tell them we will add another, say, 20% to their tips if they manage to get the guests to make another booking with us before they leave. It would sound so much better and less pressurized coming from the staff rather than from you or me. Do you see? It would be sort of, 'Thank you so much Mr So and So for visiting us here at Mogololo. I hope you have enjoyed your stay and I really look forward to seeing you again. Would you like to come back and and see us?' That sort of thing."

"Yes…" said Ralph rather hesitantly. "But could we be sure they would do it properly? Talking the guests into making another booking, I mean."

"With a bit of coaching, yes, I'm sure I could encourage them. For Grace and Miriam it would come naturally. Jackson would take a bit of proper guidance, you know what a loose cannon he can be. Edison would be fine, and the girls who do the rooms, they come into contact with the guests sometimes and as we'd be promising the prospect of more money, it wouldn't be a problem getting them on board."

"What about the kitchen helpers?"

"Mmm, they don't have much face-to-face time with the guests do they? Perhaps we could get Miriam to train them to be waitresses as well as kitchen girls?"

"It would be good if they smiled a bit more," grumbled Ralph.

"You're right," agreed Ella. "I think that's because Miriam gives them a tough time. I'll have a word and explain to Miriam that if this is going to work and they all benefit, then everyone has to be more 'guest-friendly.'"

"But they only get the bonus when a guest makes another booking?"

"That's the idea, yes."

"So if it doesn't work and no one makes a return booking it won't cost us anything."

"Correct."

"Well I'm all for more smiles and great guest relations, so yes, let's do it."

With that, Ella got up from her seat and leant over the coffee table, completely forgetting that Moses and his cameras were there. She held Ralph's face in her hands and kissed him, deeply. It was a kiss that was much more from a lover than simply a colleague and Ralph responded enthusiastically. Until, that is, he remembered Moses. He tactfully and quite reluctantly eased himself out of the embrace, clearing his throat as he did so, "Er…Moses? Can I trust you to leave that last bit out…?"

"Oh shit," muttered Ella, "I'd completely forgotten Moses was there."

Moses quietly chuckled to himself, "Mr Invisible. That's me."

"It's OK," Ralph reassured Ella. "I'll have a word with

Danny and remind him we're looking for a family audience, he's not making an adult-movie. But I, for one, really enjoyed it!"

Ella's red face was a picture as she attempted to move back into the 'professional management' persona she thought was needed. "Well, I'll see if everyone's ready for a game drive, shall I?"

The Land Rover was loaded with guests, film crew, sundowner drinks and snacks, Edison perched on his little seat over the front bumper and Ralph pulled out of the camp. He gazed up at the sky and was aware that the clear blue that had been above them in the earlier part of the day was now dotted with clouds, not the usual white, cotton-wool variety, but clouds that were tinged with grey and the breeze was freshening, too. He made a comment, as much to himself as the others on board the vehicle, "Could be the rains are coming soon. It's about time, the land could do with it, the animals, too."

"Will it rain while we're out on our drive?" asked one of the guests, anxiously.

"Hard to say," said Ralph. "The only predictable thing about our weather is that it's unpredictable. Could be in twenty minutes, twenty hours, or twenty days. It'll rain when it's ready. But don't worry, we've got ponchos to keep you covered if it does start chucking it down."

The thought of rain was quickly forgotten as Edison signalled that there were elephant off to the left. Ralph brought the vehicle to a halt and all eyes were on the elephants. They were three young adult males and Edison recognised them as a group of boys-about-the-bush that he had seen before, and they could be stroppy. Once the Land Rover was stopped, Edison skipped around to the back of the vehicle and hopped up to the top level. He didn't want to be over-exposed at the front with this unpredictable group of hooligans.

As they watched, the watchers on the Land Rover could see why Edison was taking evasive action. Two of the massive animals began squaring up to each other, heads slightly lowered, trunks overlapping and their tusks clacking against each other like very clumsy sword fighters. They pushed against each other, grunting and snorting as they took strain. There was no real malice in their contest, just a struggle to show, 'I'm the strongest, and you'd better accept it'. But, of course, neither would back down.

"This sort of rough and tumble can go on for hours," explained Ralph to the party in the vehicle. "Just establishing supremacy for when the time comes to challenge the big alpha male elephants for breeding rights."

"But can the aggression spill over and threaten us?" asked one of the guests, nervously.

"No, not really, but Edison's right to be on the safe side. One of them could say 'Enough's enough,' and turn our way and give us a slap with his trunk. In a playful way, of course!" joked Ralph.

While the two sparring elephants continued their push-of-war, the third was busy stripping bark from a tree, gouging at the surface with his tusk until enough had peeled away for him to grip the end of the bark with the tip of his trunk and pull away a strip about a metre long. He then fed this into his mouth and proceeded to grind away with his molars, while his tusk went scraping along the edge of the peeled-away bark to strip off the next piece.

"How much nourishment is an elephant going to get from a strip of bark?" asked one of the guests.

"Not a great deal," replied Ralph. "I can't quite remember the figures, but Elephants can stuff something like 150 kilos of fodder into their mouths each day, but an awful lot of it comes out the other end, too. They are not very efficient eaters I'm afraid, in terms of turning what they eat into usable energy and reserves of fat."

Just as Ralph had finished this digestive point, the elephant seemed to get bored with stripping bark and eating it. Instead, he put his massive head against the trunk of the tree and began slowly rocking backwards and forwards and on each forward push he seemed to put more effort into it. After a dozen or more forward pushes, the tree had had enough and very slowly, but inevitably, it crashed down. Now the elephant could get at the youngest, freshest leaves that had been at the top of this tree that had previously been out of reach. The other two elephants broke off from their rather half-hearted battle against each other and came to enjoy the fruits of their fellow elephant's labours by stripping away leaves and stuffing them in their mouths. But before long, and well before they had eaten all of the foliage, they all seemed to get bored with this activity, and they moved off, silently and steadily into deeper bush, away from the Land Rover.

"Wow," exclaimed one of the game viewers, "that was spectacular. But so wasteful. Why didn't they eat all the leaves on that tree that elephant had pushed down?"

"Who knows?" said Ralph, who had never figured it out for himself. "Elephants are destructive. They push over a lot of trees and you're right, they never eat everything they could. But don't forget, a lot of the trees survive, they still have lots of roots clinging on to the earth and the tree on the ground provides lots of shelter for other animals. Nature just has a way of balancing everything out."

With his little elephant lecture over, Ralph looked up at the sky and frowned,

"Folks, I think we may be in for one of our famous showers. If you grope around under your seats, you should find some rain ponchos. Just to get them ready in case the rain comes. Frankly, we could do with it!"

"Couldn't it wait until we get back to the lodge?" grumbled one of the guests. As if in response to this lighthearted comment, there was a sudden crack of thunder and a rumble, resonating around the hills in the distance.

"Not so sure the weather has a specific timetable," grinned Ralph, starting up the engine. "But we'll start heading back now. We may be lucky. We may be wet."

Just a few kilometres away, at Mogololo Lodge, the rain had already arrived. It had started slowly, but ominously. Great big rain drops, splattering the dry dust in ones and twos. Would it come to a real storm? Would it pass over? Would it decide it couldn't really be bothered to rain after all?

The birds knew. They had all taken what shelter they could, roosting in trees that gave some degree of cover from the rain they instinctively knew was coming, and as they fluffed out their feathers they grew more and more silent, waiting for the storm.

Jackson was in the open-fronted workshop, wrestling with the Land Rover wheel that needed repair. He'd managed to deflate it completely and was attempting to remove the chunky tyre from the steel wheel.

While he worked, the rain drops gathered in frequency and intensity. This was going to be a real African rain storm. It hammered on the tin roof of the workshop, drowning out the sounds coming from the pathetic little radio Jackson was listening to; he was singing along to the local pop music while he'd managed to get two tyre levers under the rubber rim and was concentrating on getting the third in place so he could persuade the tyre to separate from the wheel. He was kneeling on the edge of the tyre to depress it and give him space to get his tyre lever in position and so was completely oblivious to the silent approach of a stranger behind him. There were no introductions. Jackson never knew what hit him. It was actually a pick axe handle, swung hard enough at the base of his skull to knock him senseless, but not so hard that it killed him.

But Jackson was out cold, just the clatter of a long tyre lever on the cement floor of the workshop to mix with the hammering of the rain on the tin roof.

The stranger was not alone. There were two of them. "OK. Now find the woman," said the one with the pick axe handle, "The big man said there would only be this one guy here while the party was out on a game drive."

"The office must be over there," muttered the second, indicating the main lodge building through the rain. This second man was clutching a bag under his arm and both he and the pick axe man made a dash through the rain to get on to the verandah of the lodge. They looked furtively around. No one was venturing out – the rain was now in full force, darkening the air and hammering the dusty ground, quickly creating little streams and puddles in the red earth that soon became sloppy mud. The two men looked for signs of life. No one came to challenge them. The one nodded to the other to follow as he crept towards the open door. Inside, he scanned the room that was used by guests for lounging, reading and relaxing, with the bar in one corner. Another door, also open, was beyond the bar and the pick axe man could hear something coming from inside – the tapping of a computer keyboard.

The two men approached silently then burst into the office, completely surprising Ella who screamed with fright. She jumped up from her office chair and, still screaming, backed away – but she had nowhere to go. The man with the bag grabbed her, the pick axe man stuck his big black hand over her mouth and gripped her face hard, and with wild, staring eyes commanded her, "If you scream again, you will be hurt. Do you understand? I will hurt you."

A terrified Ella did as she was told but still attempted to struggle free. Her struggles were futile, she was held too tightly. From his bag, the second man took a roll of broad duct tape and roughly strapped Ella's hands behind her back. With that done, he tore off a strip of his tape and stuck it over her mouth. Poor Ella was panting with fright and still struggled and tried to kick herself free but both these intruders were far too strong for her. The bag man took a none-too-clean empty 10 kilogramme maize meal sack from his bag and put it over Ella's head.

"OK" said pick axe handle man, "Let's go. Pick up her legs". And with him holding her upper body and the bag man carrying her lower legs, they bustled their way out of the office, Ella still struggling as much as she could and as they rounded her desk, all the papers and the laptop she was using went flying to the floor. The bag man hesitated, just for a second.

"Leave it," said pick axe man, "They'll know she's gone anyway, let's get out."

So, carrying a still-struggling and terrified Ella under their arms, they made their way through the lodge, out onto the verandah and beyond into the rain.

They splashed their way past the parking area and another fifty metres to where they had parked their beaten up old Toyota saloon. Still holding the top half of Ella under his arm, pick axe handle man fumbled with the boot catch, raised it up and they bundled Ella into the boot and slammed the lid down. The two men got into the front of the car, started it up and headed off back the way they had come, away from Mogololo. No one could hear Ella's muffled cries of terror and anguish, or the thumping of her feet inside the boot.

Chapter Thirteen

The rain had turned many of the tracks through the game reserve into slippery mud slides but Ralph was used to it and controlled the Land Rover very skillfully as they slowly made their way back to the lodge. The guests were huddled under their ponchos, Danny and Billy made sure their camera and recording equipment stayed dry, while they suffered the inconvenience of getting wet themselves, and Ralph and Edison just got on with it; Edison even pointing out the odd giraffe or kudu who seemed oblivious to the drenching downpour.

Ralph attempted to lighten the mood by telling stories of other rainstorms he had experienced at Mogololo, but no one seemed too interested, so he cut his monologue short and just concentrated on steering the party back to the Lodge.

The light, already compromised by the heavy clouds and still falling rain was all but gone by the time they pulled into the parking space at Mogololo.

"OK Folks," shouted Ralph, "Use your ponchos to get back to your bungalows, then let's hope the rain's stopped by the time dinner is ready. See you whenever you're ready for drinks."

The guests, as well as Danny and Billy, did as they were told and dashed to the dry havens of their bungalows. With Edison still on board, Ralph drove the Land Rover round to the workshop where he could get it under cover and attempt to dry it out for the morning.

He was just turning in to the workshop entrance, his mind elsewhere, when Edison shouted "Ralph!"

Ralph stamped on the brake, stopping just a metre from Jackson's unconscious body. "Shit! Jackson!"

Jackson was still slumped over the Land Rover tyre he was attempting to remove before he was laid low with the pick axe handle. Edison was the first to get to him. "He's breathing, there's blood on the back of his neck. Jackson, hey Jackson! Can you hear me?"

Moving Jackson's body a little was enough to bring him round. He groaned and slowly opened his eyes.

"OK Jackson," said Ralph. "What happened?"

More groaning from Jackson, who now tried to sit up. "Why does my head hurt?"

"I think someone jumped you from behind. Can you not remember?"

"Oh, no. My head really hurts! And my neck."

"Come on Jackson," urged Ralph, "What were you doing?"

"I was still fixing this tyre, getting it off the wheel rim. That's all." Jackson tried feeling the back of his head, "Ow! What hit me?"

"We'd better find out," said Ralph. "Can you just sit there

for a bit Jackson. We'll bring you some water. Edison, we'd better check the Lodge."

So Ralph and Edison made their way through the rain that was thankfully easing off now, up to the main Lodge building.

Ralph called out, "Ella! Ella! Where are you?" No reply. They walked through the lounge, past the bar and into the office where Ella could have been working. He took in the mess of the usually tidy office.

"This isn't right," commented Edison, rather unnecessarily.

"Go and see if Miriam saw or heard anything," suggested Ralph, while he picked up the laptop that had been knocked to the floor in the struggle. He stood by the door of the little office, confused and with a rising sense of dread that something bad had happened while they were on their game drive.

Edison came back just a minute later. "No, neither Miriam nor the girls saw or heard anything. They were in the kitchen and the noise of the rain was pretty loud."

Ralph remembered poor Jackson. "Edison, could you get one of the girls to go and help Jackson; get him some water, give him some sympathy. I don't think he needs hospital, his skull is probably made of iron, it would take more than a knock on his head to do any permanent damage."

"Sure, but what about Ella?"

"I know. Or rather, I don't know. I'll check our bedroom, but I can't think she'd have left the office like this. No, I've got a horrible feeling about this Edison."

"Sure. I'll get Jackson seen to, then I'll look around outside."

"Thanks."

Ralph went off to look in their bedroom, but as he thought, there was no sign of Ella. Her little car was parked around the back on the store room, where it usually was. He found it really difficult to concentrate, to marshal his thoughts logically and sensibly. He had unsubstantiated visions of Ella being attacked, hurt, attempting to fight back and being hurt even more. They weren't good thoughts. He made his way back into the main lodge, just as Edison was coming back.

"I found the tracks of two people and a car; it must have been hidden around the back of the water tank, beyond the parking area," explained Edison. "Two men's footprints. They were slipping and sliding a lot."

"But no girl's footprints? No Ella?"

"No."

Ralph thought for a bit. "They could have been carrying her?" he suggested.

"Perhaps," agreed Edison.

Ralph pulled his thoughts together and worked out what he should do. "Look, Edison, can you hold the fort this evening? I'll have a word with Danny and explain what's happened – or what we think has happened – and he'll help with the guests' hospitality, I'm sure. I'll take Jackson with me into town and we'll go to the police."

Edison groaned, "Good luck with that," he said dismissively. "We know what we think of the police around here, don't we?"

"Well maybe now that Masiwa has gone, things might have bucked up a bit. And at least I can get Jackson looked at by someone who knows about first aid!"

"I thought you said his skull was made of iron?' joked Edison, trying to lighten the mood.

"Well, even iron can be cracked if you hit it hard enough!"

On the way into town, the headlights of Ralph's truck were startling the night jars and owls that were foraging in the shallow muddy pools of the dirt road. The rain had stopped and the night was clear and calm. Calm that is, apart from Jackson's running commentary on what he intended to do to whoever had whacked him over the head.

"I think they must have used a baseball bat Mr Ralphie," he suggested. "Or maybe a crowbar, or a knobkerrie like my grandfather used to have."

"Well, let's leave all the investigations to the police, shall we, Jackson?" said Ralph, whose thoughts were much more with what had happened to Ella rather than his over-excited junior ranger.

"So you didn't hear a car at all then Jackson?"

"No, Mr Ralphie. The rain was so strong, beating down on the tin roof. I heard nothing. Just you and Edison waking me up and me having a big headache."

"Well, I'm sure the doctor in town will be able to see to that, Jackson. Now, let's have a bit of peace so I can concentrate on getting us to the police station in one piece, shall we?"

They arrived at the police station to find just a desk sergeant and a constable on duty. They both looked surprised to have customers at that time of the evening in such a small, sleepy town. The sergeant recognized Ralph from the previous encounters with Inspector Masiwa.

"Mr Henderson," he said, "How may the Hoedspruit police be of service to you?"

"We've had an incident at Mogololo," started Ralph, "One person attacked and one person missing."

"Attacked?" said the startled Sergeant.

"Me!" offered Jackson, showing the sergeant the bloodied back of his head.

"And did you see this attacker or attackers?"

"No. I was busy bending over a tyre I was changing. If I had seen them coming, I would have fought them off."

"OK, Jackson, I'm sure you would have seen them off," said Ralph, wanting to get the conversation with the sergeant back to the missing Ella. "But our Lodge manager, Ella Moffat has been abducted."

"Abducted!" exclaimed the sergeant. "How do you know?"

"Well, whoever thumped Jackson here must have wanted him out of the way; Ella would have been in the office and when we came back from our game drive at sundown, the office was in a mess – as if there had been a struggle – and Ella's not at the Lodge. Anywhere."

"And she has not gone for a drive on her own, or to run an errand, or a walk?"

"First, it was pouring with rain. Second, her car has not moved. Third, Edison, my chief tracker, found two sets of male footprints and the tracks of a car that had been hidden behind our water tank. So the answer, Sergeant, is no, she did not leave the Lodge of her own accord."

"I see. You will have noticed, Mr Henderson, that since the recent and sudden departure of Inspector Masiwa, we are understaffed here at the police station." Turning to Jackson, he continued, "Are you able to give a description of your attackers?

"No, I told you. They jumped me from behind. I didn't see anything or anyone."

"And Mr Henderson, have you tried reaching your Lodge Manager through her cellphone?"

"It was still on her office desk when I discovered she was missing."

"I will take a statement from you now, Mr Henderson, and telephone the report through to Nelspruit and request they send up a team to follow up and start a search for Miss Moffat. Can you give me a full description?"

"Better than that," said Ralph, taking out his phone from his shirt pocket and thumbing through the screen, "I took this picture of her last week. If you've got an email address, I'll send it to you now."

"Isn't technology wonderful," said the sergeant, genuinely impressed that Ralph had the forethought to share a recent picture of Ella.

Having written out his statement, emailed Ella's picture from his phone and listened in on the sergeant's relaying of the incident to his superiors in Nelspruit, Ralph realized there was no more he could do at the police station, so he took Patrick to visit to Ella's doctor friend. As Ralph had thought, Patrick's injury was quite superficial and he had mild concussion (much to Patrick's disappointment that he wouldn't be able to capitalize any further on his celebrity status). In fact Ella's medical friend was far more concerned about Ella's disappearance than Patrick's injury and promised to follow up on Ralph's behalf back at the police station in the morning.

With that, Patrick and Ralph returned to Mogololo. And waited.

Chapter Fourteen

Locked in the boot of the old Toyota, Ella was fighting her rising panic. Her breath was coming in short, quick gasps and she knew from her physio training that wasn't good. She tried so hard to tell her brain to slow down, to try and breathe more normally but she was so uncomfortable and the rest of her body wouldn't listen to what her brain was trying to say. The inside of the old maize sack was scratchy on her face and smelled foul. The tape that had been so roughly stuck across her face and mouth was pulling at her skin and she so wanted to scratch her nose!

'Think, think', she told herself. But it's so hard to think when your hands are bound behind you and you're lying scrunched up in the boot of an awful old car; the floor is uneven and your knees are scraping on something sharp and one shoulder is bashing on the inside of the boot lid while the car's terrible suspension complains about the ruts and potholes they seem to be travelling over, and the other shoulder is going numb from her own weight lying on it.

She manages to control her breathing a little better and begins to count to try and bring down her heart rate,

'thousand one, thousand two, thousand three…' It seems to help and although the discomfort increases with every lurch and bump of the journey, the panic subsides. There's no chance of relaxing but Ella realizes there's no point in trying to struggle while she's enduring this hellish journey. 'Thousand eighteen, thousand nineteen, thousand twenty ...' "Oh sod it!" she attempts to say out loud, but the sticky tape across her face doesn't let her, so she lets out a groan of frustration instead. It doesn't help much.

She has no idea how long she's been a captive passenger in this moving metal coffin. It seems like hours; in fact it's just a little over forty five minutes. She senses the car is slowing but if anything, the bumps get even worse. The engine strains as the driver has it in the wrong gear; even Ella can tell the car is just about on its last legs as both suspension and steering complain with metallic insistency that this journey could well be one of its last. Eventually, it stops.

Car doors squeak open and slam. Footsteps shuffle around the car and Ella tenses herself ready for the boot to be opened. It flies up and through the loose mesh of the horrid sack over her head Ella can sense it is dark. Although the smell of the car boot and the sack itself are strong, she is also aware of woodsmoke and burning paraffin. The two men don't speak but she can hear voices in the distance and music – music coming from cheap radios or TVs all tuned to local African stations. It quickly dawns on her: she's in a township.

One man takes her arms, the other her legs and they heave her out of the boot. Ella cries with pain through the sticky tape covering her mouth as her hip is bashed against the boot catch but the men offer neither help nor sympathy. They lift her easily between them and make their way quickly into a building. One of them kicks the bottom of a door and it swings back easily, then the other closes it behind them. Ella is now shaking with fear at what will happen. She's dumped, not too gently, into a plastic chair. With her hands taped behind her and her legs strapped together and a bag over her head, she's in no position to resist. She slumps forward, and sobs, uncontrollably, involuntarily, and she hates herself for it.

One of the men orders the other, "Go and get the big man. I'll wait with the woman." Ella hears the other man leave and the door slam behind him. Her sobs have subsided and she steels herself to be strong, even though she's terrified by what has happened already and what might still lie ahead of her. She could hear the man moving around the room. He lit a cigarette and Ella was aware of the smell of the smoke, mingling with the other smells of the room, not particularly pleasant ones. Through the rough weave of the sack over her head she could sense there was a light coming from somewhere, but it wasn't an electric bulb, more than likely it was a paraffin light, maybe two of them. She thought to herself, 'Here I am, a prisoner, kidnapped, and I'm wondering whether there is just one light or two, illuminating this prison I'm in. Why am I not thinking how I'm going to get out of this? How am I going to escape?'

She couldn't continue this train of thought for long because the door crashed open and she was aware that two people had entered.

"No one saw you take her?" snapped a new voice.

"No, no one", came the reply.

"And she didn't give you any trouble?"

"No Boss."

Ella thought hard. She knew that voice. She recognized the arrogance, the assumption of authority, the bullying nature of his tone. It was Masiwa, the policeman. She corrected herself: the ex-policeman. The jigsaw pieces slotted themselves together. Masiwa wanted revenge, and by taking her, this was how he was doing it. Although she had a flicker of relief at solving the puzzle, the dread inside her came flooding back. She knew Masiwa would be ruthless; he'd lost his job, what else was there for him to lose? By taking her, he thought he had leverage and a blackmail weapon. Ella felt more afraid than ever.

"Take off her hood," commanded Masiwa. One of the men took the sack from Ella's head. "So, Miss Moffat, isn't it? I understand you are the one responsible for arranging my recent dismissal from the police force."

Ella struggled to speak, but failed. Instead she made a growling noise and tried to use her eyes to inflict as much damage as she could into Masiwa's soul; if he had one, of course. It was a futile attempt at challenging Masiwa, but it was all Ella had at her disposal. Sadly, all it made Masiwa do was laugh.

"Miss Moffat, it is no good attempting to shame me into letting you go, or for you to try to attempt escape. You don't even know where you are, do you?"

Ella gave another snort through her nose and struggled against the tape across her mouth.

"Now, what I am going to do," explained Masiwa, in a tone he thought would sound reasonable, if Ella didn't already know he wasn't to be trusted, "Is that I shall remove the tape from your mouth in a minute and I will make a short video of you, and you will talk on the video to say you are unharmed and being well cared for. Do you think you can do that for me?"

Ella's response to this was to struggle in the chair and be as angry as she could. It didn't help.

"Then," continued Masiwa, "I will send the video to your friend Mr Henderson, and he will pay me a sum of money in consideration of your safe return. If he does not pay me the money, well …" And Masiwa left the unspoken threat hanging in the air.

"Bring another lamp in here", ordered Masiwa, "I need Miss Moffat to appear as good as possible in her video performance."

One of the men, the one who had been carrying the bag when they abducted Ella from the Lodge, did as he was told and brought in another paraffin lamp – Ella noticed there appeared to be no mains electricity in the room where she was being held. He held it high to one side of where Ella was sitting. Masiwa was busy fiddling with his mobile phone, finding the video setting.

"Now Miss Moffat," he said, "I want you to just tell Mr Henderson that you are unharmed … at the moment … and you want him to do as I instruct him. Is that clear?"

Ella growled through the tape across her face.

"Ah, but of course!" Masiwa added. Then, to the other thug, the one not holding the lamp, he commanded, "You are going to take that tape off her face when I tell you. But get the roll of tape ready to go back over her mouth after I've stopped recording. OK?" The thug grunted, found the roll of sticky tape and ripped off a strip, lightly attaching it to the thigh of his filthy-looking jeans, ready to go onto Ella's face when Masiwa asked for it.

"OK, take it off." Ella steeled herself for the pain and shock of the heavy duty tape being ripped from her cheeks and mouth. She squealed with pain, followed by a gasp of anger.

"You bastard policeman!" she managed to shout, "You shit!"

Masiwa just laughed. "Miss Moffat, call me what you like, it doesn't change the fact that you are here and you're not going anywhere until Henderson pays up for your release. Now, in just a moment, you will tell him that you are unharmed and that he should do as instructed. OK?"

Ella glared at the fat ex-policeman as he attempted to clumsily frame her head and shoulders in the viewfinder of his mobile phone and said to her, "Go ahead."

Ella said nothing for a few seconds, then taking in a deep breath, blurted out, "Ralph! I don't know where I am, in a township, I think. But they wouldn't dare kill me! Don't give in to them! But find me! Please!"

Masiwa stopped recording, slowly walked the two paces towards Ella and slapped her, hard, across the face. "Not what I asked for! Now we do it again and you say you are unharmed and if he wants you back he should do as he is instructed. Do you understand?"

Ella had screamed, involuntarily, at the slap Masiwa had given her and now sat, slumped in her chair, fighting back tears and sobs. Masiwa continued, in what he considered to be a more conciliatory tone, "You see, you need to realise Miss Moffat, you are not among friends at the moment. You are, not to put too fine a point on it, a hostage. My hostage. And the more you resist and play games, the more uncomfortable, and painful, it will become." He loomed over her, with malice and venom oozing from his massive bulk, "Do you understand!"

"Yes," whimpered Ella.

"Right, then we will continue. I am recording …now."

Ella stared at Masiwa, saying nothing.

"Miss Moffat," said the big policeman, "You still have not fully understood your position. You have no bargaining power. You have no one to help you. I suggest you do as you are told. Now. I have stopped recording while you gather your thoughts and when I drop my hand, you will speak as I have told you. You need to impress upon Henderson that he should follow my instructions or you will be in more danger than you are at present. Are you ready?"

Masiwa held up his arm, and after a second or two, he dropped it.

"Ralph," said Ella to the camera phone. "I'm OK. At the moment. Don't know where I am, but I think I'm in danger if you don't do what he says." Then Ella's emotions took over, "For God's sake Ralph, help me … please!…" And the sobs poured out of her.

"Excellent!" gloated Masiwa after he had stopped the recording and checked it back. "Worthy of an Oscar, I think." Then to his two thugs he said, "Tape up her mouth again. No, give her somwater first then tape up her mouth. OK?" And with that, he walked out of the hut and into the night.

A minute or two later, one of the Africans brought a battered tin mug up to Ella and held it while she greedily slurped at the water; most of it spilled down her front but she was past caring about her appearance and almost said thank you to the man who had given her the drink. But she didn't. Then the other guy roughly applied the adhesive tape across her mouth and they both left the hut. As Ella's face was wet with the water she'd attempted to drink, the tape didn't stick too well this time, so Ella was not as uncomfortable as she had been but she still felt bereft, exhausted, alone.

At Mogololo, the evening mood was particularly sombre. Although neither Edison or Danny discussed the strange disappearance of Ella in front of them, the guests seemed to be aware of something not being quite right. They ate dinner but didn't linger. Edison promised them a special game drive in the morning and they all retired for the night. Edison waited up for Ralph and Jackson to return from town.

Ralph drove as quietly as he could into the camp, so as not to disturb the guests.

"Anything?" asked Edison as Ralph wearily climbed up the verandah steps.

"No," responded Ralph. "Only that the Hoedspruit police have passed it up the line to Nelspruit. Too big and awkward a situation for them to handle."

"And is Jackson OK?"

"Big lump on his head, bit of minor concussion, but the Doc said he would get over it. The doctor was actually more worried about Ella. Shit, Edison! Who's got her? Where is she?"

Edison didn't reply but quietly went to the bar to pour Ralph a generous shot of whisky. Ralph sipped at it gratefully. "God, what a way to end the day," he sighed as he slumped further into his chair, cradling the glass on his chest.

"I'll look after the early morning game drive," volunteered Edison. "You'd better be here for the police. I assume they want to visit?"

"Yes, I guess it will be the Nelspruit lot," said Ralph. "So we'd better leave the office in the mess we found it. They might want to fingerprint things."

Ralph was busy staring into his now empty glass of

whisky, wondering whether to have another, when there was "ping" from his shirt pocket.

"Odd," he said, fishing out his phone, "Wi-fi doesn't usually reach this far."

He looked at the screen of his phone and scrolled through to his email inbox.

A couple of clicks later and all the colour drained from his face. "Oh Shit! Edison!"

"What?"

"It's Ella. Someone's got her!"

Edison quickly came over to see what Ralph was looking at.

Ralph clicked on the video start icon and even though the connection to the Lodge's wi-fi was slow, he could make out Ella the distress she was in and the message she was being forced to deliver. The video kept stopping and starting while the fairly feeble Mogololo wi-fi connection tried to cope with the size of the video file and catch up with itself, but Ralph got the message. "Bastards!" he snarled.

"They must be making demands," said Edison, being the calm, logical man he always was. "What does the email itself say?"

Ralph clicked again. "OK, it says, '500,000 rand in cash. In 24 hours. Wait for another mail to tell you where. Do not involve the authorities. Reply to this mail that you understand.' But there's a spelling mistake in 'authorities', not that it's important."

"And who's sent it?"

"It's from a Hotmail account: Max334455@hotmail.com"

"Max? Could be anybody."

"Could be … but I've got a sneaky suspicion I know who Max is going to be. It's that crook Masiwa, isn't it?" said Ralph.

"He's the most obvious," agreed Edison.

"Half a million rand," muttered Ralph. "He could have made it five million, ten million, I've hardly got a couple of thousand spare at the moment."

"But you've now got a lead to give the police, haven't you?" said Edison

"Or, for the sake of Ella, do we keep it to ourselves?" said Ralph.

Ralph thought to himself for a few seconds, then said, "Is there a way of finding out where emails are sent from?"

"No good asking me," said Edison. "I track animals for a living, not electronics." Then he had another thought, "Danny might know, but you are going to let the police know you've had a demand, aren't you?"

"Edison, you know what I think of the police, don't you?" said Ralph dismissively. "And tomorrow morning we'll have strangers from Nelspruit up here going through the motions and filling out forms and probably doing sod all to help find Ella."

"Ralph," cautioned Edison, "You ought to let them handle it their way."

"Maybe you're right," sighed Ralph. "After all, I haven't got half a million bucks, have I?"

"Will you reply to that mail?"

"I'll sleep on it. No I won't. I can't imagine I'll be sleeping at all tonight. But I'll think about it. Go on Edison, you go to bed. I guess Grace will be worried sick about Ella, too."

The pins and needles in Ella's legs just wouldn't stop. Like a torture of electric shocks, her shins and ankles jerked uncontrollably, but were so strongly tethered by the wrapping tape they hardly moved a millimetre.

She groaned in a mixture of extreme discomfort and frustration but the sensation wouldn't go away. In an attempt to distract herself from what was happening below her knees, she tried to assess her situation: she was a hostage; she'd been assaulted; she desperately wanted to wee but wasn't about to ask; she was in a room that she had worked out must be in an African township or village; it wasn't a nice room; she was terrified of what was going to happen to her next. The floor was rough concrete, dirty and uneven. Her flimsy plastic garden chair rocked annoyingly on the bumpy floor and there were all sorts of creepy crawlies living in the cracks of the breezeblock walls. It wasn't a nice place.

Then she made a list of the more positive things: she didn't appear to be injured; Masiwa was going to be in touch with Ralph to exchange her for a ransom; she was sitting on a chair rather than just dumped on this disgustingly dirty floor of this room; she was going to survive this.

Her positivity didn't last long. She knew Ralph didn't have any spare funds in reserve, so whatever Masiwa asked for he wouldn't be able to raise. Nor was Masiwa to be trusted. A shudder of despair ran all the way through her, and the tension that was in her shoulders, back, arms and legs made the pins and needles even worse.

She almost gave in to another bout of silent sobbing, when the door to the room opened, quite quietly, and one of the thugs who had abducted her came in. The light was very poor, just the one paraffin lamp had been left in the corner, but Ella sensed there was something different about this guy. He must have been in his early twenties Ella guessed, dressed in the standard uniform of scruffy jeans and trashy T shirt. The trainers on his feet must have been third or fourth hand and this time, when Ella looked at him, his eyes were wide and stary.

There was also a smell about him. As well as the usual African male smell that Ella was completely used to (more their diet than an issue of personal hygiene), there was another smell sensation. As he stepped slowly into the room, Ella realised what it was: marijuana! The guy was stoned out of his mind.

Ella wouldn't say she was experienced in the ways of marijuana; there were a one or two times in her student days when she and her friends had experimented and coughed their way through a couple of joints, but she clearly remembered the smell and this young African, stumbling in this room, brought those memories flooding back.

After some effort, he spoke, "Ya, my name is Eric. Like Eric Clapton the guitarist, you know?"

Ella's eyes followed him as he attempted an appalling attempt at air guitar, mimicking Eric Clapton's uncopy-able style. She wasn't at all reassured by this opening gambit of his and attempted to shrink further away from him in her plastic garden chair.

"So, I think you and me should make some music, like Eric Clapton, yeah?" He shoved his hand into the back pocket of his jeans and fished out a vicious-looking flick knife. The blade sprang open and he leant down to Ella's ankles and started to cut through the strong adhesive tape that had been binding her legs together. Ella yelped as the blade cut through the material of her trousers and knicked her skin. Eric looked surprised and almost apologetic at her reaction. "Oh, so sorry, Miss Moffat" he grinned, then continued to release the sticky tape.

It was a huge relief when Ella was at last able to move her legs, but now Eric was waving the knife closely in front of her face. "Now I'm going to unbind your arms from the chair and we make nice jicky-jicky, yeah?"

Ella froze at the thought of what his words implied. His drug-addled eyes were still dangerously unfocused and even though he was obviously high, Ella knew there was no chance of her escaping from him. All she could do was emit a low, desperate and pleading moan. Eric took this as a sign of encouragement. "Yes, baby. Come to Eric, yeah?" He released her arms and pulled her roughly out of the chair and on to the floor of this squalid room. The concrete floor was rough, dirty and sticky. Ella kicked and thrashed as much as she could but he was so much stronger, even under the influence of the drugs he had smoked. He knelt across the tops of her legs and fiddled with the belt buckle of her trousers, still hanging on to the frightening knife in his right hand. He managed to undo the belt and was struggling to shift her trousers down her legs. He got them down as far as her knees and grabbed at the delicate lacy material of her knickers, ripping the flimsy fabric and hurting Ella in the process. Ella was thrashing around and hitting out at him with her bare hands, until Eric turned particularly brutal, "Don't struggle white bitch! We make jicky-jicky and you make Eric happy, yeah?" He was still kneeling over her and started to undo his own jeans; Ella caught sight of a huge, erect black penis and uncontrollable sobs began to wrack her body, almost suffocating her with the tape across her mouth. She could hardly breathe but tried so hard to scream, she had never been as terrified in her life and all she could think of was "Ralph, I'm so sorry! Ralph, come and save me! Ralph! Ralph! Ralph!"

But it wasn't Ralph who saved her. The door to the room crashed open and Maswia burst in. With a roar he took a flying kick at Eric and the boy was booted across the room and into the corner. Maswia picked up the knife he had dropped and slashed it across Eric's face, instantly drawing blood in a thin line across his cheek and upper lip. "You stupid idiot! I told you to look after the woman, not to rape her! She's no good if she's damaged!" He kicked the cowering Eric once more for good measure, connecting with his rib cage which made the boy groan with agony. "Get out of here!" he commanded. Slowly, the now humbled young thug dragged himself to his feet, managed to hoist up his jeans and clutching his damaged ribs with one arm and dabbing at his bleeding face with the other, did as he was told and slunk from the room.

Masiwa then turned to Ella, still shivering on the floor, trying to get her trousers back around her waist and sobbing through the sticky tape across her face.

"Now Miss Moffat," he said, staring down at her on the ground, as she curled into as protective a foetal ball as she could, "That was most unfortunate, and I am glad that I came to your rescue when I did. It was never my intention that you should be harmed in this process. I merely wish to have sufficient capital to start a new life, far away from here. Mr Henderson is going to assist me in achieving this aim."

He leant down and helped Ella to stand. With a small degree of compassion, he also took off the adhesive tape that was covering her face. Ella sobbed and stood, shoulders slumped, in front of him.

"Now," continued Masiwa, "Do I need to restrain you again?"

Ella shook her head in compliance, she was crushed, no fight left. All she could do was sob, and sniff, and despair took over. She managed to cover herself as best she could, with no buttons left on her bush shirt, her trousers filthy from the struggle with the drugged thug, and her soul in a dark, dank place. Masiwa left the room, locking the door behind him.

Chapter Fifteen

The early morning game drive had left the Lodge and Ralph was in the kitchen. The mood was sombre.

"How could this happen Mr Ralph?" pleaded Miriam.

"Miriam, I don't know. But I've had a message from the man who took Ella. I'm sure it's that policeman, ex-policeman, Masiwa. They are asking a great deal of money for the safe return of Ella."

"Aish!" said Miriam, "What does money matter? You need your Miss Ella back safe and sound!"

"I know Miriam," soothed Ralph, "But things often get difficult where people, especially bad people, are involved, don't they? And I haven't got anywhere near the amount of money they are asking. We'll have to see what the police from Nelspruit say when they get here. Now, I'm going to rouse Danny and see if he's got any ideas where the email message came from. The guests will be wanting breakfast in a couple of hours. You'll be ready, won't you?"

"Of course Mr Ralphie!" Miriam replied, trying to put on a brave face. "Breakfast will always be ready!"

Ralph showed Danny the email and played the video for him four or five times.

"Bloody awful lighting," muttered Danny. "Sorry Ralph, I shouldn't be flippant at a time like this. It's obviously been taken in a hut, or a shack, not a house. There's no plaster on the back wall, no paint, the chair Ella is sitting on is one of those one-piece plastic moulded chairs you can pick up anywhere. Not much to go on really."

"But can you tell anything about where the email was sent from? Not just the email address, but where whoever sent it is located"

"Oooh, I can't, no. But I know a man why might. He's a mate of mine in Cape Town, a real geek who I'm sure is a hacker. He never admits it, of course, but I'm sure he has ways of getting into big servers and behind firewalls and all that IT stuff. It's way beyond me, but if anyone can pinpoint where this came from, he can. Forward it to me and I'll send it on to him. He owes me a favour and I'll make sure he keeps it to himself."

"Thanks Danny."

"Don't worry Ralph. We'll get her back, safe and sound."

"I bloody hope so, Danny. I hope so."

An inspector and sergeant from Nelspruit arrived, accompanied by the local policeman Ralph had met the previous evening. Ralph showed them around: the office where Ella was taken; the tyre tracks where the kidnapper's vehicle had been parked; then he brought them back to the lodge and showed the email and the video he had received. He played them the video three times.

"Can you forward it to me please, Mr Henderson?" asked Inspector Coetzee, the senior policeman from Nelspruit, writing down his email address for Ralph. "It would appear you have made an enemy. This wouldn't be a haphazard kidnapping. Who have you been upsetting?"

"Inspector," began Ralph, "You must have heard of our involvement with the dismissal of your Inspector Masiwa from Hoedspruit."

"Not 'my' inspector," cut in Coetzee, "But yes, I had heard."

Ralph continued, "It was Ella who originally confronted him and it was she who sent a short video of his threatening behavior to a recent guest of ours who had senior connections in the Ministry of Justice. I have put two and two together and I'm convinced it's Masiwa who has taken Ella. Do you know where he lives?"

The Nelspruit Inspector looked directly at the local policeman, "Well?"

The local policeman, in awe of his superior from Nelspruit nodded, "Yes sir. I know where Inspec…I mean ex-Inspector Masiwa lives."

"Well, I agree it points to him. Not enough to arrest him yet. But when we're finished here we'll go and have a conversation with our ex-colleague. Mr Henderson, have you replied to his email?"

"Not yet."

"Will raising half a million rand be a problem?"

Ralph snorted. "Inspector, raising a thousand rand is a problem at the moment, let alone five hundred thousand."

"OK, but we should keep a conversation going for the time being. You'd better do as he says and just reply that 'you understand' and leave it at that. I'll get our people in Pretoria to see if they can find who opened the Hotmail account and where it was sent from. OK? I don't know anything about this modern technology myself, I don't know whether it's possible for us to find out, but we'll try."

Ralph nodded and decided not to tell Inspector Coetzee that Danny's friend in Cape Town was also tracking down the location of the sender. No point in not having two strings to your bow, he thought.

"What should I do about getting the money?" asked Ralph.

"If you can raise it, that would be good," said the Inspector. "We can then mark the notes invisibly so it can be tracked and traced. But I guess the important thing is the safety of Miss Moffatt, isn't it?"

"Absolutely," agreed Ralph.

"Well there's not much more we can do until there's another email from the kidnapper. We'll go and talk to Masiwa and see what he was doing yesterday afternoon. Stay positive Mr Henderson. We'll get her back safely."

Ralph just nodded, not feeling as positive as he wished.

They swapped mobile phone numbers, Ralph explaining that coverage at Mogololo was very patchy, but he would endeavour to keep his phone in a spot where there was at least one bar of signal so he could hear when it rang, and the police party left.

He went to look for Danny and found him, huddled over laptop screens with Billy. They were reviewing footage for the programme, logging shots they liked and deleting the duff ones.

"No news from your geek in Cape Town, I suppose?" asked Ralph. "I've just had the police here and they are getting on to their people in Pretoria to see if they can track and trace the location of an email."

"Bet my mate can do it quicker," replied Danny. "Let's have a look." And he opened his email account on his laptop and checked his inbox. "Bingo! IP address, blah, blah, co-ordinates blah, blah. Yes. He's done it. But he does caution that IP addresses are constantly changing and shifting so it's not 100% reliable but he's tracked it down to a place near Acornhoek, he says, 'Sigagula' does that mean anything to you?"

"It's only thirty minutes away, maybe forty," said Ralph. "Well done Danny. Great work. There's a sort of very unofficial settlement there: shacks, a few mud huts, no roads or services. It's pretty isolated. But I'm not sure there would be an internet connection."

"Don't be so sure. I read the cellphone companies were climbing all over themselves to get coverage for the tourists throughout the area, and if they manage it for the tourists, then there will be spill over coverage for the locals, too." said Danny. "I wouldn't assume there wouldn't be any internet Ralph."

"Well, I'm supposed to wait for the next demand anyway," said Ralph. "Meanwhile, I'd better think how I'm going to scrape half a million rand in cash together."

"Yeah," sighed Danny. "I can help with about ten grand Ralph, but that's about it I'm afraid."

"Nice of you to offer," said Ralph. "But I reckon I've got to think bigger, somehow."

"Good luck."

Ralph found he was unable to concentrate on anything other than frantically worrying about Ella and how he was going to raise 500,000 rand in cash. He dismissed the idea of going to the bank; his last encounter with the local manager had been far from fruitful. He didn't have any really rich friends who might have that amount of spare money. He seriously considered the idea of forging the notes: he could photocopy a 100 rand note, duplicate it a few hundred times on A4 paper and cut out the photocopied images, put them in bundles with genuine 100 rand notes on top, bound up with strong rubber bands and make it look like the real thing. Then he realized it wouldn't fool even the dumbest of crooks for more than two minutes, and the Reserve Bank of South Africa would probably issue a warrant for his arrest for forging the notes anyway. No, he was stumped.

His attention from this problem was suddenly diverted by an electronic beeping from his mobile phone, not the normal voice call ring, but an email alert.

It was "Max334455" again. Ralph read and re-read the mail. He tapped a few instructions into his phone, then dialed a number on it: Inspector Coetzee from Nelspruit. Ralph waited for the connection to be made.

"Inspector Coetzee? It's Ralph Henderson from Mogololo. Yes. I've had another email. I've just forwarded it to you. It seems a pretty bizarre demand. Why don't you read it and then call me back? … OK. I'll be here, waiting."

Ralph pondered the email instructions again: 'get half a million rand in used bank notes, packaged in bundles of 25,000 rand each, put the bundles in a shoe box. On the road to Hoedspruit airport there is an advertising sign for Kentucky Fried Chicken, put the box behind the pole that supports it. Do it in three days or the woman will be hurt. Email you understand and email again when you have left the box in place.'

In just a few minutes, Ralph's phone made its electronic music.

"Mr Henderson, Coetzee here. I got the mail. Much as I expected, really. Using a location that's out in the open is pretty standard. Any thoughts on getting the ransom together?"

"Haven't made any progress on that Inspector. But now this has come, I will. Did you talk to Masiwa?"

"Yes, not my favourite person, I have to say. I only had a few dealings with him when he was in the SAP, but he's an arrogant shit, isn't he? I'm afraid he has a very strong alibi for the time when Miss Moffat was taken. He was in the Hoedspruit hospital, complaining of stomach pains. I checked the record when he was admitted to casualty, saw a doctor and then when he was checked out and I'm afraid he's ruled out from any personal involvement with the abduction. The stomach pains miraculously disappeared by the time he actually saw a doctor, so he was wasting medical time all afternoon and early evening."

"Doesn't mean to say he didn't get others to do it, though, does it?" suggested Ralph.

"No. And it's strange that his mystery illness came and went at such a convenient time. You haven't responded to this latest email yet, have you?"

"No. Should I?"

"Yes, you should. Might be an idea to ask for reassurance that Miss Moffat is OK. Keeping up a dialogue is important."

"Let's just say," said Ralph, "That I do manage to get the money together, and it's put where he wants it. What do you do about keeping an eye on it?"

"The wonders of technology Mr Henderson. We'll put a tiny tracking device inside one of the bundles of money, or the shoebox itself perhaps. They won't notice it for a while and we'll be alerted the minute the tracker is moved. Then we'll have them."

"Sounds a bit James Bond, doesn't it?"

"Leave it to us Mr Henderson. Stay in touch." And the connection was broken.

"Right," said Ralph to himself. "Just the small matter of raising half a million."

Once the morning game drive was over, guests had been breakfasted and checked out of their lodges and waved goodbye, Ralph and Edison were having coffee on the verandah.

"So what have you thought about raising all this money?" asked Edison.

"I've thought of little else Edison, but haven't got any answers. Any ideas?"

Edison sat still, in the quiet and thoughtful that he did, giving respect to Ralph's question before he answered. "Well," he began, "Over the last few months we have had a number of guests who are evidently wealthy. And Ella made a big impression on most of them. Would it be an idea to send emails to them, explaining the situation you are in, and asking that they might lend you the money? You could always reassure them that the police have a way of tracking the notes, so their money would be safe."

Ralph pondered on Edison's suggestion. "Hey, that's a great idea Edison. The only danger is that the news about Ella's kidnap might get out. But, hell, we're in enough shit as it is – and I can always make a special plea for keeping it quiet. Good thinking Edison!"

Edison smiled, embarrassed at Ralph's praise. "In the meantime," he said, "Shall I get Grace to look after the office, and the new guests' arrival? I think we have four coming in later today."

Ralph stood up and gave Edison a playful pat on the shoulder. "Couldn't run this place without the pair of you. Thanks Edison."

Ralph fetched his laptop and started composing emails, being as clear and concise as he could, but still keeping a dramatic sense of urgency and desperation in his communication.

The first he sent was to Patricia Maxwell, who had been so helpful in solving the Masiwa problem in the first place.

Subject: Desperate Situation

Dear Patricia,

Something dreadful has happened at Mogololo, but with your help we might be able to resolve it. Two days ago, while I was out on a game drive, Ella was kidnapped from the Lodge and I have received a ransom demand for half a million rand. I know this may sound like one of those scam emails but I promise I have never been more serious in my cry for help.   I don't have half a million rand, or anything like it.

I am writing to just a few guests who I feel will be sympathetic to my cause and may be able to help me raise the money and the police have advised me that going along with ransom demands in the first stage is the best policy. (They also assure me that they will be able to retrieve the money once Ella is returned to us so I am asking for a loan, not a charitable donation).

Like me, you can probably guess who is behind this kidnap – although he allegedly has an alibi - but the most important thing is for us to secure Ella's release before any harm is done to her.

As you can imagine, the kidnappers have instructed not to involve the police but I ignored this and I am working with a very helpful and sympathetic Inspector Coetzee from Nelspruit.

Patricia, I have just three days to raise the money, and I am desperate to get Ella back safely. Please can you help?

Sincerely,

Ralph Henderson.

Ralph sent similar mails to another seven recent guests who he thought might be sympathetic, but he was really pinning his hopes on a positive response from Patricia. The one nagging doubt he had was that Brian, her husband the lawyer and advisor to the Minister of Justice, wouldn't want to be associated with kidnappers and ransom demands.

So Ralph waited, and fretted, and stared into the distance, and willed his email inbox to ping and give him a reply.

The next 24 hours were torture for Ralph. The more time went on the more his imagination conjured up the most dreadful thoughts of what might be happening to Ella, where she might be, what she was eating, if anything.

He checked his phone every minute and his laptop every five minutes, just in case the technology didn't do what it was supposed to do and send emails to both. Fortunately, Edison remained his usual calm, placid and sensible self, getting on with the everyday tasks at Mogololo and ensuring that what guests there were received the best experience of life in the game reserve. He looked after the game drives, with Jackson perched up front, Grace cared for the guests' comfort and Miriam made sure they were all well fed. The team tiptoed around Ralph, knowing how stressed he was and did their best to shelter him from the day-to-day trivia.

Ralph's phone gave the unmistakable squawk of an incoming mail. The screen told him it was from Patricia!

'Dear Ralph, I'm devastated to hear the news of Ella. Please call me as soon as you get this.' And then there was her cellphone number.

"Patricia, this is Ralph Henderson," he announced as soon as the call got through.

"Oh Ralph!" responded Patricia, "Is there any more news on Ella?"

"Not since two days ago, no."

"Oh you poor thing. You must be at your wits' end."

"Yes, it's not easy," said Ralph, holding his emotions in check.

"Well look, I want to help.," said Patricia. "I can let you have three hundred thousand rand. I can transfer it to your account today."

Ralph's heart almost leapt out of his rib cage. "Patricia, that's terrific! Thank you so, so much! I want you to know it's just a loan, of course."

"Of course it is. And this is just between you and me. Brian mustn't know anything about it. But listen, have you let Ella's family know she has been abducted?"

"Oh shit," groaned Ralph. "Sorry Patricia. No, I hadn't thought. I'd better go and let her mother know, hadn't I?"

"Yes, you had. Now, give me your bank details and I'll do the transfer."

Once Ralph and Patricia had sorted the bank transfer, Ralph thought about the meeting he must have with Ella's mother. He had met her just a few times and after the initial suspicion that Mrs Moffat had shown about her daughter going off to help run a game lodge with a man she hardly knew, she had actually grown to like Ralph. But that was in the days when life was fun and free from dealing with crooks and kidnappers. This meeting would be different.

He told Edison and the team that he had to go to town and on the drive he tried to compose the best way to deliver the news to Mrs Moffat. When he arrived at the coffee shop she ran, fortunately it was a quiet time with hardly any customers.

Mrs Moffat looked up from the cake display she was arranging. "Ralph! I didn't expect you. Good lord, you look terrible. What's happened? Where's Ella?"

Ralph's prepared explanation fell to pieces. He almost fell to pieces himself and he was sobbing his heart out as he tried to explain the sequence of events. Mrs Moffat was stunned, shocked and speechless. She tried hard to absorb and compute all that Ralph had told her in his disjointed, distressed way. She was silent for a while, then a barrage of questions came tumbling out.

"Didn't the rest of the staff at the lodge see anything? What about this Masiwa character? How do you know the video was genuine? What are the police in Nelspruit doing? Should we tell the papers or keep it quiet? Oh Ella! Where are you?"

Ralph tried to soothe Ella's mother and was silently so relieved that she wasn't blaming Ralph for what had happened, although he did feel totally responsible for the situation they were in.

"Mrs Moffat," Ralph said…

"Oh call me Jean, for goodness sake!"

"Jean, we're doing all we can at the moment. I'm trying hard to raise the ransom money. I've got three hundred thousand and while I'm here in town I'm going to ask the bank for a personal loan. Not sure they'll give me one but I've got to try. And I'm waiting to hear from some other people who might be able to help with the cash. So as long as we play the kidnapper's game the police say we're doing all we can at the moment. We've tracked the location of where the email was sent from: Sigagula, not far from here, actually."

"So why aren't the police going through every hut and shack to find her?"

"I guess they are being as cautious as they can until they are sure they know where she is. Going in mob-handed might panic the thugs and they'd kill her."

"Oh Ralph! Heaven forbid!"

"Sorry Jean, I didn't mean to alarm you. But I'm sure Coetzee knows what he's doing. And he did caution us to not breathe a word to the media. That could really panic the bastards. So, I'm afraid it's sit tight and tough it out."

Jean thought for a moment, "Let me help with some of the ransom money, then."

"Jean? Could you? Oh, it would be such a relief to know we've got it together."

"I've got a hundred thousand in the building society. You

can have that."

"And if I can get a hundred thousand from the bank, we're there."

"Are you going to tell the bank what you need the money for?"

"Well I can't raise it on the business, we're maxed-out on our overdraft as it is. But I was going to string them a line about needing it for a deposit on a new property I want to buy in town."

"Ralph, they'll never buy that. Nor would you be able to arrange it in two days."

Ralph looked crestfallen. "Any ideas then?"

"Say you need a personal loan to buy an engagement ring," said Jean with a wry smile. "Not that I'm dropping hints, or anything."

"Good idea," said Ralph. "On both counts."

After Ralph had given Jean his bank details, Jean made him a cup of coffee, explained to her staff that she had to go out for a while. She went off to her building society and Ralph headed to his bank. To his great relief, the manager he had seen some months before who had given him such a hard time was on leave, so Ralph's request was dealt with by a charming young lady who, when Ralph crossed his fingers and told his little white lie about the engagement ring, got quite emotional and immediately agreed to Ralph's romantic request for the money. The interest rate was pretty crippling but Ralph consoled himself with the thought that it was only for a few days and everyone's money would be back where it belonged very soon.

Leaving the bank with his current account balance looking healthier than it had ever been, he called Inspector Cotezee.

"Mr Henderson, how are things?"

"No more emails, but I thought I'd let you know I've managed to raise the half million. I'm a bit nervous about asking for it all in cash without raising suspicions at my bank branch. Do you think you could help me sort it out in person? You're going to need to have the cash to mark it anyway, aren't you?"

"Yes. That's good about the money. You must have friends who think very highly of Miss Moffat to risk their cash on her behalf. Yes, I can be in Hoedspruit in about an hour. Do you want to hang on there for me?"

"Sure. I'll be at the Crumbs Coffee Shop. Ella's mum runs it. I'd like you to meet her anyway."

"In an hour then."

Ralph's coffee intake that day rose to previously unheard of levels. So he was buzzing by the time Inspector Coetzee had been introduced to Jean Moffat and they had gone over the current situation, which, until Ralph confirmed back to the Max334455 Hotmail account that he had the money ready, hadn't changed.

The Inspector and Ralph went on to Ralph's bank and requested a meeting in private with the most senior member of staff. Inspector's Coetzee's warrant card caused something of a flutter among the junior bank staff and gave them instant access to a small room and they waited just a moment for the assistant manager to join them.

"Oh, Mr Henderson," she said, quite taken aback. "You were here just a little while ago."

"Yes," said Ralph, "But I'd better let Inspector Coetzee explain why we're here now."

In his rather officious, methodical, yet calming way, the Inspector explained the situation to the wide-eyed bank employee. He impressed upon her the need for discretion and secrecy, and he requested the half a million rand in notes to be bundled as instructed by the kidnappers. "Better not make them brand new notes, it will look too suspicious."

"Gosh, Inspector," said the bank lady. "That's a lot of cash. It will take twenty minutes or so, and there's a bit of paperwork. I'll get right on it. Can I get you coffee?"

"Not for me thanks," Ralph said, fearful of what even more caffeine might do to his system. The Inspector just shook his head politely.

Ralph and the Inspector sat in the anonymous little

meeting room at the bank, waiting for their money. Ralph asked, "So you mark the notes with some invisible ink or something, do you?"

"Something like that," said the Inspector, "Then when suspicious amounts of cash start to turn up, we have special ways of identifying the notes."

Ralph thought the Inspector obviously didn't want to give away too many trade secrets, but he was more curious about the tracking device that had been mentioned. "So what about this tracking thing, then?" he asked.

"It's tiny," said Coetzee. "Our geeks will hide it in the shoebox bottom and put a false floor to the box on top of it. It runs on a little watch battery, the whole thing is smaller than a credit card. They'll never spot it."

"And it just sends out a signal to let you know where it is?"

"That's it. We'll be on it the minute it moves."

" As long as we're not putting Ella in any more danger," muttered Ralph.

"Don't worry Mr Henderson," assured Inspector Coetzee. "We'll be putting her welfare first, I promise."

The banking lady came back with a canvas money bag under one arm and a sheaf of papers in the other. "Rather a lot of paperwork, I'm afraid," she apologized. "It's more than the usual amount of cash we deal with in one transaction." Ralph just shrugged and started scribbling his signature on the forms that she put in front of him.

"I guess I'll have to ask you to give me a receipt for the cash, as well," Ralph said to the Inspector.

"Don't worry," smiled Coetzee. "We're good at paperwork in the SAP. You'll get all the receipts you want. We'll go back to the Hoedspruit station now and sort it out. But we'll do it in private, OK? I'm still suspicious about Masiwa, even though he had an alibi, and he may still have friends in the SAP here, so I'm trusting no one, OK?"

"Fine by me," agreed Ralph.

They left the bank and made their way to the South African Police station in Hoedspruit. Ralph thinking that he had spent too much time there this year already, what with the rhino poaching, Edison's false arrest and now Ella's kidnapping. Inspector Coetzee was as discreet as he had promised and the papers were dealt with quickly.

"Right, you get back to your Lodge. I'll go back to Nelspruit and get the money in the shoebox, with the tracker, and call you when it's ready. I think it's best if you put the money at the drop yourself as they might be looking, so we could meet between Nelspruit and here for a handover?"

"And once I've put the box where they want it, I just leave?"

"Yes. They won't know we've put a device in the box. We're dealing with pretty thick crooks here Mr

Henderson, not masterminds who win chess championships. The money will lead us to Miss Moffat. I promise."

Ralph sighed wearily, and nodded. What else could he do?

Chapter Sixteen

At the Lodge, everyone was keen to know if there was any news, Ralph reassured them as much as he could, but by now he was so tired himself through lack of sleep and constant worry he found it hard to be positive.

"So," he said, "I'll wait for the call from Nelspruit, get the shoe box with the money, put it where the kidnappers have told me to put it and wait to be told where to pick up Ella."

Edison took all this in and said, "Ralph, let me meet the Inspector on the road and deliver the shoebox of money to where the thugs want it. You've done enough running around for a while."

"You know Edison," said Ralph, "I'll take you up on that offer. Thanks."

So when the call came from Nelspruit, Edison went off to meet the Inspector at Hazyview, a small town on the road between the bigger metropolis of Nelspruit and the struggling little community of Hoedspruit. He called Ralph to tell him all was well and made his way back to Hoedspruit and on to the road that led to the town's little airport. There was the Kentucky Fried Chicken hoarding, standing high above the ground, supported on two iron girders that had once been railway tracks. He was to place the shoebox right at the base of the pole nearest the road and put a rock on top of it to conceal it. This he did. He looked around for signs of anyone watching him, but even with his years of experience in bushcraft he wasn't aware of anyone spying on him. He got back in his beaten-up old car, turned round and headed back the way he had come.

A few minutes later, however, he stopped. He called Ralph to tell him the shoebox of money was where the kidnappers had instructed them to leave it and told Ralph he was just going to the shops in Hoedspruit before they closed and then he would head back to Mogololo.

But shopping was the last thing on Edison's mind. Although the light was beginning to fade in the late afternoon, he turned his car around again and went a little way back towards the airport. He parked next to a roadside fruit stall that was shut up for the day, locked his car and walked a little way off the road, into some scrubby bushes. Silently and quite invisibly, he moved towards the Kentucky Fried Chicken sign and stopped about two hundred metres before it, squatted under a bush, watched and waited.

After about an hour, watching the occasional cars buzz by on the airport road, with none of them showing any signs of slowing down or stopping, he became aware of the noise of a small motorbike, its engine struggling and straining as if it was being ridden by someone who wasn't at all used to riding a motorbike.

Then, through the twilight, Edison saw the rider bouncing over the open ground. He wasn't using the road at all. He wasn't going fast but a lot faster than Edison could run, so all he could do was attempt to take pictures of the motorbike rider on his smartphone. Edison recognized the rider from his bulk and awkwardness. It was Masiwa, no doubt about it. Masiwa stopped by the pole, tried to lean over and retrieve the shoebox but couldn't manage to hold the bike upright at the same time. Edison thought about sprinting over, but realized it was too far; Masiwa would get away easily. Masiwa dropped the handlebars of the bike, picked up the shoebox, had a cursory glance inside, seemed satisfied, and stuffed the box in a rucksack he had been carrying over one shoulder. He now put the rucksack on his back properly, picked up the bike again, clumsily managed to get it in gear and wobbled off, going further away from Edison, and not heading back to the road. Edison thought Masiwa must have been suspicious he would be watched from the road, that's why he came cross country. Not so stupid after all, Edison said to himself.

It was dark by the time Edison made his way back to the Lodge. Ralph and Danny were still sitting on the verandah, they each had a can of beer but neither of them were that interested in finishing them. Edison quietly joined them and sat down.

"It's definitely Masiwa, Ralph," he said. "I watched him pick up the box just 30 minutes ago. He came on a motorbike across country so I couldn't follow him. All I could do was try to take his picture but as evidence, I don't think it's really worth that much." Edison showed Ralph the screen of his smartphone with the pictures he had taken.

"Could be anything," agreed Ralph, passing the phone on

to Danny. "Don't suppose you've got any magic software that can enhance pictures like these, have you, Danny?"

Danny stared at the pictures. "Not much to work with, is it? No, don't think there's anything there. Just Edison's word, of course."

"And Coetzee's magic tracker," said Ralph with a bit more enthusiasm in his voice. "I'll call him."

"Bit late, isn't it?" cautioned Danny.

"Bloody hell Danny! This is Ella's safety we're talking about. I don't care how late it is!"

"OK, sorry, sorry," said Danny.

"Oh Danny," apologized Ralph, "I'm sorry. Didn't mean to snap. I'm like a bad-tempered baboon. Sorry."

"Maybe you should give Coetzee a ring then."

Ralph needn't have worried about disturbing the Inspector's leisure time. The conscientious policeman was at Nelspruit Police Headquarters, monitoring the signal being received from the tracking device when he took Ralph's call.

"Yes Mr Henderson," he said, "I'm looking at the trace of the tracker right now. It looks like it's going over open ground. Not on a road or a track."

"Yes, Edison saw the shoebox being collected by someone on a motorbike," said Ralph. "He's convinced it was Masiwa. What direction is it heading?"

"Going north, away from the airport road. Could be heading for Sigagula, near Acornhoek?"

"Yes, that makes sense," Ralph agreed, but not letting the Inspector know they had linked Sigagula to the location the emails had been sent from."

"Hang on," said the Inspector. "It's stopped. But it' still in the middle of nowhere. No houses, tracks or roads, or anything. I've got a car with two officers on the way. They'll be at Acornhoek in fifteen minutes or so. But why has it stopped in the middle of nowhere, out in open bush?"

Masiwa had had enough of motorbikes. His sense of balance was awful and coordination of steering and adjusting speed at the same time, then changing gear with his feet was proving too much for him. When he had ordered his two thugs to "get me a motorbike", he thought riding one would be a straightforward and smooth exercise, something that someone of his stature and authority would take to with ease. He was very glad he didn't have an audience of people watching him as his technique of controlling the bike was not improving.

He brought the motorbike to a jerky and very dusty stop in the middle of the veld and just managed to get both feet on the ground without toppling over.

It was now completely dark and even though he was really in the middle of nowhere, Masiwa wanted to check the ransom money. He clumsily took the rucksack from his back and unfastened the clips and pulled out the shoebox. He had a little torch that he held between his teeth and looked carefully at the bundles of money. He made a decision that the shoebox had done all it needed to do, so he put the bundles of banknotes straight back into the rucksack, counting them as he pushed them inside. Happy that the money added up to half a million, he casually tossed the shoebox to one side, refastened the rucksack clasps and struggled into the shoulder straps. Putting the torch back in his pocket he wrestled with the motorbike controls once more and wobbled forwards, engine screaming for him to change gear, which he just about managed without stalling, and lurched forwards once more. A few moments later he reached a track which became a dirt road and riding a little more carefully now, he made his way to the settlement of Sigagula. The African night was still and quiet, apart from the spluttering of Masiwa's complaining machine.

Sigagula was a ramshackle collection of huts and shacks on the side of a hill. There was no electricity, water supply or sewage, it was a haphazard arrangement of informal housing that was under constant threat of being demolished by the council and all the residents moved on, but many in the council realized that drastic action like that would only move the problem elsewhere so as long as the residents didn't cause too much trouble, they were pretty much left to their own devices. Which suited the residents just fine. Some had jobs, most children attended school, there were goats and chickens and generally, everyone knew everyone else. Apart from one larger hut that was set apart from the others. Sigagula residents knew this hut was the property of Masiwa and they all left it well alone. He hadn't built it himself, but had 'acquired' it a year ago in return for turning a blind eye to the previous resident's misdemenour over some theft from a supermarket. The previous resident was no longer in the area. The other Sigagula people also knew that this wasn't Masiwa's 'proper' home, he had another house elsewhere in one of the Hoedspruit suburbs where his family lived, but they knew this was the property where a lot of his shadowy dealings and assignations took place. They left it well alone.

Masiwa rode up to the back of the hut and dumped his complaining motorbike. He entered the first room of the hut and barked at his thugs, "Get rid of that motorbike. It has done its job for me, I don't want to see it again. Is the Moffat woman OK?"

"Yes Boss," came the muted reply.

Masiwa pointed to the padlock holding the door to the room where Ella was being held, "Open it."

One of the young thugs fiddled with the padlock key and unlocked the door.

Masiwa took a lantern in with him. Ella was cowering in the corner, disheveled, distraught, dirty.

"Ah Miss Moffat," Masiwa announced, in his most condescending manner. "You'll be pleased to hear we will return you to Mr Henderson very soon. He has very sensibly complied with my request and supplied the money."

Ella slowly looked up at Maiswa, with a dull look in her eyes, but she said nothing. Masiwa glanced down at the tin plate on the floor. It had a congealed mess of something on it that might have once masqueraded as food, but any appetite appeal had long since gone. There were flies crawling over it, even they weren't that interested in eating.

"You did not want the food my boys made specially for you? Shame." He grunted at the thug standing behind him to clear the plate away. "Just a little while longer Miss Moffat, we will have you back at your home." Ella still said nothing, there was no spark of rebellion, or even anger in her eyes; just a blank, mid-distance stare. Masiwa left the room, taking the lantern and all the light with him, Ella heard the rattle of the bolt and padlock on the other side of the door and she slumped her shoulders, sighed and silently sobbed.

It was around midnight when Inspector Coetzee drove into Mogololo. There were still some lights on in the main guest area, moths were flitting suicidally close to the lamps, and Ralph and Danny were sitting slumped in the easy chairs.

"Mr Henderson," said the Inspector as he walked towards them. "My men found the shoe box, empty, in the middle of the veld, a couple of kilometeres from the KFC sign. The kidnapper must have either found the tracker, or decided to dump the box anyway. I'm so sorry, the trail has gone cold for the moment."

Ralph grunted, "Well, it was a good idea, wasn't it? We didn't have any others. Now what?"

"We wait, I suppose. No emails from them?"

Ralph looked at his phone, "No bloody wi-fi again!" He jumped up and moved towards the office where the wi-fi router was kept. "Sorry Inspector, I didn't notice the thing had gone off. I'll restart it and see if I can connect."

After fiddling with the device for a minute, Ralph sat, mesmerized by the twinkling LEDs on the little black box, willing it to burst into life. The lights settled, confirming it was healthy and working fine again. Ralph turned his attention to the screen of his phone and thirty seconds later, "Ping!" Notification that emails were coming in. Yes! One from Max334455!

"It was sent two hours ago," said Ralph. "It says, 'Miss Moffat will be on the R40 between Hoedspruit and Klaserie, at midnight. Collect her at your pleasure.' What a bastard!"

The Inspector looked at his watch. "We'd better go now then. I'll radio for assistance."

Danny volunteered, "I'll drive Ralph, you look too bushed to be in charge of a car."

"Thanks Danny," said Ralph, wearily, "Let's go then."

It took twenty long minutes to reach the R40. They had to take it slowly on the dirt roads as a whole selection of creatures liked to use the warmth that the tracks had built up during the day and retained through the night. There were nightjars and eagle owls, small buck, a honey badger and clouds and clouds of moths and flying insects.

Inspector Coetzee had already alerted his team to start searching the road but nothing had come back to him yet. On the way to the R40 he drove in front, so that if a message did get through to him, he'd be able to alert Ralph and Danny.

After what seemed like hours to Ralph, they eventually reached the T junction with the R40. Once they'd stopped, Coetzee ran back to Danny's car to say he was going south, as his officers in the patrol car were covering the road north.

"OK, just let's go!" said Ralph irritably, frustrated at any more delay. They headed out onto the tarmac surface, refreshingly smooth after the corrugations of the dirt. But Coetzee kept his speed down, as they all attempted to peer into the dark of the roadside, inky black with shapes of trees and bushes making their search all the more difficult. "I knew I should have brought the searchlight we use for night-time game drives," muttered Ralph, more to himself than to Danny.

"Don't worry Ralph, we'll find her," said Danny, in as reassuring a voice as he could manage.

They were travelling really slowly which was frustrating, but Ralph and Danny realized it was a sensible pace as they had no idea where Ella might be, they had to search as carefully as they could. The road was empty, which was hardly surprising as it was now well past midnight. Coasting around a bend, they were coming up to the entrance to a farm. Coetzee put on his hazard lights and pulled in to stop, with Danny close behind him. There, propped up against the short wall of the farm entrance was a pathetic, bedraggled figure, feet bound together and her hands bound in front. It was Ella.

Ralph was out of the car even before it was properly stopped, "Ella!" He rushed up to her before Inspector Coetzee got there, dived onto his knees and tried to both hug her and assess her condition at the same time. "Darling Ella! Are you hurt? What has Masiwa done to you? Did he mistreat you? Here, let me get you up." Ralph awkwardly helped Ella to stand and the Inspector had one of those clever folding tools that had a lethal-looking knife blade that he used to get rid of the strong tape that had bound Ella's hands and ankles. Now Ralph hugged Ella properly, but she was strangely unresponsive, merely sobbing quietly but not seeming to gain any comfort from Ralph's embrace.

"Before anything else I think we should get her to hospital in Nelspruit," said Inspector Coetzee.

"Couldn't we just take her to Hoedspruit, Inspector?" said Ralph. "She's got a good friend who is a doctor. It would be much better if she was checked over by someone she knows."

"It's one o'clock in the morning, Mr Henderson!"

"I know, but her doctor friend has been as worried as we've been. Well, almost. He won't mind being woken up. And there's Ella's mum, she's in Hoedspruit, too."

"OK. Look, you take her to the doctor. I'll head back home, but I'll be back in the morning to take a statement," said the Inspector. "Good to have you back in safe hands, Miss Moffat."

Ella didn't acknowledge the Inspector's kind words. She stood, still with Ralph's arms around her, still staring blankly. She hadn't said a word since she'd been found.

Chapter Seventeen

Ella's doctor friend, David Millard, initially not happy at being rung up at one o' clock in the morning, was so relieved that Ella had been found when Ralph told him the news, he immediately agreed that Ella should be brought to his house. Danny drove, with Ralph and Ella in the back seat, Ralph with a protective arm around Ella's shoulder and gently stroking her hand, talking soothingly to her, reassuring that it was all over, it would be all right now, there was nothing more to worry about. But his words didn't seem to be getting through. Ralph had so many questions he wanted to ask, but was aware that Ella was in shock and wasn't yet ready to talk about what had happened.

They reached the doctor's house and David was waiting on the porch to greet them. He helped Ella out of the car and both David and Ralph supported Ella and slowly walked her into David's house. David's wife Suzie was busy with coffee and biscuits but now, for the first time since her rescue, Ella spoke, "Water?" she croaked.

"Of course darling," said Suzie and went off to the kitchen to get some.

Ella greedily gulped a whole glass of water and held it out for more.

"Hang on, Ella", said David. "I'd like to check you over before you get awash with water." And he gently led her into his surgery room.

While David and Ella were in the surgery, Ralph called

Ella's mum.

She lived just minutes away, so before Ella and David reappeared, she had joined the small group in the Millard's house. In the rush, she had just thrown on a track suit over her nightwear and was still wearing her slippers. "Ella? Where is she?" Jean breathlessly asked.

"With David," explained Julie Millard. "He's examining her, shouldn't be long now."

In fact, it wasn't long at all. The surgery door opened and David led Ella out. Jean Moffat rushed to her and embraced her daughter. Ella, wrapped in her mother's arms sobbed on her shoulder. Ralph looked to David for signs of Ella's condition. David silently indicated that Ralph should come into his surgery.

Once the door was closed, David explained. "A few bumps and bruises, but nothing broken," he started. "But I have to tell you there was an attempted rape. Ella has closed up, shut down. I'm sure she will recover Ralph, but right now she's in shock and won't open up about what happened. I was getting one word 'yes' or 'no' answers. I gather one of the thugs who took her was high on drugs, was pretty rough and tried to force himself on her. There was no actual penetration, it was lucky the gang boss came in and stopped him. But right now Ralph, Ella is too fragile and damaged from the trauma to really talk about it. So we're all going to have to tread very carefully. I'd say she needs some professional counselling, but the best place for that would be Jo'burg."

"Bloody hell," said Ralph, slowly taking in what David had just told him.

"You'll have to take it at Ella's pace, I'm afraid Ralph. I've given her a sedative so she should sleep tonight. Are you going to take her back to Mogololo?"

"If she'll come."

"Well, good luck. Let's see how she's doing with her mum."

Ella was, in fact, still clinging to her mother's velour tracksuit top. The sobs had subsided a bit, but she was still not talking.

Ralph quickly took stock of the situation. "Jean", he quietly said. "Would it be best if Ella went to your house tonight?"

"I wouldn't let her go anywhere else," she replied, looking at Ralph as if he was stupid.

"OK," said Ralph. "Danny will drive us to your house. I'll go back to the Lodge. But I'll come back in the morning because I'm afraid the police will want to interview Ella. I'd like to be there."

"That's fine Ralph, but Ella's welfare comes first," said Jean firmly.

So they gently took Ella to Danny's car, dropped her and her mother off at the Moffat's house, and drove back in the pitch dark to Mogololo, without a word exchanged between the two of them, all the way there.

Exhausted, Ralph collapsed into bed and didn't wake until Miriam was calling outside his door at eight thirty in the morning, "Knock, Knock Mr Ralphie! It is morning. We need you."

Ralph roused himself and realized how late it was. Late for him, anyway.

"Thanks Miriam. Be there in a minute!" he called.

All the staff were anxiously waiting for news of Ella. Ralph told them what had happened in the early hours and that Ella was safe. The collective sigh of relief was audible but Ralph did caution them that Ella was very upset and was staying with her mother in Hoedspruit for the time being.

"Grace?" Ralph asked, "Could you handle what guests we have booked in for the time being? Until Ella comes back to us?"

"Of course, Mr Ralph. But I don't think we have any guests this week."

"Well, that's a relief in many respects," said Ralph. "Not so good for our financial future, but I wouldn't be much use to guests at the moment anyway. Can you let me know when the next booking is coming in?"

"Of course," said Grace and she went off to the office to check.

"Edison, I'd better get off to Ella's mum's house. I'll call

Inspector Coetzee on the way. Will you be OK here?"

"That is an unnecessary question Ralph," said Edison very calmly.

"Of course it is. Miriam? If Mr Danny hasn't made an appearance by about ten o'clock, perhaps you would take him some tea and wake him up."

Miriam giggled at the thought and hid her smiles behind her hands. Happy that the Lodge would be in good hands, Ralph showered and was on the road in no time. Miriam had thrust a packet of sandwiches into his hands as he got into his vehicle and he was enormously grateful for her thoughtfulness as he'd completely forgotten about food. On the road into town he called Inspector Coetzee's mobile number and relayed what David Millard had told him about Ella's condition. Coetzee was sympathetic but impressed upon Ralph how important it was that he questioned Ella immediately as he was determined to get the kidnappers; they couldn't let any trail go cold on them. He promised he would be sensitive, but was firm in his insistence that there would be no delay.

Ralph was nervous as he walked up to Jean Moffat's front door, not at all sure how he would be received, either by Jean or Ella.

He needn't have been concerned about Jean's reception; she hugged him and kissed him generously on both cheeks. "Did you sleep at all?" she asked him.

"A little bit," replied Ralph with a sigh. "How is she?"

"Just waking," said Jean. " I took her some tea twenty minutes ago. She slept right through but I'm not sure about the quality of sleep when sleeping pills are involved. But she's having a shower now. She still hasn't said much."

"No, David told me we must let things go at her own pace. But I'm afraid Inspector Coetzee will want to talk to her this morning. He's on his way here now."

"Oh dear."

"He's OK Jean. In fact, I'd go as far as saying he's the best policeman I've ever come across."

Jean raised an eyebrow, "And you have come across…how many?"

"Well, not that many. But he knows about Ella's condition and has promised to walk on eggshells."

A door opened and Ella slowly walked into the room. Her hair was wet from the shower, she wore a simple cotton print dress and Ralph saw she was carrying a rag doll from childhood.

"Ella," Ralph said softly and he went across to kiss her and put his arms around her. Ella showed no sign of response. Ralph's heart sank. The Ella he knew would light up a room whenever she entered. She would walk in with a brisk confidence and sparkling eyes. This Ella was more like a mongrel dog that had been repeatedly beaten into submission and was too cowed to make its presence felt.

"Everyone at the Lodge has been asking after you," Ralph said, with a large lump in his throat, "Grace and Miriam and Edison, Jackson, all of them." Ella looked at Ralph but her eyes showed little interest. She gave a slight nod, but nothing more. "There's a policeman coming in a little while who wants to talk to you. Inspector Coetzee. He's very nice, professional. Do you know, I haven't found out what his first name is. I must ask him. Anyway, it's important you answer his questions Ella; it's the only way we're going to catch the bastards. OK?"

Jean then joined the rather one-sided conversation, "That will be all right, darling, won't it?"

Ella looked at her mother, sighed, and nodded.

As if on cue, there was a knock at the door. Inspector Coetzee had arrived.

As he promised, he was very caring and patient, but Ella wasn't forthcoming with information. She would answer with an occasional 'yes' or 'no' but wouldn't give her own narrative account of events. During their phone call on his way into town Ralph had primed Coetzee with David Millard's medical opinion of Ella's mental condition and the attempted rape, so the Inspector was acutely aware of the situation.

"Miss Moffat," said Coetzee, fishing out a file from his briefcase. I'm going to show you a picture of someone who might have been involved in this unfortunate affair. Is that OK?" Ella nodded and the Inspector put a photograph on the coffee table in front of Ella. It was ex-policeman Masiwa's file picture. Ella glanced at it for just a second, looked Coetzee straight in the eye and said in the loudest voice she'd used since her ordeal was over, "Yes. Of course it's him!"

"Thank you, Miss Moffat," said Coetzee. "I'm going to have more questions but we can leave those for another day. Right now I want to catch this bad man." Coetzee nodded to Ralph, indicating he wanted to talk to him alone, got up and walked outside onto the porch of the house.

"Right. Masiwa it is," said the Inspector. "I imagine he's left the area, but we'll get him."

"How can I help?" asked Ralph.

"Look after that brave girl. She's been through a dreadful ordeal. She needs all the care you can give her."

"I will. By the way, what's your first name, Inspector?"

The policeman smiled, "Caleb; my father had a sense of humour. My friends call me Callie."

Ralph returned to Mogololo. Alone, of course. Ella was still being uncommunicative and withdrawn and Ralph fully understood she needed a mother's love and care rather than the rather haphazard life on a game lodge.

It might be a while before the 'old' Ella was back. If she was coming back.

It was when he drove into to Mogololo that the full impact of the kidnap and the implications for his livelihood fully hit him. He had lost half a million rand, he'd also lost the love of the woman he loved. He fervently hoped that both losses were temporary. He called Patricia to let her know that Ella was safe, but that she was far from being herself. Patricia was sympathetic and very tactfully didn't mention the money that she had lent Ralph to help with the ransom. Ralph, however, had too much integrity not to mention it himself. He pledged to Patricia that he would work tirelessly, with the police, to secure the return of the money. Patricia, of course, insisted that Ella's return to health was the most important issue.

With that awkward phone call out of the way, Ralph went to find Edison.

He found him in the workshop, tidying tools that looked to be pretty tidy already. "Edison," started Ralph, "I can't remember when I've felt worse. It was almost better when those bloody kidnappers still had Ella."

"The police have accepted it's Masiwa then," said Edison quietly.

"Yes."

"What about the two who took Ella in the first place?"

"Haven't really thought about them yet," said Ralph. "Although the one who attacked Ella is going to wish he'd never been born."

"Attacked?"

"Yes, while she was being held, one of them tried to rape her."

"Oh, no!"

"Fortunately, Masiwa actually stopped it. Ella's not talking about it, but it seems that Masiwa didn't want her damaged. I don't think he stopped his thug from altruistic or humanitarian reasons. It appeared completely commercial. Don't spoil the goods. That sort of thing."

"Look Ralph, we're not busy at the Lodge, are we? Why don't I pop into town and see what I can pick up on the grapevine?"

"Hey, Edison, I don't want you getting involved with these gangsters."

"Don't worry. I can be like a shadow; I'll just look and listen, see if anyone is suddenly spending money, that sort of thing."

"Hmmm," started Ralph. "We really ought to leave it to the police, you know."

"We will. I'll just pass on to them any little snippets of news I pick up along the way."

"Well we're certainly we're not busy," sighed Ralph. "Lord knows what I'm going to do to fill my time. OK then. Off you go…but be careful, OK?"

For his undercover investigations, Edison had dressed very

carefully, or rather, 'dressed-down' very carefully. He wore the tattiest t shirt he possessed and the scruffiest jeans that were torn at the knee, worn out trainers and a floppy sun hat that a guest had abandoned many months ago. He looked just like the garden boy he was intending to be.

He drove to town and parked his car in the shade on a side street. He didn't go to the main shopping area, but started ambling through the more run down backstreets where there were cheap shops and a couple of bars. It was early afternoon, a little after lunchtime, so he looked into one or two of the bars and chose the busiest. He bought himself a beer and sipped it straight from the bottle, like most of the other customers were doing.

Looking around the place there were maybe a dozen or so drinkers, all male apart from one over-made-up female wearing a dress far too tight for her. She might have been attractive once, thought Edison, but time and booze hadn't been kind to her. Edison quickly summed up what her reason for frequenting the bar was and carefully avoided any eye contact with her. Through his dark glasses he scanned the other customers; all black, like himself, evidently not working and clustered in groups of twos or threes. Thankfully, apart from a glance when he walked in, they seemed to be ignoring Edison. He started an elimination process of who would not have been able to carry out an audacious raid and kidnap. The two guys in the corner to begin with: they must have been in their sixties or older and wouldn't have been strong or fit enough to carry out a violent, physical attack. Then there was a group of three at the bar: young and fit enough to be thugs thought Edison, but he felt in his bones they just didn't look either intimidating or criminal. He glanced over at another group of three, sitting at a table, they were playing their own version of draughts using beer bottle tops as counters and seemed to be making the rules up as they went along. Conversation was animated and not always good-humoured as there were constant disputes over breaches of their self-made rules. Studying their body language Edison could judge that they could have violent streaks in their character, they could well be prepared to work outside the law, could they be kidnappers?

He realised his bid to become an undercover detective was hardly likely to reap quick success. Sipping his beer he tried hard to think of other ways in which he might discover who was responsible for the raid on Mogololo. Masiwa was evidently long gone now, but his henchmen might know where he had been headed, but how was he going to discover who those henchmen were? Maybe they'd made a run for it as well? Or perhaps they'd just hung around. His initial thought of finding someone who was splashing out unusual amounts of cash was still his best bet, but he now understood it wasn't going to just fall into his lap or be someone walking round with a sign round their neck: 'retired kidnapper – lots of money to spend'.

Feeling depressed and bereft of ideas, he was staring into space, he had not noticed there was someone joining him at his table.

"Hi, I'm Suzie, what is your name?" It was the smudged-make up girl in the too-tight dress.

"Oh, Edis ... or, just Ed, that's my name," said Edison, trying not to encourage the conversation.

"Do you want to buy a girl a drink, Ed?"

"Not really. I'm finishing this one then I'm off," he said, waving his half-finished beer bottle and quickly judging that the girl had already been drinking for quite a while.

"Going far?"

Edison really didn't want to keep this lady talking, so he was about to leave his beer and walk out when he noticed a new customer entering the bar. It was someone he knew slightly, a second hand car dealer who had a sales lot just around the corner. His cars were often sixth or seventh hand, but Edison had bought from him in the past and regarded him as being as straight as you could ever expect from a used car dealer. Edison tried hard to ignore the approaches of the persistent Suzie and was keen to hear and see what the used car dealer would do.

He breezed up to the bar and instantly got the attention of the bartender.

"Hey Joe! Howzit! Get me a beer, Bro. And get one for these fine guys too," indicating the small group to his left. They greeted him warmly and gratefully.

"Had a good morning Thabo?" asked the barman while he cracked off the tops of the beer bottles and slid them in front of the customers.

"Pretty good Joe, " he grinned, "Sold two vehicles for cash, just like that!" snapping his fingers to confirm his great salesmanship. "They were fighting each other as to which cars they wanted to buy."

Suzie, hearing that someone was buying drinks, abandoned her attempts to sweet-talk Edison and glided, somewhat unsteadily, to Thabo the car dealer.

He saw her coming, "Hey, Suzie!" he deposited a slobbery kiss on her caked cheek, "What are you having, darling?"

Edison, watching this scene play out before him quickly put two and two together: two customers, both paying cash, too good to be true, he thought…but might it be? He waited, patiently, watching as Thabo pulled out a big wad of money and peeled off a one hundred rand note to pay for the round of drinks. That just about sealed it for Edison - it had to be the two thugs who were assisting Masiwa. They'd had their pay off from the ransom money and were going to spend it as fast as they could.

Edison stayed in his corner, listening, watching, thinking. He needed a chance to talk to Thabo in private, but didn't want to barge in on the party at the bar that seemed to be getting louder and louder. So he waited, eking out the last few drops of beer that remained in his bottle.

A chance presented itself when Thabo made to go to the gents toilet. Edison followed him at a discrete distance and when Thabo had finished and was washing his hands Edison said, "Hi, Thabo, Edison Ngoveni."

"Ah," said Thabo, "Yes, I remember you; Volkswagen Citi Golf, wasn't it? Silver?"

Edison smiled, "Yes, that's the one. Still going strong."

"Good. Any time you want a trade-in to upgrade, come see me. Got a lovely Mercedes that would suit you, very low mileage."

"It's more your customers I'm interested in than cars, Thabo. The two guys who paid cash this morning, what do you know about them?"

"I thought you were in the game lodge business, not private detective?" said Thabo, very defensively.

"Sure. I am. But we had a bit of bother at the Lodge recently and there were two guys involved and I wondered if your customers might have a connection."

"Look. I sold two cars to two guys. OK? I didn't ask too many questions. Their cash looked good. It is good." Then the car dealer thought for a moment, "Isn't it? Hey! It's not forged notes is it?" He dug in his pocket and examined the wad of notes carefully. "They're used notes. Can't be a problem with them, surely."

Edison very politely explained, "Actually, if it is the same people who…er…caused the problem, the police invisibly marked the money. Would you be prepared to come to the police station with me to check?"

"No! Not a chance," responded Thabo. "I'm not handing over forty grand to the police! You think I'm crazy?"

"Well, they might come looking for you," suggested Edison. "Look, did your customers leave names and addresses with you?"

"No. They wanted a quick cash deal and just drove the cars away. They didn't even haggle over the prices"

"At least you can give me details of the cars," said Edison.

"Sure. That's easy," said Thabo. "Come back to the dealership with me and I can give you makes and numbers."

"Thanks," said Edison. "Can we go now?"

"Hah!" laughed Thabo, "And I thought I was having a good day until just ten minutes ago!"

Armed with the details of the two newly sold cars, Edison went to the police station and explained his story and suspicions of the new owners of the two second hand cars. The officers at the station all knew about the Mogololo kidnapping, and that their own disgraced ex-inspector Masiwa had been involved. Descriptions and numbers of the cars were circulated and the policemen were very interested in the wad of money that Thabo had in his pocket. Edison didn't like to relate that as soon as he had acquired the makes and numbers of the cars, Thabo would be going straight off to his bank to deposit the cash into his account, knowing that even though he might have to declare the transactions to the tax man by passing the money through his bank, at least it wouldn't be confiscated by the police as potential evidence. The notes would get combined with a mass of money in the bank branch, so it was going to be impossible to trace them back to Thabo's Five Star Auto Dealership.

Feeling that he had achieved quite a lot through his detective work, Edison made his way back to Mogololo. Ralph was delighted to hear the story of the car deal and the two cash buyers, at least they now had a lead.

"It means you may have lost some of the ransom money, Ralph" said Edison.

"Maybe Edison," replied Ralph. "Although if they catch them both, perhaps I end up with the cars as compensation; what did you say they were, these two cars?"

"A Mazda and a Honda."

"Just what I need," sighed Ralph.

Edison, always keenly tuned in to Ralph's moods, asked the delicate question,

"What news of Ella?"

"Well, I spoke with her mother about an hour or so ago. She's still totally withdrawn, speaking in monosyllables, barely eating, vacant expression in her eyes. David the doctor called in and told Jean he was arranging an appointment with a trauma counselor, but that would have to be in one of the Jo'burg clinics and Jean's not at all happy about her moving far from her home, so that's where we are. We haven't moved forward at all, really. Edison, I just don't know what I can do to help."

Edison, in his quiet and sensitive way, said, "Maybe a

little prayer might be a good idea?"

"Hmmmm, can't do any harm, can it?"

Chapter Eighteen

A couple of days had passed. Ralph had driven into town to see Ella, but her withdrawal and depression was just the same. She just sat, her rag doll on her lap, rocking very slowly backwards and forwards. There was no colour in her cheeks, no light in her eyes, her hair was lifeless and lank. It was so unlike Ella.

Jean and Ralph were whispering in the kitchen. "Is she sleeping?" asked Ralph.

"Yes, but restlessly," replied Jean. "I assume she's having bad dreams about it, but I'm no psychologist. How long do we let it go on, Ralph?"

"Wish I knew. I'll go and see David. I know we don't want her to go to this specialist in Jo'burg, but just seeing her like this is so awful. Maybe that is the answer."

"Go on then, see David," said Jean, very flatly.

Ralph had to wait a while for David to finish with his regular surgery patients, but eventually, Ralph was in his room, sitting on the hard backed chair that was normally occupied by the sick, infirm and hypochondriacs of Hoedspruit.

"I've had a chat with the counselor in Jo'burg about Ella," started David. "She says she's handled similar cases and is confident she can help."

A 'she', you said?" asked Ralph.

"Yes, Anne Gray, graduated from Stellenbosch the same year as me. Very bright."

"So she's a proper doctor as well as a counselor?"

"Oh yes, she's nothing to do with alternative, hippy, save the gay whale communes or anything like that," said David with a smile.

"Well that's a relief."

"She recommends a first meeting with Ella next week," explained David. "She can do Monday afternoon, for an hour at two o'clock. Depending on what she determines during that hour, she'll be able to suggest a course of therapy that will suit Ella."

"If Ella co-operates," cautioned Ralph.

"Well, that's what Anne does best," said David, "Draws out the demons and helps the patients overcome them."

"OK. I'll tell Jean," said Ralph, not over-enthusiastic that things were going in this direction, "I guess it will mean Jean taking her."

"Yes, she'll have to."

"I've got a brother who lives in the northern suburbs," said Jean, once Ralph had relayed the conversation he'd had with David. "The coffee shop can look after itself for a few days. We'll drive up on Sunday afternoon."

"Jean, I wish there was more I could do," offered Ralph. "But I feel I'd only get in the way."

"Yes, at the moment, the way Ella is, I think you would," agreed Jean.

During this brief exchange in The Moffat's sitting room, Ella had been sitting in the same chair she'd occupied since she came home, slowly rocking back and forth. Ralph went over to kneel in front of her. He took her hand in both of his, "Ella darling," he said softly. "We're going to make you better. We're going to get you back to the Ella we all know and love. If you can, just remember how much I love you. Have I told you that enough times? Probably not. But I do, really, really, do love you. And I need you back in one piece." He softly kissed her cheek, his moist eyes leaving one of his tears at the end of her eyebrow. Ella didn't respond, just rocked slowly, rocked slowly, rocked slowly.

Ralph drove back to Mogololo with a very heavy heart. He felt he ought to be going to Johannesburg too, to support Jean and Ella, but he had responsibilities back at the Lodge; so many people were dependent on Ralph for their livelihoods and their families' futures, he had to keep the show on the road.

As he pulled in to the little cluster of buildings that made up Mogololo, Danny and Billy were busy loading up their vehicle with flight cases, lighting stands, coils of cables and all the complicated kit that film crews always travel with.

"Hi Ralph," called Danny. "Any news?"

Ralph brought Danny up to date with Ella's condition but shook his head glumly over any further progress on catching Masiwa or his thugs.

"Look Ralph," said Danny. "We're sort of done for the time being. I've got masses of great material, Billy's got another production he has to move on to, and now that Ella's…well…now she's back, I ought to be getting back to base, too. "

"Yeah, sure," Ralph replied, rather half-heartedly. He had got used to Danny being around and had rather liked it.

"I need to get on with editing the material for the pilot, to show the commissioning editors at the TV stations, but I'm only a phone call away if you need me."

"Of course," said Ralph. "And I can't thank you enough for your help Danny. Look, if you get a chance, perhaps you could stay in touch with Ella's mum, Jean? She's going to be somewhere in the Northern Suburbs, where her brother has a place."

"Absolutely."

Ralph read out Jean's mobile phone number and Danny keyed it into his phone's contacts memory; they hugged, then Danny and Billy drove away from Mogololo. Still feeling pretty sorry for himself, Ralph headed for the

little office but before he got there, his own phone chirped its annoying alert noise that a call was coming in. Ralph recognized the number.

"Hi Callie," Ralph said, "Any news?"

"Well, yes, actually," responded Caleb Coetzee. "One of our patrol cars picked up one of the characters who'd bought the Honda for cash. He's currently in one of our interview rooms here at Nelspruit, telling his life story to one of my sergeants."

"Hey, that's good," said Ralph. "What about Masiwa?"

"Well, so far, this suspect hasn't been forthcoming about Masiwa's whereabouts. It's quite possible he really doesn't know. So I imagine he's either a remarkably good actor or, more likely, he's just a pretty unintelligent heavy who Masiwa picked up to snatch Ella in the first place. He's admitted he was paid twenty five thousand for the job and he's spent twenty of that on the car he bought. I'd say he was done; from what I've seen it's a bit of a wreck, but that's another issue entirely. In the meantime, he's more than happy to be telling us what Masiwa told him and his mate about Mogololo and how to get Ella while you were out on your game drive."

"Have you got his mate?"

"Not yet, but we now know where he lives, so we'll pick him up some time today or tonight, I'm sure."

"It's Masiwa we need."

"I know, I know," agreed the Inspector. "We've checked

out his home, of course, but we knew he wouldn't still be there. He could have gone to Jo'burg, Cape Town. He might have left the country although getting through a border post would be difficult for him – he hasn't got a passport."

"With half a million bucks of my money, getting one wouldn't be too difficult for him," said Ralph.

"That's true," agreed the Inspector with a resigned sigh.

"So what happens now?" asked Ralph.

"Well, we pick up the accomplice who kidnapped Ella, interview him and continue our search for Masiwa."

"Well, thanks for the call anyway," said Ralph, his mind already wrestling with the problem of how he was going to deal with the Masiwa situation, as well as the awful prospect of the potential financial ruin he was facing.

He was standing in a shady spot on the verandah, facing the bush beyond the thin line of electrified fence that kept the main camp of the Lodge safe from the larger animals when he spotted a massive bull elephant come ambling slowly towards Mogololo. The elephant was totally relaxed, secure in the knowledge that he was not under threat from any creature, apart from unscrupulous humans. So Ralph just stood and watched, as the elephant grazed on young leaves on the trees that had sprouted, following the recent rains. The rhythm of the probing trunk, gripping the ends of branches and stripping away the leaves to then deftly rearranging the foliage into a bunch that could be easily transferred into its mouth, then chewing, chewing, and dropping any of the woody twigs that the elephant couldn't be bothered to crunch into a mess that could be swallowed. It became mesmerizing, watching this vast, graceful animal satisfy itself with the business of gathering forage and eating. It actually helped soothe some of the stresses Ralph was feeling.

Then the elephant realised some of the leaves it really fancied were too high for its trunk to reach, so it decided to vary its diet and try some grass instead. It deftly kicked with its front foot against a clump of grass to loosen it, wrapped the very tip of its trunk around the grass and pulled. The grass came away, but being a fussy eater the elephant wasn't just going to stuff it straight in its mouth; it knocked the tuft a couple of times on the ground, to get rid of most of the earth that had come away with the roots and then it was ready to eat. It did it again, and again. But after four or five mouthfuls, the elephant got bored and having shown off both its strength to break off branches and then its trunk handling skills to to anyone who happened to be watching, it moved on and drifted silently away.

"Good for you, matey," Ralph said to himself, wishing that he was an elephant and all he had to do was wander through the bush, filling his stomach.

During the rest of the day Ralph tried to keep himself busy, checking paperwork in the office with Grace, making sure Miriam had enough supplies in her kitchen, ensuring the store cupboards were safe from cheeky vervet monkeys who were always trying their luck. His heart wasn't really in it but for the sake of morale of everyone at Mogololo he tried hard to be positive and upbeat. He was going through a pile of overdue, unpaid invoices, wondering which ones he could hold off from paying longest, when Grace came across to him, "Mr Ralphie," she started, "We have just had an email; an enquiry for a party of eight persons who want to arrive tomorrow. Shall I tell them no, we cannot accommodate them at such short notice?"

"Absolutely not, Grace!" responded Ralph. "We need the money! Tell them they are welcome. Where are they coming from?"

"It's an enquiry through a big hotel in Sandton, it appears they are from the Netherlands but they are coming into Nelspruit airport from Johannesbsurg and please can they be collected?"

"Hmmm," thought Ralph. "I wonder if they are friends of Jan and Esther? Bit odd that it's such a last-minute booking but we'll make sure they have a great time, won't we? I'd better go and warn Miriam she's going to be a lot busier than she expected. Grace, can you make sure the room girls double check the lodges to see everything is perfect? Then you'd better do an inspection yourself. OK?"

"Of course, Mr Ralphie."

"Good, let's all work to keep the Lodge going, just the way Ella would like it!"

The party from the Netherlands arrived via a minibus that Ralph had arranged from the airport at Nelspruit. There were four married couples, and yes, two of them were very friendly with Jan and Esther. Four of them had been at a medical conference in the city, with partners tagging along for the ride, but the last two days of the arrangements had all changed and rather than sit through presentations on topics that were of little interest to them they had decided to take Jan and Esther's recommendation and make a trip to Mogololo.

"Well I'm delighted you took Jan and Esther's advice," said Ralph once he had heard the brief explanation of why the booking had only been made at the last-minute. "And that we happened to have a convenient gap in our booking schedule, of course." (Ralph wasn't at all sure whether his pretence that Mogololo was always busy was received with the credibility he had intended, but the Dutch guests were too polite to comment.)

"Esther said to be sure to give her regards to Tanya," said one of the Dutch ladies.

"Ah, Tanya hasn't been around for a while," said Ralph." In fact she left us shortly after Jan and Esther's visit. "But Grace will look after you admirably."

Grace blushed with embarrassment and made signs that the guests should follow her and she would take them to their rooms, with Jackson helping with luggage.

Ralph felt strongly conflicting emotions over the arrival of these new guests. He was happy that Mogololo would function normally as a game lodge again after all the disruption of the past few days, but he also felt pangs of guilt that he was here, carrying on with business, while the woman he loved was still badly damaged and was being taken to a strange environment where there would inevitably be more pain and distress for her to endure. He also didn't particularly like to be reminded about Tanya who, as far as Ralph was concerned, was consigned to the trash bin of his personal computer screen. But the responsibility of keeping the Lodge running was at the forefront of his mind, so he determined that this new party of Dutch guests would have a great time.

And they did. Once they were settled and Miriam had fussed around them and made sure they tasted all of her cakes and biscuits and had copious amounts of tea, they went on their first game drive. Having eight passengers in the vehicle was a bit of a squash but as they all knew each other well enough, it wasn't really a problem. Like all first-time visitors to the bush, they were enthralled with the sights, sounds, smells and vastness of the area.

With Edison perched on his usual spot right at the front of the vehicle, guiding Ralph to where he thought there would be interesting game, they traversed the dusty tracks for a couple of hours, stopping every now and then to take photos of giraffe, zebra, wildebeest, baboons and elephants. Conscious that his guests were probably feeling cramped after being bumped over the sandy tracks for quite a while, Ralph stopped on the top of a mound with great views into the distance over unspoilt bush.

"Drinks time, ladies and gentlemen!" Ralph announced. "Not quite sundown yet, but I'm sure you'd all welcome some refreshment. Feel free to stretch your legs, but please don't wander off. I don't want to lose any of you!" And with that friendly instruction delivered, Ralph and Edison set up the camp table, unpacked the cool box and started pouring drinks for the party.

Once everyone had their drink, with most of the group chattering away to each other in Dutch, one of the men, not engaged in that discussion, started talking to Ralph.

"So, has this always been your life?" asked the guest, "I'm Henrik, by the way," he added, politely offering his hand for Ralph to shake.

"Well it was my grandfather's farm, then my father's, but I'm not cut out to be a farmer, so I turned it into a game lodge a little more than a year ago. Wildlife has been my passion since I was a boy, so I guess I'm living the dream now. Not that it doesn't come with its headaches and dramas," said Ralph.

"Oh, in what way?"

Ralph was very cautious with his reply," Oh, you know, the bureaucracy of having to deal with local government and parks board officials, poachers, keeping one step ahead of the creditors and the bank, that sort of thing."

"Very different from my life," laughed Henrik.

"What, you mean the medical world?"

"No that's my wife, Greta, she's the doctor," said Henrik, "I run an internet company."

"What, designing websites and stuff?"

"Not exactly," started Henrik, "It's more to do with data management and analyzing where traffic is coming from, and spotting future trends."

"Oh, I'm afraid you've lost me already," laughed Ralph. "I can deal with tracking hyenas but I don't have a clue about tracing what internet users are up to!"

"It's not so tough really," smiled Henrik. "I've got some very clever brains on my team, they're just kids really, but they have the ability to send out a mass email and within seconds, they can tell who has picked it up and with a bit of data mining, they can tell where those people might be located. It all helps to build patterns for our clients who are desperate to know their customers better."

"Well I prefer to know my customers face to face," said Ralph. "Your world is very different, but I'm grown up enough to realize it's probably the future."

"Well," said Henrik," finishing off his beer and gazing at the seemingly endless vistas around him, "I think your world has a lot going for it too."

As Edison and Ralph packed away the coolbox and table, Ralph was thinking over his conversation with Henrik; how the internet world was opening new avenues of commerce and communication, and he had the germ of a thought that might, just might, be a route to finding

Masiwa.

Once back at the Lodge, Ralph showered and changed at top speed and, checking his watch, he saw he had around twenty minutes before he needed to greet and welcome everyone for dinner. He made his way to the office and logged on to the internet. First of all, he created a brand new gmail account for himself, carefully masking any hint of his own identity, he called it 'gameboy88@gmail.com'. Then he wrote an email to the account that Masiwa had used. He was gambling that Masiwa hadn't created the account just for the kidnapping of Ella, but used the address more frequently. He wrote, 'I am planning an operation where your skills and contacts could be very useful. If you are interested in making some easy money, respond when you receive this.' In the subject panel he wrote, 'A proposition for you.' He was relying on Masiwa's greed and ego that we would reply, and then, with Danny's contact in Cape Town, he might be able to identify the area from where Masiwa had sent the mail. It was a long shot, but he had nothing else to lose.

He also wrote a brief email to Danny, telling him he was trying to make contact with Masiwa and hoping that if he replied, could Danny's geeky friend could help them locate where Masiwa was sending mails from?

Feeling he had done just about all he could do for the time being, he checked his watch and was happy to see he was still well in time to meet his guests before dinner. Saying a private prayer for Ella, he stitched a smile on his face and went to greet them.

Chapter Nineteen

The Dutch visitors' trip came and went in a flash. They stayed for two nights and were full of praise for everything Ralph and his team had done for them. Ralph had really enjoyed their company, especially Henrik's and was genuine in his entreaties for them to all come back and visit Mogololo again , and to stay longer next time.

Having waved their minibus goodbye, the black cloud of his situation came to rest over Ralph's head again: Masiwa was still somewhere out there, with the best part of half a million rand that Ralph was responsible for; Ella was not the girl she was before the kidnap took place; with too many blank spaces in the bookings diary he was teetering on the brink of financial collapse; his own resilience was at an all time low. It didn't look good.

Edison saw how his friend and boss was in danger of sinking into deep depression and was determined not to let it happen. "Hey, Ralph," he started, "That visit from our Dutch friends was good. They had a great time. We looked after them well. It was the Lodge at its best."

"Would have been better with Ella here," mumbled Ralph.

"Yes, well she will be here again soon, won't she?"

"Edison, I just don't know," sighed Ralph.

"Oh come on, be positive," urged Edison.

"I'm trying, really I am," promised Ralph, but Edison

wasn't convinced.

"You've got a lot of people here at the lodge depending on you," he said. "You have to be strong for their sake. Come on, I'll help however I can."

"Edison," said Ralph, smiling for the first time since the Dutch people left, "You should be president of this godforsaken country. I'd vote for you in a flash."

Before Edison could respond, the alert went off on Ralph's phone. Ralph looked, pressed the screen and a grin began to grow over his face. "Got you!" he said.

"Got who?" asked Edison.

"Masiwa. I sent him an email – anonymously, he wouldn't ever know it was from me - tempting him with some scam, appealing to his greed and his ego, and he's responded, look." Ralph showed his phone screen to Edison and there, an email from Max445566, 'Interested. Tell me more.'

"So what?" asked Edison, more than a little confused.

"Well now I've had a response, I can forward it to Danny's computer wizard friend in Cape Town; he has a way of locating where emails are sent from. Don't ask me how he does it, I don't even want to know. But once we know whereabouts Masiwa is hiding, we can get Callie Coetzee on the case and catch the bastard!"

Edison furrowed his brow, shook his head and muttered, "I'd rather deal with a herd of angry buffalo than a computer."

Ralph hurried off to his office to use the computer there, to download the mail from Masiwa and send it instantly on to Danny. Once that was done he sent a text message to Danny, telling to watch out for the mail and he was hoping that Danny wasn't miles away from his base out on location somewhere.

He was in luck. Danny responded immediately and passed on the mail to his pet computer wizard. So now Ralph had the torture of waiting for an answer. He idly pondered what the computer wizard in Cape Town might be like. Probably still a teenager, Ralph thought; spotty, sloppy T-shirt, training shoes with no laces, oversized jeans that seem to defy gravity how they manage to stay above his non-existent hips, a diet of junk food and fizzy drinks, yet with a brain that can compete with and beat the best that silicon valley in California can produce. Or it could be a girl, of course.

His pointless conjecture was brought to an abrupt halt by Miriam asking him questions about what would be needed in the way of food for the rest of the week. Ralph was about to tell her to talk to Grace about it but remembered that there was a degree of jealousy between Miriam and Grace over territory within Mogololo: Miriam was catering; Grace was housekeeping. So Ralph just said, "I'll check the bookings diary and get back to you Miriam, OK?"

"But Mr Ralphie, the bookings diary is right there. I see it," said Miriam, pointing to the book.

"Of course, sorry Miriam," said Ralph. He flipped through the pages. "Hmmm, doesn't exactly look like you'll be busy for the rest of the week, Miriam. Sorry. Not a single guest till a party of four next week."

"OK, well I will go and see my sister in Hoedspruit," said Miriam. "She has been in the hospital and now she is getting better. But my cooking will help her get strong more quickly."

"I'm sure it will Miriam," said Ralph kindly, "Give her our best."

While this exchange was going on, Ralph was keeping an eye on his computer screen for any signs of an incoming mail. Yes! A mail from Danny. Ralph opened it and saw Danny had simply forwarded the result from his Cape Town computer friend. Ralph read it as fast as he could, then had to re-read it as he'd missed some important bits. 'Hotmail firewall, blah blah, security protocols, blah blah, coordinates of sender location, blah blah, Soweto. Soweto? Soweto!'

"Brilliant!" exploded Ralph. "But where in Soweto?" He read the mail again and copied down the coordinates that were in the body of the message. He clicked out and went on to his search engine and typed in the coordinates, realizing as his fingers typed clumsily on the keyboard that it would have been easier to copy and paste, but too late now. He was almost breathless with excitement as he clicked 'search' and drummed his fingers on the desk as he waited for his painfully slow internet connection to give him an answer. Eventually the screen came up with the answer: Hoof Road, Eldorado Park, Soweto, Johannesburg. "OK Mr Masiwa. Now we know where you are, the police are coming to get you."

Ralph tried calling Insector Coetzee but only got his voicemail so he left a message asking him to urgently call back. He didn't elaborate in the message, not wanting to spoil the surprise that Ralph had done, what he modestly thought, was brilliant detection work, albeit of a pretty dubious legal nature.

He didn't have to wait too long for Callie Coetzee to call back.

"Mr Henderson," he began, quite formally, "I got your message, how can we help?"

"I know where Masiwa is," Ralph said without any more preamble.

"What? How do you know?"

"Perhaps I'd better not go into too much detail, but I can vouch for the accuracy of my information. He's in Soweto."

"Soweto?" responded the Inspector. "Quite a big place for him to hide."

"Well, I don't have a specific address, but I know it's Hoof Road, Eldorado Park, Soweto."

"OK," said the policeman, quite guardedly. "Now I may have a bit of a problem following this up personally. First it's way out of my area, and second we've had an instruction from the chief of police that we have to put all our resources at the disposal of a state visit to the area that's happening next week."

"State visit? What state visit?" asked Ralph.

"The Chinese are coming, hadn't you heard?"

"No, I hadn't heard, and frankly I don't give a shit. So does this mean there's nothing you can do about Masiwa?"

"No, not at all," said Coetzee. "I'll pass it on to the Jo'burg police and get them to follow it up."

"But they won't know the first thing about the case!" complained Ralph.

"I know, and I'm really sorry, but there's nothing else I can do,"

"Well there's something I can do," said Ralph and cut the connection.

He sat at his desk, fuming, furious that having identified where Masiwa was, today, right now, the police couldn't follow it up. Or rather, they would follow it up, but at a snail's pace. He knew full well that any request from Nelspruit police to the Jo'burg force would not get treated with any real degree of urgency, so the chances were that Masiwa could move on at any time…unless…unless.

"Edison!" he yelled. "We're going to Jo'burg!"

Ralph frantically packed a bag, not really knowing how long they might be away. He was about to head for the parking area, suddenly changed his mind and dashed back to the his office; he dialed in the combination of the safe and fished out a cardboard box that looked vaguely medical and then repacked his bag so that the box was at the bottom.

"Edison? Are you ready?" he yelled.

They took Ella's little VW car. It was more than four hours drive to the massive, sprawling Sodom and Gomorrah that was Johannesburg; the greedy, gaudy, commercial centre of South Africa. Gold was discovered on a farm in the 1880s and the scrabble for mining claims and all the exploitation and corruption that goes with a gold rush explosion was soon vividly apparent in the way the city mushroomed. The original city centre was quite neatly laid out in a grid pattern, but the lust for gold and space soon had the metropolis spreading out in all directions. The South Western Township, Soweto, had been established by the British administration in the 1930s, but with the arrival of the Boer-controlled nationalist government of 1948, the forced separation, apartheid, meant Soweto grew and grew. Ralph had heard that around 2 million people lived in Soweto, how on earth were they going to find Masiwa?

Ralph was driving quite fast, the wide, four lane toll road allowed him to cruise and eat up the kilometres, but Edison, always cautious, kept urging him to beware of speed traps, and of the many unlicensed and crazy drivers that he knew were in charge of beaten-up cars and vans, and the heavy goods trucks that were often not safe to be on the road, all in Edison's personal opinion, of course. But Ralph indulged him and made sure they were travelling at speed, but not recklessly.

They stopped for cokes and burgers when they refuelled. Edison offered to drive but Ralph was quite happy to continue. It was now getting late in the afternoon and the traffic was building as they got nearer and nearer the city. It was slow going through Pretoria, even though the highway now had more and more lanes. Ralph expected there to be open farmland between Pretoria and the northern suburbs and tried to reassure Edison that the traffic would improve. It didn't. It got worse. What used to be open country was now covered in warehouses, office blocks, shopping malls, housing complexes and traffic, traffic, and more traffic.

"How do people do this every day, Edison?" mused Ralph.

"Why do they do it is more of a question," said Edison. "The time they waste going up and down this road every day. They could be with their families, not stuck in little tin boxes, pouring out smoke."

"Or they could be out in the bush, like us."

"Perhaps it is a good thing they stay here, and leave the bush for the animals, and for you and me. It would not be so good if everyone here came to visit us in Mogololo."

"Well, not all at the same time, anyway," agreed Ralph. "But I wouldn't mind just a dozen or so of these poor people paying to visit us."

"But only the nice ones, eh?" said Edison.

"I guess we just keep going south on this highway until it tells us to head west for Soweto," Ralph said.

"You mean you don't even know where we are going?"

"Well, I have a fair idea, but I've never set foot in Soweto. Have you?"

Edison laughed, "Ralph, I've never been as far as Johannesburg! This is an entirely new adventure for me."

"Not so sure 'adventure' is the right word, Edison. We're coming to catch a slippery bastard and try to recover a great deal of money."

"You're right, Ralph. Is 'experience' better?"

"Much better. Ah! There's an off ramp that says Soweto," said Ralph, preparing to change lanes and take the exit.

"OK," said Edison. "Soweto's pretty big, I hear. Where do we go now?"

"Look for signs that say, 'Eldorado Park' I guess."

So they drove into Soweto, looking for signs that might help but after twenty minutes of aimless driving, they didn't find any. Dusk had now completely taken over from the bright light of the day and the haze of pollution from traffic fumes, dirty industry, dust and coal fires hung eerily in the air. Edison's natural caution led him to say, "I'm not comfortable here Ralph. Do you think it's wise we should continue?"

"Come on Edison," Ralph said. "I'm not giving up now. Look, we'll have to do that thing that most men resist at all costs: we'll have to ask someone for directions. It's best if you do it, rather than me."

Edison smiled at Ralph, "You mean because I'm the same colour as everyone else here and you are not?"

"You know what I mean," laughed Ralph. "Exactly that! Try that guy with the shopping bags over there," pointing to a single figure walking ahead of them.

Edison had a brief conversation with the man and there was a deal of pointing this way and that way, then some laughter and a handshake with the double grip that came naturally to all Africans.

"So?" asked Ralph when Edison got back in the car.

"He is a Shangaan, like me," explained Edison. "He says it's not far, back that way and then go left for a few kilometres. But he did say that Hoof Road was a long, long road."

"OK, well we'll just hope we get lucky," said Ralph, heading in the direction Edison was pointing.

They found Eldorado Park and soon discovered they were on Hoof Road. It was a wide main thoroughfare that seemed to run right through Soweto, although the section in Eldorado Park was pretty easy to identify. Ralph drove carefully up and down a few times, with both Edison and he searching for anything, something, that might look like Masiwa could have a connection to. There were dozens of side streets, Hoof Road itself was a proper, tarmac road, but all the offshoots were potholed dirt roads, with ramshackle homes, mostly home-made with building blocks and tin roof, and an electricity cable snaking to the shack from a nearby pole. Occasionally there would be a 'proper' house, professionally constructed and even architect-designed, but the majority were dirt poor and didn't look like they could withstand either a rainstorm or a puff of strong wind, but most of the population lived like this, and although they always aspired to something better, they knew they were more fortunate than many of their people who had no roof over their heads at all.

"It's hopeless, Edison," said Ralph, eventually pulling in to the side of the road. "I don't think we'll find him just aimlessly driving up and down."

"I guess you want me to start asking questions then?" Edison said, "See if anyone has noticed a big man, new to the areas, with lots of money?"

"I think we'll have to, Edison. You OK to do that on your own? I mean, I'll come with you if you like."

"No, better for me to do it alone. But I'm not going far from the car, just in case I ask the wrong people. So don't go to sleep, OK"

"Sure," said Ralph. "I've got your back."

Edison got out of the car and ambled over to a place by the side of the road that had one of the few streetlights giving a fairly pathetic attempt at illuminating the area. He wasn't there long before a cyclist came wobbling down the road. There were no lights on his bike, of course, and it looked like it had already had a hard life of being pedalled over rough and rocky tracks. Edison greeted the guy riding it with a cheery wave, the cyclist came to a wobbly stop and they soon struck up a conversation. Ralph could see there was some head scratching on the part of the cyclist and some helpful miming from Edison in trying to describe Masiwa, but the head shaking of the cyclist seemed to show that he didn't know what Edison was talking about. Then there was a sudden change of body language and some pointing and arm waving and more pointing and some laughing and Ralph thought this looked more positive. Edison shook the cyclist's hand and waved him away as he continued his laborious pedalling and Edison crossed the road to come back to Ralph in the car.

"Well?" asked Ralph.

"He says there is shabeen near here, and the madam who runs it also has some rooms to rent for sleeping. The guy didn't know, of course, but it might be worth a look?"

"Best suggestion we've got, I guess," said Ralph, starting the car. "Which way?"

Following Edison's directions, it was no more than a kilometre from where they had parked, and was down a side track off Hoof Road. Like all unofficial drinking dens, the shabeen had no sign outside, but the thumping bass of music coming from the neglected looking building gave a very strong hint as to which place it was. There were a couple of groups of men hanging around outside, each holding a bottle of beer and shouting animatedly at one another, there were the gaudy flashing colours of a cheap set of disco lights and a fierce-looking woman hovering around the door, attempting to get the men to keep the noise down; she was evidently the owner. Ralph and Edison watched and waited.

After an hour there was no sign of Masiwa and both Ralph and Edison were getting hungry, restless, uncomfortable and tired.

"This isn't getting us anywhere, is it?" said Ralph, as much to himself as to Edison.

"No," agreed Edison. Then he had a thought, "You know the way you made contact with Masiwa was through an email…"

"Yes, so what?"

"You could send him another one, arranging to meet."

"We could, but it's bloody risky, Edison."

"Are we not taking a risk sitting outside an illegal shabeen right now?"

"Point taken."

"So, will you do it?"

"OK. Now we know that Masiwa is somewhere in this area but he has no idea where we are."

"More importantly, he has no idea who we are," interrupted Edison.

"So if I sent an email suggesting we meet in one of the suburbs of Johannesburg, that would sound plausible, wouldn't it?"

"And we know how greedy Masiwa is…"

"Right, let's get out of here and find a cheap hotel for us and I'll send an email to him, inviting him to meet to discuss the proposition. And the meeting will be somewhere anonymous like a shopping centre."

"As well as finding a cheap hotel, can we also find something to eat?" pleaded Edison.

They went to an area of the suburbs known as Rosebank. Ralph didn't know Johannesburg well, but he once had a friend who said he had come from Rosebank. It was an urban and residential sprawl of townhouses, offices, shops, car showrooms, some old established grand properties and many, many more scruffy shacks and shelters that cropped up on any unclaimed space. They found a budget hotel for the night and to Edison's relief, a steakhouse from one of the renowned South African chains where Ralph was able to log on to the free wi-fi in the restaurant while they were waiting for their food.

"Right," said Ralph, "From Gameboy88 to Max445566, 'Proposition for you. Need to meet to outline business plan. Suggest Mug and Bean, Oxford Road, Rosebank' …

what's tomorrow's date Edison?"

"The twelfth, I think."

"OK, '…11am, 12th September.' See if he responds to that," said Ralph, pressing the 'send' button on his phone.

"So there's no way of him knowing it's us?"

"He'd have to be psychic to link us to a meeting in Rosebank. He won't have a computer geek like Danny's friend to track down a location of where an email came from, and I am rather expecting his ego and greed to get in the way of much rational thinking."

Their food arrived and they both attacked it like hyenas piling into a carcass, but with considerably better table manners. Just as Ralph was mopping up the last of his gravy with some bread, his phone pinged. He pressed the screen and there was a new mail in his inbox.

"Got him!" he exclaimed. "He says, 'I will be there.' I guess we'd better make a plan then."

"Can we not have pudding first?" asked Edison with a smile.

Chapter Twenty

Ralph and Edison were up early and were both nervously excited at the prospect of trapping Masiwa. They went to the coffee shop to check it, approaching very cautiously just in case Masiwa was also doing a recce of the place, but there was no sign of him.

"Pity it's got three different ways in and out," said Edison.

"But it's not so big that we'd never spot him."

"But have you thought what we do when we confront him?"

"Not really. If it wasn't for the bloody Chinese visiting Kruger, I'd leave it all to Callie Coetzee, but he's not around, so we'll have to wing it on our own."

"Well he's not likely to just put his hands up and surrender and say sorry, is he?" said Edison rather scathingly.

"No, and I suppose he just might have someone watching his back, as well," said Ralph as an afterthought.

"Someone we would never have seen before," added Edison.

"I do have something of an idea though."

"Yes?"

"A while back, one of the Park rangers gave me a tranquilizing dart that was coming up to its expiry date.

He said they always destroyed them when they reached the date, but a chemist friend of his said that was just for the drug company to cover themselves; they go on being effective for years after. Anyway, I just happened to bring the dart with me."

"And you're going to shoot Masiwa with it, like he was an elephant needing a collar?" asked Edison, astonished at the idea.

"Not exactly," replied Ralph. "You are. Not that you'll need a gun, of course."

Edison groaned, "Come on then, what's your plan."

"OK. We'll wait for Masiwa to go in. Let him stew for maybe ten minutes; once we know where he's sitting, I'll sneak in, using the door that he can't see, I'll sit down opposite him, he'll be shocked to see me, he'll probably jump up, but I'll be ready for that, I'll be as nice as pie towards him, I won't let on that we know it was him all along, and I'll ask him what he's doing in Rosebank, or some such rubbish. Meanwhile, you've come in another entrance and while he's talking to me, you get behind him and put the needle in his neck. The drug should take effect in about five or ten seconds."

"It's mad Ralph!" laughed Edison. "What about the other customers?"

"They'll be shocked, sure. But none of them will want to get involved."

"But those darts have enough drug to bring down an

elephant! Aren't we going to kill him with an overdose?"

"Nah, we'll get rid of at least of half the chemical first. What we put in him won't kill him."

"And if it works, and if he's unconscious, what do we do then?"

"Well, I'll give Callie Coetzee a call to say we've got Masiwa and that should give him enough incentive to get the local police to come and get him."

"Ralph, I still think it's crazy," said Edison. "It's going to cause a big fuss in the café."

"It probably will, yes, but if we get him, it will be worth it," said Ralph. "Edison, he's had half a million bucks of my money, poor Ella is still in a bad way, and the police in Nelspruit are farting around with a visit from the Chinese. We've got to do this ourselves!"

Edison put up his hands in submission, "Okay, Okay. Let's start with the tranquillizer drug. I don't want to be on a charge for murder again."

So, sitting in the front of Ella's VW, Ralph studiously read the instructions that came with the tranquillizer drug. As Edison had said, one dart was enough to bring down an elephant and keep it asleep for twenty minutes, so Ralph found an empty water bottle in the back of the car and carefully began to release at least two thirds of the liquid into it. He held up the dart to the light, guessing that what was left in the syringe would be enough to send Masiwa to sleep.

"That's a pretty nasty-looking needle," commented Edison.

"Masiwa's got a nasty-looking thick skin," replied Ralph. "Sure, he's going to make a fuss once you stick it in him, but he won't be expecting it. I will. So I'll be able to grab his arms; once you've got the stuff inside him, you can also hold him down, and within ten seconds, he'll be gone."

"Bad choice of word, 'gone'", said Edison.

"All right, 'asleep' then," smiled Ralph. He looked at his watch, "Okay, it's an hour and a half before he's due. Let's move the car into the shade, somewhere that we can see the entrances, but he won't notice us."

"OK, but shall we get a couple of takeaway coffees first?"

They waited, as patiently as they could, both keyed up by the anticipation and danger of what they were about to do.

"Is this what criminals feel like before they go on a smash and grab robbery?" asked Edison.

"Edison, I've never done a smash and grab robbery! How would I know?" said Ralph. "I did nick a packet of sweets from a corner shop once, but I was only twelve at the time, and got such a spanking from my father when he found out, I've been on the straight and narrow ever since."

Edison just smiled and continued gazing out of the car windscreen, occasionally scanning from one side to the other, as if he was back in the bush, looking for signs of leopards. "I wonder what direction he will be coming from?"

"Hard to say. I imagine he's blown some of my money on a car for himself," said Ralph. "Not that many car parking spaces left around here now," he added, "so we have no idea where he'll pop up from. Good thing he's hard to miss."

Edison checked his watch again, "Shouldn't be too long now. If he's coming, of course."

"He'll come."

And five minutes later, he did. Swaggering along the road, oblivious of other pedestrians, Masiwa headed for the Mug and Bean café. Both Ralph and Edison had spotted him at the same time and both slid a little further down in their seats, just to be sure Masiwa didn't spot them. They watched surreptitiously as Masiwa strode in to the café, then gasped as ten seconds later, he came out again. He looked around the area. Ralph and Edison held their breaths, thankfully Masiwa went back into the Mug and Bean and this time he stayed there.

"Now we need to know where he's sitting," whispered Ralph.

"Why are we whispering?" asked Edison, also in a whisper, "He can't hear us!"

Ralph ignored the jibe and concentrated on trying to see through the large windows into the interior. "I've got him!" he said, now in a normal voice. "Can you see him? He's gone for a table near the side. He's ordering now. Enjoy your coffee Masiwa, it may be a while before you have another."

"OK," said Edison, "So you will go in the same door that he used, and confront him. I will use the side door on his blind side."

"That's the plan," said Ralph. "God! I wish my heart would slow down a bit!"

"Mine too," agreed Edison. "We're not cut out for this type of work Ralph."

"No, once is going to be quite enough for us."

Ralph gave Masiwa a few more minutes then, "Come on, let's go." He made sure he had his mobile phone, he locked the car and waited until a big truck was passing by before crossing the road so that the truck would shield him from Masiwa's view in case he was looking out of the café window. Keeping his head down, he took a deep breath and entered the Mug and Bean. It was quite busy, which suited Ralph. Masiwa was busy fiddling with his mobile phone so he didn't notice Ralph was coming towards him until he was three paces away.

"You!" he spluttered, attempting to get up at the same time.

"Yes, Mr Masiwa," said Ralph, smiling as he spoke, "I've come for our meeting. Please sit down."

But Masiwa did not sit down. He attempted to reach across the table to grab Ralph, spilling his coffee mug onto the floor. A waitress screamed. Other customers looked around in shock. Ralph avoided Masiwa's lunge, but then grabbed his arms. Edison was already in the café and rushed up to the side of Masiwa and stuck the dart into the side of his gross neck. Maswia roared like an injured buffalo and tried to release himself from Ralph's grip. Edison had dropped the now-empty dart and held Masiwa from behind. Tables and chairs went flying in the struggle, customers were shouting, the staff were retreating behind the counter, the manager half-heartedly told them to stop or she would call the police. Masiwa continued struggling and trying to kick out at both Ralph and Edison. He connected with Ralph's shin which made Ralph cry out in pain, but both he and Edison hung on to the big man. After what seemed like an age to Ralph and Edison but was actually only ten or fifteen seconds, his roars turned into grunts, and the struggles became completely un-coordinated and with both Ralph and Edison quite breathless with exertion, Masiwa slumped, in a most undignified way to the floor.

Ralph and Edison pulled him to one side, Ralph feeling for a pulse in his neck.

"It's Okay, Edison," he said, "You didn't kill him."

"What is going on!" screamed the manageress. "I'm calling the police."

"Please do," said Ralph. "This man is a criminal and we want him taken into custody."

"Are you under cover cops?" asked one of the middle-aged lady customers, eyes wide-eyed in amazement.

"Not exactly, madam," replied Edison, " But we are helping them do their job."

One of the waitresses was calmly putting tables and chairs back where they belonged and was clearing up spilt coffee and broken china. "Would you like some coffee?" she asked sweetly.

"That would be nice," said Ralph. Then, looking down at the unconscious Masiwa, "I don't think our friend needs any, though."

The café was still in a sense of shock, with the manageress on the phone explaining to the police just where they were in Rosebank. She evidently wanted to be the one in charge, "Right," she announced to the café in general, but to Ralph and Edison in particular, "The police will be here in just a minute, so don't you go anywhere!"

"Madam, as I said earlier," Ralph said very reasonably, "That's just what I want."

Ralph then pulled out his phone and called Callie Coetzee. Fortunately, he responded within seconds.

"Callie? It's Ralph Henderson. We've got Masiwa. We're in a café in Rosesbank and we've managed to…er…sedate Masiwa."

"What?" came the incredulous response from the Inspector in Nelspruit. "What do you mean by 'sedate' exactly?"

"Well, I happened to have a tranquillizer dart, and we gave some of the drug to Masiwa. He's out for the count on the café floor."

"Oh God, what have you done!"

"It's all right, we haven't killed him, but the local police are on their way now. It would be really good if you could let someone in authority know in Jo'burg that Masiwa's a wanted criminal, otherwise they just might lock up Edison and me instead."

"OK. I'll make a call," said Coetzee. "Did you talk to Masiwa before you drugged him?"

"No, he was not in a talkative mood. He just wanted to fight."

"Hmmmm. Stay there. I'll ring you back once I've spoken to my contact."

"Your coffee?" smiled the waitress sweetly, offering two mugs to Ralph and Edison.

The siren of the police patrol car started in the distance and built in intensity as it came closer and closer to the café. A pair of muscle-bound constables strode into the Mug and Bean and took in the sight of Masiwa slumped on the floor, next to a table where Ralph and Edison were casually sipping their mugs of coffee.

While one policeman checked that Masiwa was breathing, the other listened to Ralph's story of Masiwa being a kidnapper and blackmailer and how Ralph had tricked him into a meeting and Edison had drugged him with the tranquillizer dart and if they'd like to contact Inspector Caleb Coetzee of Nelspruit police he would verify the story. The policeman listened, open-mouthed, to Ralph's account. He was more used to attending small-time burglaries, traffic accidents and domestic arguments than major crime like kidnaps and blackmail.

"So how long will this man be unconscious with this drug inside him?" asked the policeman?

"If he was an elephant, and if we'd given him all of the drug in the dart, maybe fifteen or twenty minutes," Ralph replied, very casually. "But we only gave him about a quarter, but I've no idea how long he'll be out. You might like to handcuff him as a precaution?"

"Now listen Mister," said the Policeman, very full of his own importance. "You don't tell me what to do. I'm just assessing the situation and as far as I'm concerned, you and your mate here are the ones who are under suspicion for causing a disturbance and illegal handling of drugs. See?"

"Call Inspector Coetzee, please," said Ralph, very reasonably. "I spoke to him a few minutes before you arrived and he was calling a colleague in Johannesburg to verify my identity and explain the case."

"Ah, identity. Ja. Can I see some?"

Ralph wearily got out his wallet and showed the constable his ID card.

"Hoedspruit?" commented the constable, in his thick Afrikaans accent, "That where you from, eh?"

"Yes, I run a game lodge on the edge of Kruger. Our friend on the floor used to be an Inspector in the police there, but he got fired for being a very bad policeman and he attempted to get revenge on me by kidnapping my girlfriend and lodge manager and extorting half a million rand from me. I haven't got the money back, by the way."

The policeman scratched his head and wondered just what he had got himself into by responding to this call.

"So you saying this man used to be in the SAP?"

"That's right."

"I'm calling my boss. You stay there." And with that, he went out to his patrol car and contacted his police headquarters on the radio. He was gone quite a while. His partner, having convinced himself that Masiwa was alive and apart from having a strange drug coursing round his body, was uninjured, was standing by Ralph and Edison and was intrigued to hear more about Masiwa's police record.

"So how did he get fired?" he asked.

"He came to the Lodge one afternoon, drunk, and he threatened my partner. Fortunately we had a film crew there at the time and although Masiwa didn't realise it, the whole confrontation was recorded on video. We sent the video to a contact in the justice department, someone quite high up, and Masiwa was sacked. I didn't think at the time he might be vindictive and revengeful. He's caused me a great deal of trouble, I can tell you."

The policeman thought for a while, "I guess we'd better get an ambulance for him, then. I don't fancy trying to pick him up."

"Good idea," said Ralph, "As long as he stays in your custody. Apart from getting him jailed, I want my money back!"

The other policeman came back into the café. "Okay," he said. "I spoke to my boss who had been alerted by the serious crime people about this Thabo Masiwa. So your story checks out. It's still not right that you do this drug thing all by yourselves though. You should have left it to our guys, you know?"

"If I had left it to you, I don't think we would have caught him, do you?" said Ralph, dismissively. "We found out he was staying somewhere in Soweto and we set up this meeting. He thought we were going to get him involved in some scam where he would make money. Talking of which, can we make sure he's still got the ransom money I paid him?"

The policemen searched through Masiwa's pockets and came up with a wallet stuffed with hundred rand notes, car keys and another key that looked like a hotel room key, it had a number 11 on its tag, but no clue as to which hotel it might be.

"No hotel card?" asked Ralph.

"If he's in Soweto, it's more than likely a shabeen with rooms, it won't be the Hilton, you know," said the policeman.

Ralph and Edison described the place they had been looking at the previous night, thinking that Masiwa might make an appearance.

"I know it," said the second policeman, "It's known as Mama Maisie's, off Hoof Road, right?"

Edison nodded.

"Well," said the policeman. "It's not really our area, but once we've got this lump of shit safely off to hospital, we'll take a trip down to Soweto and see what we can dig up. Okay?"

"Good. Can we come?" asked Ralph?

"I need you to make statements, Sir," said the policeman, with a very officious tone of voice.

"Certainly," said Ralph, "But I'd still like to know my money is not all spent yet!"

"Ja, ja, well, it's a bit irregular, but I guess it should be all right."

"The police in Nelspruit marked the banknotes with some invisible dye before Masiwa picked it up," said Ralph, being as helpful as he could.

"Sure," said the policeman, as if it was a common occurrence that he was involved in the recovery of half a million rand of ransom money.

Just then the ambulance arrived and the two crewmen bustled in to attend to the still-sleeping Masiwa. Ralph explained what had put him to sleep and handed them the empty dart syringe. The ambulance men were aghast at what Ralph and Edison had done. "You could have blerry killed him, man!"

but they were also quite entertained at the situation, with an overweight snoring ex-policeman at their feet. So they heaved him on to a stretcher and carted him off to their ambulance.

The two policeman had a short conference about what to do next; they agreed that one constable would accompany Masiwa to hospital, while the other would drive to Soweto, with Ralph and Edison following.

Ralph was amazed how the traffic seemed to part in front of them like the Red Sea for the Israelites when he was following the police patrol car with its lights flashing and siren blaring, so the journey to Eldorado Park, Soweto didn't take too long.

When the policeman confronted a formidable-looking woman who must have been Mama Maisie herself she didn't look at all pleased.

"What you doing bringing my establishment into disrepute?" she challenged.

"It's already in disrepute Mama," said the policeman with a smile. "It's Okay, we don't want to check your licence or your cash receipts this time. It's one of your rooms we want to look at, Number 11."

"Oh, that's Big Boy Max's room, I guess," said Maisie. "He's been here a couple of nights, says he's moving on tomorrow."

"Well I don't think he'll be sleeping here tonight," said the policeman. "Along here is it?"

They headed down a dim corridor, with doors either side, Mama Maisie following with keen, proprietorial interest. "What's Big Boy done then?"

"Never you mind," said the policeman as he fiddled with the lock of Number 11.

They piled into a very small room: an unmade bed, a small table and chair, clothes haphazardly dumped everywhere. They were searching for a bag, rucksack or suitcase and eventually Edison lifted up the single bed and there was a bag underneath. It seemed empty.

"Shit!" said Ralph. "Where's my money?"

"Money?" exclaimed Mama Maisie, suddenly becoming very interested. The others ignored her.

Edison said, "I wouldn't leave a stash of money lying around here, would you Ralph?"

"No," replied Ralph. "Let's look a bit deeper."

So they searched again, investigating all the nooks and crannies in this none-too-clean room. They searched around the door frame, under the bed, they carefully felt every part of the empty bag, the chair was turned upside down. Nothing. Eventually, Ralph got on his hands and knees and crawled under the table.

"Bingo!" he shouted. There, under the table top, stuck with some industrial tape, was a small key. It had a four figure number on it. Ralph showed it to the policeman.

"I reckon that comes from Jo'burg Central," he said.

"Central what?" asked Ralph.

"Central Station, of course. It's a left-luggage locker key."

"Let's go to the station, then," said Ralph.

The policeman gave a strict warning to Mama Maisie to leave the room as it was. Not to let it out to anyone else, and not to move any of Masiwa's belongings.

"I don't reckon she would have tidied it up anyway," muttered Edison as they made their way back out into the sunshine of Soweto.

Outside, standing on the potholed dirt track, the police constable had a pang of doubt about what the morning's events had led to and the speed at which events were unfolding.

"Listen man," he said to Ralph and Edison, "This is getting bigger than my normal cases of traffic accidents and shoplifters. I'm going to put in a call to my sergeant at the station to see what I should do with this, ja?"

Ralph shrugged his shoulders and waited patiently as the policeman got on his radio to talk to his superiors. It took a while as he was passed up the line from uniformed sergeant to detective sergeant to detective inspector. He was getting a few of the important facts wrong and Ralph tried to interject and correct him but the policeman resisted his attempts to help until finally, and reluctantly, he handed the radio over to Ralph.

"This is Ralph Henderson. I'm the victim of this character Masiwa's kidnapping and extortion. Who am I talking to?"

"Detective Inspector Pinaar, Meneer. I took the call from Caleb Coetzee about your case. We don't normally approve of individuals taking the law into their own hands especially when it comes to attacking suspects with dangerous needles with drugs inside them. I think you need to come to the police station to give us your statement, Mr Henderson."

"Yes, I'm happy to do that but first shouldn't we go to the railway station and see what Masiwa has hidden in the locker?" pleaded Ralph.

"Ja, Ja, I understand your impatience Mr Henderson, but it's best if we follow procedure," said the Detective Inspector. "Now why don't you just follow the constable in your car back to the station and we can take your statement and then while you are doing that we can arrange for the locker to be opened."

"I'd far rather be present when that locker is opened,"

protested Ralph.

"You don't trust the police, Mr Henderson?" countered the Inspector, quite aggressively.

"Masiwa was a policeman," said Ralph very reasonably. "He's the policeman who started all this. He took half a million rand of my money. What do you think?"

"Mr Henderson," said the Inspector, "We are the Gauteng Division of the SAP. We have standards. We have integrity. I can understand your, shall we say, reluctance, given your recent experiences with ex-inspector Masiwa, but we are different. But look. Come to the station for your statement and then you can go with one of my men to see what's in the locker. Is that OK?"

"Fine," said Ralph.

The statement-taking was a fairly long and tortuous process, with Ralph and Edison being separated so both their statements could be given individually. Then there was the typing up, and the signing and the counter-signing and then the two statements were compared for the verification of the versions of the story both Ralph and Edison had given. Ralph was becoming more and more impatient with the methodical but painfully slow way in which these things were done. He was more used to making instant judgements and decisions on given circumstances and acting, decisively and confidently and to hell with the consequences. Police work wasn't like that.

Eventually, DI Pinaar was satisfied that he had a definitive record of the events leading up to the incident in the Mug and Bean. He painstakingly compared the report from Callie Coetzee with the statements that had just been given and was nodding his head in agreement, then shaking his head in amazement at what he was reading. "Yerrer, man!" he exclaimed. "He's a bad Oke, this Maswia, eh?"

Ralph nodded, reluctant to get into a lengthy discussion as he wanted to move on to the Railway Station and establish whether or not Masiwa had stashed his money there.

"Okay," the Inspector eventually said. You go with the constable to open up this locker. Whatever is inside it will be evidence, of course. But if it is the cash you paid over for the ransom money, then the courts will get it back to you, eventually.

"Horrible word: 'eventually'," grumbled Ralph.

"Ja, but we have to go through the due process," said the Inspector, rather pedantically.

Ralph and Edison carefully followed the police car through the built-up sprawl that the city of Johannesburg had become. It had once been a vibrant and affluent city, boasting properties that newly rich entrepreneurs had built for themselves to show off their wealth. Today it was a mess of over-development, decay and neglect. Some areas tried hard at rejuvenating themselves, and attempts at style were thrown up against the faded Victoriana of what had gone before. To its credit, it was now a much more cosmopolitan city than a few decades earlier when it was under the cruel grip of apartheid and a ruling class that was for the few and not the many. Ralph and Edison found the traffic tiresome and were grateful that having a police car ahead of them managed to make progress a little easier than would otherwise have been the case. They made their way through Parktown and Hillbrow, with Edison commenting to Ralph, "I'm glad we didn't have to come looking for Masiwa round here, Ralph. Not sure we would have got out alive."

Eventually, they pulled up at the main railway station, the police car parking wherever it wanted, Ralph was a little more circumspect and found a space for Ella's car where there was no danger of getting a parking ticket.

The police constable was striding across the railway station concourse, with a sense of purpose and importance as he headed toward the left-luggage area. Ralph and Edison walked briskly behind him, both marveling at the scale of the building with its high arched ceiling. It was a mad bustle of people coming and going, catching trains, leaving trains, meeting people, coming to work, going home after work, travelling on business, travelling to families, everyone had a story, but there was no time today to dig into their personal histories.

The constable seemed to know where to go which was good news for Ralph and Edison as they were totally out of their depth and comfort zones in this environment. The noise, the bustle, the chaos of constant arrivals and departures was making them both long for the peace, quiet and calm of Mogololo.

"Do people do this every day?" wondered Edison.

"Isn't that what you said about the traffic on the freeway yesterday?" responded Ralph.

By now the constable was searching for the locker that the key he was clutching would open. There were hundreds of lockers but he found the right one and with a mechanical clunk, the key opened the door. A scruffy black rucksack was inside.

"That's the rucksack Masiwa had when he picked up the shoebox with the ransom money," offered Edison.

"Right, follow me," said the constable, taking charge of the rucksack. He strode off towards the ticket office with Ralph and Edison in his wake. Pushing past some would-be passengers queuing up for their tickets he demanded the railway official behind the counter gave him an office "for some important police matter". The railway official wasn't happy and called for his supervisor to deal with the policeman. Negotiations were short and quite blunt; a small office was found. Edison, Ralph and the policeman crowded into the room, the railway supervisor also wanted to stay, very curious to discover what was going on, but the policeman ordered him out.

With the rucksack on the table, the policeman opened the straps and delved inside. He methodically took out bundles of money.

"That looks like the money we got from the bank at Hoedspruit," said Ralph.

The money kept coming. The constable was wide-eyed with amazement. He, personally, had never seen so much money before.

"I think you should start counting it," suggested the policeman.

After the piles of money were stacked on the table, the policeman fished around all the other pockets of the rucksack. He found a small handgun, and yet more bundles of money, different from the piles that Ralph and Edison were now methodically counting.

It took a while, but they eventually came to a figure of four hundred and twenty thousand rand of the money that Ralph declared was the ransom, together with another hundred and thirty five thousand rand in the rubber bands of the second stash.

Ralph breathed a very audible sigh of relief, "Thank God for that."

The policeman suggested they should write down exactly what they had found in the locker, so there would be no disputes later, and sign statements for one another. The railway supervisor was summoned back to bring blank sheets of paper and pens and they duly made brief statements of what had been in the rucksack and Ralph and Edison signed their copy and the policeman signed his and they exchanged papers.

"So that's that?" asked Ralph.

"I guess so," said the policeman. "There is the issue of the man in custody in hospital, of course."

"Just don't let him go!" pleaded Ralph.

"No, we don't like policemen who turn into criminals. We'll look after him, don't worry."

Ralph didn't really like the implication of the emphasis the policeman had put on the phrase 'look after', but didn't comment. They said their goodbyes and went their separate ways.

"It's been a busy day, so far," volunteered Edison.

"Hmmm," said Ralph. "And I'm not sure it's over. Edison, would you mind if I called Ella's mum to see if we can see Ella, while we are here?"

"If you hadn't suggested it, I would have," said Edison.

Ralph called Jean on his mobile and although he didn't go through all the detail on the phone, he said he had news and could he come and see Ella, and her, of course. Jean explained that Ella had seen the consultant a few times, and although the consultant said they were making progress, she didn't really see any signs herself. So she cautioned Ralph not to expect too much, but yes, of course he and Edison should come.

Chapter Twenty One

Driving north from the centre of Johannesburg, following Jean's directions, Ralph brooded on the events of the past couple of days. They'd trapped and captured Masiwa, like a rogue buffalo; that was certainly progress, but the cloud that still hung over him was the thought that Ella was still damaged and didn't seem to be healing.

Travelling through the northern suburbs, the traffic was still dense but instead of smoke-belching trucks, overcrowded buses and beaten up, clapped-out vehicles, the roads were now dominated by the smart cars of the affluent. They cruised through tree-lined areas where properties were huge and ostentatious but largely hidden behind high walls, with coils of razor wire or even electrified cables on top of the walls. Remote controlled gates were all sternly shut to keep out intruders or prying eyes.

"Are people happy, living like this? Behind fortresses that they can't see out of?" asked Edison.

"Paranoid, aren't they," agreed Ralph. "But everyone has a story about how either they or someone close to them has been attacked or car-jacked or robbed in their homes, so they think this is a way to deter the bad people. Not sure if it works, though."

"I'd rather take my chances with the lions and the hippos," muttered Edison.

Ralph found the house Jean's directions had guided him to. The property, like so many of the others, was protected by high walls and an automatic gate (closed, of course). Ralph spoke into the little microphone sticking out on a stalk, and a few seconds later, the gate slid back on its runners. Ralph slowly drove up a brick-paved drive and was impressed by the immaculate lawns, borders and the imposing house that stood at the top of the drive. Jean came out to greet them. She hugged Ralph and held on to him for a second or two longer than was customary, Ralph reading into the gesture that she was stressed and deeply concerned for her daughter's welfare. She greeted Edison rather more formally with a handshake, but was genuine and warm with the smile she gave him.

"Come on in," she said, "My sister-in-law is here. And Ella, of course."

The house was spacious, airy and tastefully furnished. Ralph cynically suspected the hand of an interior designer rather than Jean's brother and sister-in-law, but quickly dismissed the thought. It was Ella he had come to see. She was sitting, quietly, in a deeply cushioned chair that seemed to make her smaller than she really was.

Ralph beamed and went across to kiss her, "Hello Darling. I've missed you."

Ella turned her head to face Ralph and gave him a half smile. But it was a smile with her mouth, not her eyes. Ralph's heart sank but he was careful not to show it. He was kneeling on the floor so he was at Ella's level and said to her, but also included Jean, "Well, the big news is we've captured Masiwa. Edison and I tracked him down to Soweto, then we tricked him into meeting us in Rosebank. Edison used a tranquillizer dart on him, now the police have him in custody and we got the ransom money back. Well the police have it now, but that's another story. And we actually found more money than he got from us, but that's another story as well. I'm sorry, darling. I'm rambling, aren't I? Most importantly, how are you?"

Ralph had been holding her hand while he had gabbled on about the events of their day, Ella looked down at their hands and slowly withdrew hers, "I'm Okay", she said.

"Well," piped up Jean's sister-in-law who had been introduced as Sally, "Who'd like some tea?"

Ralph realised neither he nor Edison had consumed anything since their coffee at the Mug and Bean that morning, "Oh, Sally, that would be wonderful. Yes please!"

While Sally went off to the kitchen, Jean suggested to Ralph they walked around the garden, she evidently wanted to talk about Ella's progress, or lack of it, alone.

"We've seen Anne Gray the Consultant three times now," she started, "She specialises in post traumatic stress cases, but she's told me that Ella seems to be resisting opening up about what happened to her. At her last appointment, yesterday morning, it was, she tried hypnotherapy. I wasn't there, of course, but she told me afterwards it wasn't a great success. Ella got quite restless and tearful, so rather than put her through more anguish, she brought the session to an early halt."

"Oh, dear," said Ralph, "Jean I'm so sorry. So what does the Consultant suggest now?"

"We have another appointment tomorrow," said Jean. "If you're still here, you could come along if you want to? You couldn't go in to the appointment itself, that's only for Ella and the Consultant, but it might help if you meet her."

"Of course," said Ralph, "Anything to get her better."

Ralph then had a thought, and waved to Edison who had been wandering around the garden by himself and was busy selecting some long grass stems from a border. "Edison!" shouted Ralph, and Edison sauntered over. Ralph handed Edison his phone, "Could you call Grace and see if everything is under control at the Lodge?"

"Sure," said Edison, still holding the grasses in one hand while he dialed his wife's number on the keypad with the other. He had a brief conversation in Shangaan with Grace, ended the conversation, and handed the phone back to Ralph. "There's a party coming in to the Lodge the day after tomorrow, but no problem."

"Okay," said Ralph, then to Jean, "What time is Ella's appointment tomorrow?"

"Ten o'clock. The clinic is just ten minutes down the road."

Sally then called from the terrace that tea was ready, and

Ralph and Edison needed no further prompting. As they walked up to the house, Ralph asked Edison, "What's the grass for?"

"For Ella," was the cryptic reply.

After their tea and two or three pieces of very welcome cake, Ralph and Edison politely said their goodbyes. Ralph tried again to get a response from Ella; he was patient and tender but there was no light in her eyes. Jean smiled sympathetically towards Ralph, sharing his concern. "See you tomorrow my love," whispered Ralph. Then he and Edison made their way back to their Rosebank hotel.

"Another trip to the steakhouse?" suggested Ralph.

"So long as it doesn't trigger what we've been through today all over again tomorrow," said Edison.

The next day, Ralph and Edison were up and about early. Ralph telephoned Detective Inspector Pinaar to see if there was any news on Masiwa.

"Ja, Mr Henderson," said the Inspector, very cheerily. "The hospital have got him chained to his bed. He's not happy, I can tell you!"

"Did he come round from the drug okay?" asked Ralph.

"He seemed to. He didn't know where he was. Tried to get out of bed and just fell over as his legs wasn't working yet," said the Inspector in his thick, Afrikaans accent, more used to conversations in his own language. "But my guys made sure he is secure and we'll have him in our custody later on today. Got a pretty major headache apparently, but that's the least of his troubles now."

"Well, thanks for the update Inspector," said Ralph. "I'll be heading back to the Lodge later on today, but you've got my number if you need me?"

"Sure, you take care now," and the Inspector cut the connection.

Ralph and Edison drove slowly to the clinic, yet still arriving well before Jean and Ella were due. Ralph tried to read the tired and out-dated magazines, he gazed out of the window, he fiddled with his mobile phone, with his fingers he tapped out rhythms from his favourite rock songs on his thighs, his impatience grew and grew. Then he noticed Edison sitting beside him, silent, still, unaffected by the wait.

"How do you manage it Edison?" he asked.

"Manage what?"

"To be so patient all the time."

"I have realized that to get frustrated and angry with time is a very pointless exercise," replied Edison. "Nothing you do will make the sun go down any sooner or rise differently in the morning. If we have to wait for something, we are destined to wait, that is all."

"Well, it just doesn't seem to be in my genes, whatever it is you have in yours," said Ralph.

"That is because you are not an African," said Edison with a smile. "Only an African knows how to wait properly."

"Okay, I give up," Ralph replied, and jumped up out of the chair in the waiting area and walked around the room two or three times.

"And what are you doing now?" asked Edison.

"Keeping my legs from going numb with inactivity and my mind from turning to mush."

"There are those who would say your brain is already mush," said Edison. "Not than I count myself among their number, of course."

Ralph glared at him…then burst out laughing. Just then, Jean and Ella came walking slowly and quietly into the area.

"What's so funny?" Jean asked Ralph.

Ralph blushed at the insensitivity he was showing, "Sorry Jean. Something Edison said made me laugh. Good morning. Hello Ella, How are you today?"

Ella gave a half nod, but said nothing, continuing to cling on to her mother's arm.

"Hello Ella," said Edison, approaching her slowly. "I have something for you." From his pocket, he produced a delicate-looking but beautifully woven grass bracelet. "I made it yesterday, from the grasses in your aunt's garden. I hope it will bring you good fortune." He gently placed it around Ella's wrist and fastened it.

"Edison, that's lovely," said Jean. "How kind of you."

"My grandmother taught me how to weave grasses like this. She was a sangoma and had special powers. I do not think I have inherited her special powers of healing, but I thought you might like a new bracelet."

Ella still didn't say anything, but after looking carefully at the new bracelet and then raising her gaze to meet Edison's, there was a new moistness in her eyes and she whispered, "Thank you."

Just then, Anne Gray came bustling into the waiting area, "Gosh! Are you having a party this morning?" she declared. "So many of you today. Ella? Shall we go through?" Then she briskly walked off, expecting Ella to follow like a faithful puppy. Ella did follow, but at a far slower pace than Dr Anne Gray was setting and with her head down, shoulders slightly slumped, she shuffled along the corridor to Anne Gray's consulting room. Jean and Ralph exchanged glances and they both slowly let the breaths they were holding expel into the room. Then they waited, and waited.

After a long forty minutes, Anne Gray and Ella returned. Ralph looked at Ella to see if there were any signs of improvement, any spark that might have returned to her eyes, or if she'd recovered the confident way she had always held her head, but no, she still gave the appearance of a mongrel dog that had been beaten too many times into submission. Dr Gray walked along side her, gently talking to her, but Ralph could sense that whatever she was saying wasn't registering with Ella.

"Ah, Mrs Moffatt and you must be Mr Henderson," the doctor said, "Well it's slowly, slowly, but I'm sure we'll get there. I didn't do hypnotherapy today, perhaps it was a it too much to try it last time as it seemed to upset Ella. But we did go back into childhood and that seems all fine. No traumas that have imprinted themselves that I can see."

Jean Moffat snorted at the very thought of it. Ralph was a bit upset at the dismissive way this doctor was talking about Ella as if she wasn't there.

"Edison," he said, "Could you sit with Ella while Jean and I have a word with Dr Gray?"

"Of course."

"Well, you'd better come back to my room," said Anne Gray, evidently not too pleased at the prospect of this unscheduled meeting that she'd been bounced into.

Once back in her room with the door closed, Dr Gray attempted to forestall any challenging questions by announcing, "Ella is making some progress, I am sure. But these things do take time. We all have to be patient and allow her recovery to come at Ella's pace rather than rushing her. We've tried some mild anti-depressants, of course, and those take a while to take effect. Mrs Moffat? She is taking her medication at the prescribed times, isn't she?"

"Yes, twice a day," said Jean. "But they're not really having any effect."

"It's important you maintain a regular routine, of course,"

went on the doctor. "In these cases, re-establishing a pattern of daily life can do a lot to overcome the trauma of what she's been through."

"Have you handled many cases like Ella?" asked Ralph.

"Three or four, but each one will be different, of course. It's not like treating measles."

"I never thought it would be," replied Ralph, trying hard not to let his anger rise to the bait of the doctor's dismissive tone. "But I'm at a bit of a loss to see exactly what it is you are doing. Ella is still locked inside the horror of what she's been through. Is going through her schoolgirl crushes or playground squabbles really going to help us?"

"We have to try everything," said the doctor, very defensively. "There are so many things about the subconscious we really don't understand. We know the mechanics of how the brain operates by sending its signals of response to stimuli, but the emotional impact of events is not a quantifiable science. Patients need patience, if that's not too awful a pun to use. Ella still needs time."

"Hmmmm," said Ralph, not convinced.

"Come on Ralph," said Jean, rising from her chair. "I'm sure Dr Gray has other patients to attend to."

"We'll get there," said the doctor as she saw them out of the door. Ralph and Jean remained unconvinced.

As Jean, Ralph and the Doctor had walked off to the doctor's room for their meeting, Edison sat next to Ella. Ella was calm and quite impassive, Edison listened to the rhythm of her breathing for a few seconds then said, "I see you are wearing the bracelet?"

Ella nodded, fingering the delicate weaving of grass around her wrist.

"Let me tell you about my grandmother," started Edison. Ella sat passively, still gently turning the bracelet around her arm. "In my village, she was regarded as the leader, even though she was a woman. Being a sangoma gave her a privileged position as people would come to her if they were sick or their children were unwell and she would treat them with her medicines she made from the herbs and plants from the bush. But grandmother wasn't just a healer, she had a gift of wisdom that saw into people's hearts, too. She could talk to people about their personal problems, the disputes they had with neighbours, or women who were jealous of one another. My grandmother would often just sit down with people and talk and through her talking she was able to soothe bad spirits or make worries seem to diminish.

"I remember one time I was troubled that a bigger boy in the village was bullying me. I was always quite slight and skinny for my age and this bigger boy would push me over whenever no grown up was watching, or if we were playing football he would kick me, not the ball. My grandmother could see I was unhappy but I didn't want to talk about it as I thought it was telling tales and I had to sort these things out for myself. Eventually though, she got me to admit there was a problem and when I did tell her she just sat and thought about what I had said and told me a story about a boy who was unhappy because no one liked him and his mother was dead and his father was away working at the mines so he had to fend for himself most of the time. His unhappiness expressed itself in the only way he knew and that was to hurt others who could not, or would not, fight back. So I asked my grandmother, what happened to him? She said the boy who he treated worst of all confronted him one day, not with violence, but with calm, reasonable words. The smaller boy spoke of his desire to be friends, but the bigger boy would have to stop bullying, or else there would be no one in the village who would be his friend. My grandmother went on to say this was what happened. They ended up being the best of friends."

Ella looked wide-eyed at Edison and whispered, "Was the little boy you, Edison?"

"Yes Miss Ella. That was me."

"And you stood up to the bully?"

"Yes, I did."

"Tell me more about your grandmother, Edison."

"She lived to be a very old lady. She had six children of her own and I lose count of how many grandchildren and now great grandchildren. She passed away three years ago. When I was still quite young she taught me how to weave grasses, and she said if I wove a grass bracelet for a girl, I must always be sure of my feelings for that girl because in the weaving there is more than just grass."

"And did you weave a bracelet for Grace?"

"Oh yes, I have woven a number of bracelets for Grace!"

"Because you love her?"

"Of course Miss Ella."

"And now you have woven one for me?"

"Because I love you in a different way. I want you to be strong again, and be a partner for Ralph because you are good for him and without you he is like an old buffalo with a big hangover. Very difficult to live with!"

Ella laughed. She actually laughed! All the while Edison had been talking, she had been gently rolling the grass bracelet around her wrist, but concentrating on what Edison had been saying. Just as she laughed, Jean and Ralph came into view and both Edison and Ella acted like little schoolchildren who had been caught out in class.

"Ella!" said Jean, "I heard you laugh!"

Very carefully and quietly, Ella replied, "Yes Mum. I think I did."

Chapter Twenty Two

After the hospital visit, Jean and Ella went back to Jean's brother's house and Ralph and Edison got on the road for Mogololo. Ralph was excited at the change he'd seen in Ella's appearance and demeanour and wished he didn't have to go back to the Lodge to look after guests, but he knew that Mogololo was teetering on the brink of financial disaster and without him driving it, the whole enterprise would collapse and everyone involved would be out of a job. So duty came first. But at least he had some time on the road to talk with Edison.

"Edison," he said, "What on earth did you do to Ella?"

"I talked about my grandmother, that's all."

"The one we all thought was a witch when we were kids?"

"Sangoma, Ralph. Very different from a witch."

"Okay, sangoma then. But what's she got to do with the change in Ella?"

"Oh, I don't know. My grandmother was a very smart lady. She did things almost instinctively: helping people, healing them, sorting out problems. She taught me a lot of things. Like weaving grass bracelets. Maybe some of her special power has come down through the family?"

"So you're a witch as well?"

"No. I am not a sangoma. But maybe the spirit of my

grandmother saw how Ella was so troubled and helped her start her recovery."

"Oh Edison, I do hope so! I really do."

It was a long drive all the way from the Highveld of Gauteng back to the Lowveld of the game reserve area and Mogololo, but both Ralph's and Edison's spirits were lifted by their adventures with Masiwa, the police, the recovery of ransom money and the small but remarkable change in Ella. Ralph felt he didn't need to talk any more about Edison's effect on Ella, but he inwardly thanked God that his lifelong friend had such inner wisdom and strength of character to make such a difference. Modern medical thinking hadn't done much but traditional methods had.

It was dusk when they drove up the dusty track to the Lodge and they were greeted by Miriam, Grace and Jackson, all keen to hear of their adventures and news.

"Grace," announced Ralph. "I think your husband may just be a witch doctor. The best psychiatrists in South Africa haven't been able to unlock Ella's demons, but I think Edison just may have done the trick."

Grace giggled with embarrassment, "I expect he made a bracelet for her?"

"How did you know?" asked Ralph.

"Long story," interrupted Edison, wanting to stop the conversation and explanations going any further.

"So the place didn't burn down or fall apart while we were away?" asked Ralph.

"Of course not, Mr Ralph," said Jackson with hurt in his voice. "Everything is in top ship shape."

Ralph smiled at Jackson's mangled colloquialism. "That's the stuff Jackson. Miriam, don't suppose there's any chance of something to eat is there? Edison and I seem to have forgotten how to feed ourselves."

The rhythm of guests arriving, game drives, sundowners, dinners and more game drives continued at Mogololo. Whenever he got a chance, Ralph would disappear into the office to check emails and then climb the small hill behind the lodge to get a decent cellular signal and check in with Jean to see how Ella was doing.

"Certainly progressing," said Jean. "In fact we're thinking of coming back to Hoedspruit tomorrow. It's high time I got back to the café anyway."

"Hell, of course," said Ralph. "Sorry Jean. I'd forgotten all about your café. Yes. Is there anything I can do?"

"No, don't worry. You've got enough on your plate with that game lodge of yours," said Jean. "No, we'll just make our way home slowly tomorrow.'

"No more visits to Dr Anne Gray then?"

"Frankly, I'd rather Ella had another talk to Edison," said Jean. "He seems to have brightened her up a lot more than the traditional medical world."

"I'll tell him," chuckled Ralph. "Although, on second thoughts, maybe I won't. He's too important to me here than giving him ideas of setting up a counselling service to all and sundry."

"Anyway, come and see us the day after tomorrow, if you can."

"I'll be there."

As Ralph made his way back down the hill to the lodge, Jackson was just returning from Hoedspruit with the supplies Miriam and Grace needed to keep the Lodge going. One of his tasks while in town was to check the mailbox at the post office and bring all correspondence back with him. There was one package he was excited about.

"Mr Ralph!" he declared, waving a small packet in the air. "Special delivery! I had to sign for it. The lady in the post office didn't want to release it to me. I had to show her my bush shirt with Mogololo written on it before she would believe I was a trustworthy person!"

"Thanks Jackson," said Ralph, turning the packet over and over to see who it might be from. "Sunrise Productions?" he muttered to himself, "Oh! That's Danny's company." He tore at the tape to open the package and saw it was a DVD case. There was a hand-written letter with it, 'Ralph, here's a first edit of the pilot. It's looking good. Let me have any comments if there's anything you're not happy with. Hope Ella is ok. Best wishes, Danny.'

Ralph went straight to his office, trailing the others in his wake as they all wanted to see what was on the DVD. Ralph loaded the disc into his laptop and made sure everyone could see the screen, although he took the best view for himself.

The screen came alive. The opening titles were still in fairly rough outline without any of the finished animation that Danny had spoken abut during one of their long, late night chats before the trauma of the kidnap, and the music track needed more mixing, but when the live action started, they all gasped in awe at the camerawork, the subtlety, the drama of the animals, the way daily life around the lodge was inextricably linked with the flora and fauna of Africa's brilliant bush. There were behind-the-scenes sections of Miriam making her bread and her girls in the kitchen, Grace and her team doing housekeeping, Ralph and Edison preparing for game drives and the drives themselves. There were guests, of course, enthusing over animal sightings and relaxed over drinks. There were wide, sweeping shots of magnificent sunrises and sunsets. There were the natural conflicts of animal behaviour, beautifully shot and edited. And there were scenes of Ella. Ella being Ella: greeting guests, managing the team, teasing Ralph, soothing Jackson, being the perfect, charming, face of Mogololo. As Danny and Billy had promised, she hadn't been 'on camera' in the sense that she was being interviewed or asked to make specific comments, but it was clear she was the fulcrum around which the whole of Mogololo operated.

After the first giggles and comments of everyone seeing

themselves on screen, and once the part that Ella played became so evident, there was silence in the office while the programme ran through. By accident, it had become Ella's show. After twenty five minutes, the programme ended. No one spoke. No one could speak.

Eventually Ralph broke the silence, "We need Ella back, don't we?" he said.

Everyone murmured and nodded. "I'll show her this as soon as they get back. Edison, will you come with me?"

"Of course."

The next day was busy with the imminent arrival of new guests. Ralph was always on edge before a new arrival; he knew their names from the online booking form, he knew where they were from, but he never knew whether they were really interested in what Mogololo could do for them, or if they just wanted to sit around all day drinking beer, pretending they were having a 'bush experience'.

With the group that arrived that day he needn't have worried. They had all visited wildlife parks before, they were knowledgeable, sensitive to the bush and its ways, and perfect guests. The afternoon game drive went well with excellent sightings of elephant, rhino, buffalo and Edison spotted lion in the distance but they moved off too quickly for the Land Rover to catch them.

So it was a happy and satisfied group that gathered for dinner to enjoy Miriam's dishes. While they all enjoyed retelling the day's stories, Ralph excused himself and went up the small hill to get the only possible cellular signal in the camp to call Jean.

"Hi Ralph," said a tired-sounding Jean. "I thought you might call."

"How was your journey back?" asked Ralph.

"Long and tiring, but we made it."

"And Ella?"

"Well, she does seem brighter. She's taking a bit more care of herself again, she even put make up on today, and that's a first since…since, you know."

"Progress then."

"Oh Ralph, I do hope so."

"Can I come and see you tomorrow?"

"Sure. I'll be at the café in the morning. I'm getting a friend to sit with Ella. But I'll be back here in the afternoon. Can you come then?"

"I will. I have something special to show her."

"Sounds intriguing. See you tomorrow."

It was just a one night stay for the guests. Ralph took them all on a sunrise game drive which was quite spectacular. The lions Edison had spotted the afternoon before must have made a kill as Edison spotted the tell-tale signs of vultures circling in the air and then taking up positions in trees, waiting their turn to clear up the scraps after the lions, hyenas and jackals had all had their turn at ripping the carcass to shreds.

So the vultures led them to the kill, with Ralph carefully steering the Land Rover through bushes and round rocks and trying to avoid the antbear holes and bigger termite mounds until he eventually got close to the scene. The lions were still gorging themselves, ripping at fur and flesh and fighting over what they regarded as the easiest, tastiest parts. They seemed to want the softest pieces of the animal first: the guts and internal organs rather than more protein-rich muscle, but that's the way of nature. They were scrapping with one another and also keeping a wary eye on opportunistic hyenas who were slavering frantically and drooling from their horrible jaws as they trotted round the carcass and the lions, hoping the big cats would soon have had enough and leave what was left to them. The lions were having none of it, of course. Even though they had all just about eaten all they could, they still needed to put the hyenas in their place and teach them some respect.

The group in the Land Rover watched, enthralled, for about an hour and a half, until eventually Ralph declared that Miriam would be cross if they were too late back for breakfast and their bacon and eggs got cold. So they left the animals to the remains of their feast while they looked forward to their own.

"Wish all our guests were as easy and appreciative as that party," said Ralph as he waved them off after breakfast.

.

"Hope they come back one day."

Grace, who had also been waving their departure said, "It is because you are a good host, Mr Ralphie."

"Hmm, nice of you to think so Grace. But I'm not so good without Ella."

"She will come back. My Edison says so."

Happy that everything was under control at the lodge, Ralph grabbed his laptop and the DVD from Danny, found Edison and they both headed into town to see Jean and Ella.

He was nervous on the drive, fretting over whether the improvement he'd seen in Ella was genuine and would continue. As he'd gone through most of his life so far without any illness, only the inevitable teenage accidents of broken wrists and squashed thumbs, he was unused to people being unwell. And the thought of a mental instability was totally alien to him. The trauma that Ella endured was immense; could the mind, or psyche, or whatever it was called really recover from experiences like that? And whatever key Edison had managed to turn had been the beginning of her recovery, he prayed it would continue.

He stopped at a florist on the way to Jean's house and spent far too much money on an enormous bunch of flowers.

"Are they for Ella or Mrs Basset?" laughed Edison.

"Well they're not for you, that's for sure!"

Ella was sitting on the verandah of her mother's house when Ralph and Edison arrived. She stood up and waved.

"That's a good sign," said Ralph more to himself than Edison.

Ralph walked up and with great embarrassment proffered his flowers.

"Ralph, they're lovely. Thank you" said Ella quietly. "When was the last time you gave anyone flowers?"

"It's a first. How are you feeling?"

"Bit numb. But better."

"Hello Miss Ella," said Edison shyly.

"Edison," smiled Ella, "Still wearing it," showing Edison her wrist.

"I will need to make you another quite soon," said Edison. "They never last too long I am afraid."

"Shall we go inside? I've got something to show you," said Ralph.

Once they were sitting down, with Ella on one side of him and Jean on the other, with Edison standing behind, Ralph started up the laptop and played the DVD.

After a little while, he heard Ella make a little gasp as she saw herself. He gently moved his hand to hold hers. She continued looking at the screen, totally mesmerised and wrapped up in what she was watching and taking in. No one spoke, but out of the corner of his eye Ralph was carefully watching Ella for her reaction and signs of recognition. She gripped his hand tighter. He saw a range of reactions cross her face, small smiles, slight frowns, intakes of breath, and then, towards the end of the programme, he was aware of a tear that had appeared at the corner of her eye. As the caption closed the programme, he leant across and kissed it away.

"Are you ready to come back to us?" he whispered.

Ella turned to face him, and another tear began to escape. She brushed it away with the back of her hand and slowly nodded. "Yes, I think so."

"Ralph," said Jean. "That programme is wonderful. When will it be shown on TV?"

"Danny has to sell the idea to the TV station first," said Ralph. "But it is good, isn't it? And, as you've seen, there really is only one star!"

"Ella?' said Jean, "Are you really strong enough to go back?"

"Mum," said Ella. "You've been great. Really. And taking me to Sandton to see Dr Gray was an okay idea but she didn't really do anything for me. It was Edison who helped me turn the corner. And Ralph. And now seeing what Mogololo is really like, I know it's my life. I want it back."

Ralph turned to her and had tears in his eyes too, "That's

terrific," he croaked.

"Look at the two of you!" snorted Jean. "Love's young dream!"

Then Edison broke the spell by gently touching Ella on her shoulder, "It will be good to have you back Ella."

Chapter Twenty Three

The rhythm of life in Mogololo got itself back to something like normal. The rains came and with them arrived a new flush of life and fresh growth in the plants, grasses and trees. The impala, zebra and wildebeest herds had babies, the lions and other predators had more to eat than they needed. The whole game reserve looked forward to new generations of animals arriving to take their place in the great scheme of nature.

Guests arrived and departed in a steady, but unspectacular stream. Ralph was still very concerned for the future of the Lodge; the letters from the bank seemed to be arriving with more regularity, asking what was his forecast for the next quarter? What was his plan for reducing the overdraft? What was he going to do about the outstanding payments on his personal loan? He did his best not to get too concerned but the responsibility was weighing heavily on his shoulders.

He shared his concerns with Ella, who was now back to her normal self, though she never wanted to talk about the kidnap or her time locked up by Masiwa and his thugs. She was, however, curious about the personal loan.

"So you took out a loan to help pay Masiwa's ransom?" she asked.

"It was the only way I could raise all of the money. Patricia was so generous, as was your mother, but there was still a gap in the middle so I took out a loan."

"What did you tell the bank it was for?"

"An engagement ring for you," answered Ralph, looking her straight in the eye.

"Really?"

"Well it was only a little white lie," defended Ralph.

"I know," said Ella, "I was only teasing. I don't need a ring."

"One day. When we're millionaires," promised Ralph.

"And when is that going to be?" she wondered aloud.

"When Danny sells the TV programme around the world and people want to come and stay where they've seen the wonderful Ella on the box, that's when," said Ralph.

"I get the impression that these things don't happen overnight," said Ella.

"No, but you've prompted me to email Danny to see how he's getting on. I know he's as keen as we are to get things moving.," said Ralph. "In the meantime, have we got any more guests coming in this week?"

"Four tomorrow, then another two the following day. They'll all be here for the weekend," said Ella.

"Well, that will keep the vultures at bay for a while."

A week or so later, after coming back from his afternoon game drive, Ralph checked his emails and saw there was a message from Caleb Coetzee. A date had been set for Masiwa's trial and Ella, Ralph and Edison would be needed as witnesses.

"Oh shit," said Ralph. "I'd been putting off thinking about that."

"Thinking about what?" asked Ella, who was at her desk in the office.

"Masiwa's trial, darling," said Ralph. "I'm afraid you'll have to go over it again."

Ralph could see Ella tense, her eyes closing as she thought of the implications of what lay ahead. "I hope he burns in hell," she said, "And I'll help put him there."

"Good girl," said Ralph, relieved that she was facing the future with such determination.

The case was too big to be heard in Nelspruit so the proceedings took place in the Johannesburg Court. Much to Ralph and Ella's relief, Masiwa and his two thugs were all pleading guilty to the charges of abduction, false imprisonment and extortion.

"They could hardly do otherwise given all the evidence," said Inspector Coetzee when Ralph discussed it with him. "Your intervention with the tranquillizer dart will, of course, catch the media's attention, so I guess you should get ready for a lot of pestering."

"Yes," said Ralph. "Not quite sure how I feel about that. I mean publicity is always supposed to be good, but will guests want to come to a game lodge where the staff get kidnapped and the owner goes around with a dangerous dart full of drugs?"

"Time will tell," laughed Coetzee. "See you in court!"

On the first day of the trial, Ralph, Edison and Ella presented themselves in court where they were met by the prosecution team and Callie Coetzee. Surprisingly, it was the first time the Inspector had met Ella. He was gracious and generous with his praise of her fortitude and bravery. Ella just smiled, Ralph could see she was as nervous as a rabbit caught in the unwavering glare of a cobra about to strike.

When Masiwa was led into the dock, Ralph let out a huge sigh of relief.

"Look at him", he whispered to Ella. "He's broken."

Ralph was right. All of the arrogance and swagger had gone. Masiwa was scared, diminished and his spirit was crushed. It was evident that his time in jail had already been rough on him, a bruise and lump under one of his eyes told its own story. His fellow inmates would know he had been a policeman and they would not have been sympathetic to his plight; past revenges would have been meted out and Masiwa was not physically or mentally strong enough to withstand them.

The formalities began, an archaic system of legalities, with officials dressed up in traditional costumes going through rituals that had been passed down by old colonials to a new nation that forever promised fairness and justice to all but didn't always deliver.

For Masiwa, however, it was an open and shut case. Once the charges had been read and descriptions of the events had been aired, Ella was called as a witness and the prosecuting counsel gently asked her about the events of her kidnap and capture. Ralph knew she would hate having to go through the nightmare again, but although her voice was occasionally shaky, she gave a lucid and clear account. So clear, in fact, the defence counsel had no further questions.

Edison was called to relate the story of how he had seen Masiwa on a motorbike, collecting the ransom money and then how he had managed to find the car dealer who had sold two second hand vehicles to the thugs who had carried out the kidnap itself. The defence barrister attempted to query the strength of Edison's story, but Edison was solid in his evidence and Ralph could see the panel of three judges nodding in acceptance of his version of the facts.

When it was time for Ralph to take the stand, there was a significant rustling and fidgeting coming from the press gallery. As Callie Coetzee had suggested, the press were going to have a field day with someone taking the law into his own hands with a tranquillizer dart.

After the prosecuting barrister had led Ralph through the

events leading up to Ralph and Edison confronting Masiwa in the Rosebank café, the defence opposition was strong and confrontational. 'Why had Mr Henderson taken the law into his own hands? Did he hold a licence for a potentially lethal tranquillizer dart? Did he never consider the safety of innocent members of the public?' Ralph kept calm and answered all the questions with reason and patience, addressing his answers to the panel of judges as well as the terrier of a barrister who tried hard to rile him, trip him up or ridicule his rash actions in the eyes of the court.

Eventually, the defence barrister acknowledged that the judges were tiring of his aggressive style and released Ralph from the witness stand. Before he left, Ralph caught Masiwa's eye and glared at him, unblinking and unforgiving. Masiwa tried hard to avoid Ralph's stare and looked down, in shame.

At the end of the day's proceedings there was a mad media scramble. All the reporters, radio and TV crews wanted to interview Ella and Ralph. Fortunately, the prosecuting counsel had anticipated this and had set up a press conference room where Ella, Ralph and Inspectors Coetzee and Pinaar had agreed to take questions. The conference was chaired by the barrister who had led Ralph and Ella through their evidence. The room was packed; camera tripods and lights, a spaghetti tangle of microphone cables and a gang of about twenty journalists shouting questions at Ralph and Ella. The barrister managed to get some sort of order and Ralph and Ella went over their stories; the journalists looking for the most salacious and sensational angles and Ralph, while answering, was always aware that the future of Mogololo could well be in this room. He managed to play down the dangers of running a game lodge and the fact that he had taken the law into his own hands, joking that it was the fault of the Chinese: first through the poaching that had prompted Masiwa's interest in Mogololo and then the Chinese premier; if there hadn't been a high level visit by the Chinese on the day he tracked down Masiwa then Inspector Coetzee would have brought Masiwa into custody through the proper channels. Callie Coetzee glared at Ralph while he was offering this explanation and attempted to set the record straight, but the press had their story.

Completely out of his normal comfort zone, Ralph thought he had managed to fend off the media quite well, making the case for Mogololo being a highly desirable destination as strongly as he could. Ella was more reluctant to talk about her experience and the prosecuting barrister brought the conference to a close to save her any more anguish than was necessary.

They stayed one more night and the next day in court the judges deliberated on the sentence they would hand down. Masiwa and the two accomplices had admitted guilt so that was to be taken into consideration. The chair of judges gave a long and fairly rambling speech about Masiwa being a senior policeman, holding a position of trust and authority and how he had abused that privilege and brought the police force into disrepute so the sentence he would receive would reflect that. The two hapless thugs received a sentence of three years each, Masiwa was given a sentence of twelve years. He gasped in shock as this sunk in, then he was led away, out of Ralph and Ella's lives at last.

Ralph, Ella and Edison drove back to Mogololo, emotionally drained by all they had been through in court, but they had a sense of closure, now it was all over.

They had collected piles of newspapers to see how the case had been reported and most had got the story a bit mangled and gave emphasis to the things Ralph considered unimportant, but made for racier headlines. They had missed all of the TV coverage but Jean had been glued to her television and called on their cell phones to report that the story had received lots of coverage and she'd seen the press conference and Ralph, Ella and Edison leaving court and she was sure it would all die down before the weekend and when would they b

It was actually late afternoon when they arrived, hot and dusty back at Mogololo.

Grace greeted them, "Oh, I am so glad you are back! The website: it has been broken with all the people trying to book at the same time! And my phone will not stop ringing!"

"Oh?" said Ralph, "Well that's bad, in a good way, isn't it?"

"What?" said Ella.

"Well, not great that the website has crashed, but good that people want to book."

"Sounds like we're going to be busy then," said Ella with a smile. "You'd better get your spanner out and fix the website, hadn't you?"

"Well, I'll call a man who can," answered Ralph.

Chapter Twenty Four

Mogololo had never been busier. The notoriety of the trial had piqued the interest of the South African visitors in particular, but the story of the trial and Ralph's tranquillizer dart intervention had got overseas coverage, too, so visitors were booking from Europe, the USA and even some from the Far East.

They were operating just about at their limit, but the Lodge was buzzing when it was busy. Guests would share stories and new friendships were made across continents. Jackson got to take guests on game drives as well as Ralph and Edison, and Edison was training up a new bush guide, a nephew of his who was cast in much the same mould as Edison: calm, deep thinking, capable.

Ella had put the trauma of her experiences well behind her and the running of the lodge took her full attention. Jean visited more frequently, just to make sure Ella was coping and came armed with cakes from her café, much to Miriam's annoyance.

"Why does that lady bring cakes to our lodge, when she knows I am perfectly capable of making good cakes?"

"Don't worry, Miriam," soothed Ralph. "It's what ladies like Jean like to do. It's in their nature to be generous like that."

Miriam huffed and got on with pulling the messy entrails out of a chicken.

The next day, collecting post on a trip to town, Ralph noticed a very official-looking letter addressed to him. It had a government stamp and he opened it with some trepidation. He needn't have worried. It was a letter from the court, enclosing a cheque for 500,000 rand. "Wow!" whispered Ralph. "I wondered when that might happen, and I didn't expect to get it all."

He sat in his vehicle, reading the very formal, very legal letter but it did explain that the amount they discovered in Masiwa's bag at the railway station was actually more than the ransom money Ralph had handed over. Masiwa wouldn't give any explanation as to where the extra money had come from (presumably not wanting to incriminate himself in another crime that hadn't yet been discovered) so under the circumstances, the court was prepared to refund the full ransom and the remainder would go to the state.

The two cars that had been impounded, purchased by the two accomplices, would also become the property of the state. "You're welcome," Ralph said to himself as he read that bit.

Ralph was supposed to acknowledge safe receipt of the cheque, which he would do in his own time, but he went straight to the bank to deposit the half a million rand. The bank teller looked at him wide-eyed in amazement when he handed over the cheque, never having seen a transaction from the South African government to a private individual as large as that, but Ralph just smiled sweetly and gratefully pocketed the receipt. While he was in the bank he also arranged for transfers to go to Jean and to Patricia so he could bring closure to the debts he owed them. He also paid off his personal loan in full. He had just completed this when he spotted Mr Wilson, the bank manager, out of the corner of his eye.

"Ah, Mr Henderson, isn't it?" he said, "Mogololo Game Lodge. I was wondering when you would be replying to the letters I have been sending you about both your overdraft and your personal loan?"

"Mr Wilson," said Ralph, "You'll be glad to hear I've just deposited half a million rand. Does that answer your letters?" With that, he turned and left the bank, smiling a smug smile that Mr Wilson would never see.

Life at Mogololo was never normal, but a sense of order did seem to descend on the Lodge as the pattern of guest arrivals, game drives, sundowners, meals and guest departures slotted into place. Bookings had never been better and guest experiences matched up and often exceeded their expectations. The team at the Lodge got used to working at full stretch and both Miriam and Grace had hired extra hands to help with the number of meals to be cooked and beds to be changed and rooms cleaned.

Things were about to get even more hectic, however, as Danny had successfully sold the programme to the main TV station, and it had been picked up by many international broadcasters, too.

"Having you on the front page of the news certainly helped!" laughed Danny when he told him the good news that the first of the programmes was to be aired in three weeks time.

"Danny, I'm thrilled," responded Ralph. "But I'm panicking, too. We're flat out now. Lord knows what it will be like when we get another flood of bookings enquiries."

"Expand."

"Never," said Ralph. "I really don't want to be running a big outfit. Not my style. We're good at being small and if we stay exclusive, so be it."

"Well good luck with that. How's Ella, by the way?"

"Ella's great again, thanks," said Ralph, genuinely relieved that he could say that with confidence. "Back to her old self and even able to speak about what she went through. Now, if anything goes wrong at the lodge, as it often does, like toilets blocking, or running out of shampoo, or five guests arriving together when they only booked in for four, she's got a new saying: 'It's all gone Masiwa'. So it's fantastic that she has been strong enough to really get over it at last. There were times, in the early days, when she was seeing that shrink in Sandton, that I didn't think we'd get her back. It's was Edison's magic touch that did it. But I don't tell him that too often."

"Well, give her my love and a hug from me," said Danny. "And we need to fix a date for me to come and talk about the next series."

"Next?" said Ralph. "Let's get over this one first! Bye

Danny."

As he walked back to the office from the little hill where he'd been talking to Danny on his cellphone, Ella was waiting for him.

"What's that big grin for, Henderson?" she asked.

"Danny's just sold the programme to TV, here and overseas. Mogololo is going to be on the map. Big time."

"Well that's good that we'll have to find yet another gear to go on top of turbo-charged-boosty-overdrive style in the way we already run this place," said Ella as ironically as she could manage.

"Ella, my darling," soothed Ralph. "No one ever notices that the elegant swan called Ella, gliding over the surface of the smooth, glassy pond, is paddling like crazy underneath. You'll be fine!"

"Will I? Another three hours in the day would help. Can you fix that, 'Mr Ralphie'?"

I'll see what I can do. In the meantime, I've got to pop over to see the National Park Rangers in a bit, do you want to come? Get away from the office for an hour or two?"

Ella immediately melted. "Oh boy, yes please! Much as I love Mogololo, I'm beginning to get Lodge Fever."

They slipped away in the Land Rover, promising to be back in time for the afternoon game drive. Ralph thoughtfully took drinks and Miriam gave some of her famous scones, fresh from the oven.

The drive to the Rangers HQ in one of the main rest camps in Kruger Park took no more than forty five minutes. They were happy to be in one another's company, just the two of them and Ella slid across the front seat to hug Ralph's arm as he drove. As soon as they left Mogololo's dirt tracks and joined one of the main roads that criss-cross the national park, the atmosphere changes, just a little. It is more public, less intimate, there are more 'do not' signs and speed restrictions and direction posts. It is game viewing like painting-with-numbers Ralph always thought, but for those who couldn't afford the opportunity to visit places like Mogololo it was still Africa. It was still the bush in all its wild glory. The animals didn't know whether they were in the park proper, or on Ralph's territory, or on any of the other private lodges that shared the park's fenceless border.

They drove on to the Ranger's HQ and Ralph signed the documents he had been requested to put his name to.

"Sorry about this, Ralph," said his park ranger friend. "It's them blerry pen pushers in Pretoria, Man. Shish! The paperwork they make us do. While they sit on their fat arses in their air conditioned offices thinking up more forms for us to fill in. This lot is just to confirm there's no diseases you've come across on your concession in the grazers and browsers that need to be notified to the ministry. Blerry waste of time, eh?"

"Never mind, Hennie," said Ralph, "As long as they also let us get on with our jobs of minding the animals, beating the poachers and keeping the tourists happy, eh?"

"Ja Man, " said the big Afrikaaner, "Nice to see you Miss Ella."

Ella thanked him, they all shook hands and Ralph and Ella made their way back to the Lodge.

"This is a bit like the very first time you took me on a drive, when I was giving physio to that guest of yours," said Ella. "Just you and me, and the animals, of course."

"I like the idea of just you and me," said Ralph.

Just then he jumped on the brakes and they stopped in a cloud of dust.

"What?" said Ella, very surprised.

"There, through the bush," said Ralph.

"Can't see anything," complained Ella.

"Hold on," said Ralph, and he pulled the steering wheel over and headed off the track into the mopane scrub, casually pushing over small saplings, knowing they were tough enough to spring back, virtually unharmed.

"What is it?" whispered Ella, still confused.

"Rhino, I think," replied Ralph, and he slowed the vehicle and came around a dense clump of vegetation and there, just twenty metres away was a female rhino and a very new calf.

"Oh Ralph, it's just so sweet!" said Ella.

"Not sure I'd call it 'sweet'," said Ralph. "But it's lovely to see a rhino baby."

"Do you think?" started Ella, "That the father might just be your favourite rhino, the one that got killed by those poachers?"

"I guess the timing's about right," said Ralph. "They're pregnant for around fifteen or sixteen months, so it's well within the time when he was still around."

Ella was quite for a moment then said, "Gosh, fifteen months."

"Or sixteen," said Ralph. "I forget which."

"Ummm," Ella started, nervously.

"What?"

"Well, it's rather a strange place to tell you, but…"

"But what?"

Ella gently reached across to pick up Ralph's hand and she guided it to her own tummy. Ralph creased his brow and looked directly into her eyes.

"Well, we probably won't have to wait quite that long."

"What? Do you mean…?"

"Yes I'm pregnant. I think. We're pregnant, I mean."

"Are we?"

"I'm not 100% sure as I haven't been able to get hold of a

pregnancy test kit. But I'm normally clockwork reliable. Even through the aftermath of Masiwa."

"Oh my darling," said Ralph. "A baby?"

"Well I hope it's not going to be a rhino," said Ella.

"Does anyone else know?"

"Of course not, silly. You're the first," said Ella. "Though I think Miriam might have guessed."

Ralph held her close, uncomfortable as they were in the front of the Land Rover, and the female rhino continued grazing the new grass around the bushes, with her little calf bumping around her legs, trying to encourage her mother to let it suckle. Then the mother rhino caught a scent of their presence and lifted her head and peered, myopically in their direction.

"Time to retreat," said Ralph and he started up the engine and reversed the Land Rover to leave the rhinos to carry on being rhinos.

That evening, after the guests had all been wined and dined and gone sleepily to their beds, Ralph and Ella were left alone on the lodge verandah. They sat side by side for a while, gazing out into the African night, seeing the occasional firefly dancing through the air and suicidal moths making for the lanterns. Then Ralph had a thought, got up and went over to the bar, and from the back of the fridge he collected a very old, cold bottle of champagne.

He picked up to glasses and came back to Ella.

"I think this is in order, isn't it?" he said.

"It's no good trying to get me tipsy and then expecting to have your wicked way with me, Henderson," she chided. "It's a bit late for that now. But yes, it's certainly in order. I'd love some."

Ralph grappled with the cork and opened the bottle as quietly as he could, poured two glasses and helped Ella to stand. They chinked glasses, drank, and kissed. A very long and tender kiss. Ralph held Ella close then sat down, encouraging her to sit on his lap.

"A while ago," said Ralph, "I borrowed money from the bank, telling them I was going to buy an engagement ring. I think I'd better go shopping for one, don't you?"

"Are you proposing?"

"I certainly am."

"Well in that case, I accept."

They stayed, Ella sitting on Ralph's lap, as the stars began their glorious nightly show, the best cinema screen in the world, drinking a little more champagne, kissing a little more, loving a lot more.

Ralph pointed to a satellite a pinprick of light, soaring through the sky, then he quietly said, "Makes you feel very small, doesn't it? That big smudge across the sky is the milky way, and our very own planet, our great big earth, is a part of it, a tiny, tiny part."

And as they sat, blissfully happy with their news, their future and each other, the silence of the night was punctuated by a male lion, some kilometres away, roaring and grunting its presence to others, clearly stating, "This is my Africa, my territory. It's mine."

As they continued to sit quietly, not needing to speak, Ralph slowly pointed to something beyond the verandah, out in the dark, some twenty metres away.

"What?" whispered Ella.

The 'something' was large, it was obscured by the foliage of the wild fig tree but Ralph knew what it was, "Elephant," he whispered. And the massive animal quietly moved up to the trunk of the tree, slowly scratched its shoulders against the trunk, stood still and to the inexperienced eye, it became a rock, waiting for the few hours of night time left to pass before another African day would unfold itself to the world.

THE END

Printed in Great Britain
by Amazon